AN
ECHO
IN THE
CITY

ECHO

IN THE

CITY

K. X. SONG

LITTLE, BROWN AND COMPANY
New York Boston

Little, Brown and Company
Hachette Book Group
1290 Avenue of the Americas, New York, NY 10104
Visit us at LBYR.com

First Edition: June 2023

Little, Brown and Company is a division of Hachette Book Group, Inc. The Little, Brown name and logo are trademarks of Hachette Book Group, Inc.

The publisher is not responsible for websites (or their content) that are not owned by the publisher.

Library of Congress Cataloging-in-Publication Data
Names: Song, K. X., author.
Title: An echo in the city / K. X. Song.
Description: First edition. | New York : Little, Brown and Company, 2023. | Audience: Ages 14 & up | Summary: "Two teenagers come of age against the backdrop of the 2019 Hong Kong protests"— Provided by publisher.
Identifiers: LCCN 2021051672 | ISBN 9780316396820 (hardcover) | ISBN 9780316397025 (ebook)
Subjects: CYAC: Coming of age—Fiction. | Protest movements— Fiction. | Hong Kong (China)—Fiction. | LCGFT: Bildungsromans. | Novels.
Classification: LCC PZ7.1.S6755 Ec 2022 | DDC [Fic]—dc23
LC record available at https://lccn.loc.gov/2021051672

ISBNs: 978-0-316-39682-0 (hardcover),
978-0-316-39702-5 (ebook)

Printed in the United States of America

LSC-C

Printing 1, 2023

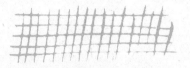

謹以此書獻給我的父母

*For my mother and
father, with love and
gratitude*

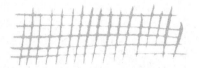

Those who
wish to fight
must first
count the
cost.

—Sun Tzu, *THE ART OF WAR*

PROLOGUE

Hong Kong

2019

Kai

THE STREETS ARE DARK, BUT I CAN MAKE OUT hazy silhouettes shifting against the glow of storefront windows. On the concrete, remnants of tear gas send whispering smoke into the night air, mixing with the sour scent of sweat and gunpowder.

I wait, afraid to run, afraid to stay. All I can do is concentrate on holding my baton, as if it were a hand grenade, and if I let it go, the whole world will come crashing down.

At the end of Kwong Yip Road, the crowd closes in on us from all sides. They rustle like a growing storm, muttering behind their makeshift shields of wooden boards and toilet lids and construction cones. One boy on the front line carries a Nerf shield, a child's toy, but his expression is as solemn as an old man's. The protests have aged us all—decades, centuries. Time feels borrowed, or in my case, stolen.

How did I end up here, on this street, on this night? I'm supposed to be the pragmatic one, the one who makes all the right choices, who never fails to find the easy way out. *You're like water,* Ma used to say, *you go with the flow.* Well, the river is supposed to lead to the sea, to infinite possibility, but instead, here's a dead end, a dam.

There's only one way out.

PART ONE

Three
Months
Earlier

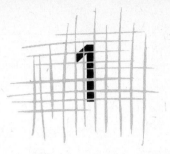

Phoenix

THE SCHOOL BELL RINGS. I ELBOW MY WAY INTO the jail-like corridors of Whitney American School Hong Kong, searching the mass of people for a blond head about a foot taller than the rest. Charlie shouldn't be difficult to find as one of the few expat kids at Whitney, and the loudest one at that. Once, I overheard him asking a question in AP Chemistry, and I'm not even *in* AP Chem. I'm in normal Chem, which happens to be in the next room over.

Today, Charlie's making himself scarce, much to my frustration. I take one more cursory scan over the crowd before heading out back to the football field. No sign of him there either. WHERE ARE YOU? I text. Charlie knows patience isn't one of my virtues. I check my phone again.

Someone grabs my shoulder. "Charlie! Finally, you—"

It's Osprei, my older brother. He raises a cool brow,

cocking his head to one side. This is his signature move that makes everyone from middle school girls to old grannies swoon, but his charm has zero effect on me. I fold my arms across my chest.

"You're not happy to see me," he notes, using Cantonese slang.

I roll my eyes. "Your powers of inference amaze me," I reply in English.

He scowls. "Inference?"

I've given myself a migraine from too much eye-rolling. "It means 'teoi leon.'"

He still looks confused. Osprei may be a pro with the ladies, but his prowess in dating doesn't translate to prowess in academia. He's twenty-one and just barely passed secondary school. He's now in year two of his associate degree and still trying to get into uni. At this rate, I'll graduate before he does.

"Some of us don't spend all our time watching American TV shows," Osprei retorts, in English now. "Some of us have lives."

"You should still be scoring higher than me in English," I point out, "seeing as you were in the States longer."

Although Osprei and I were both born in Hong Kong, we were raised in Cary, North Carolina, where Osprei got stuck with a southern drawl. (*My* accent comes straight from the set of *Friends*.) I spent all of elementary school in the US before moving back to Hong Kong when I turned eleven.

"But I guess my English is better than yours now," I say with a shrug, smirking.

"Helps to have a white boyfriend."

"Charlie's not my boyfriend!"

It's his turn to smirk. "For now."

"What do you want anyway?" I ask, wrinkling my nose. "And why are you here? You better not be dating one of my classmates again." I remember last year's nightmare when Osprei asked out my badminton friend Melody, then promptly dumped her after a week. Melody hasn't spoken to me since. (As if I have anything to do with my brother's frivolity!)

"No way," he says. "I've moved on to a more sophisticated crowd. I like a woman who knows what she wants."

"A woman who knows what she wants wouldn't want you."

He flashes his signature crooked grin at me. God, we go to the same dentist, but I swear his teeth are whiter than mine. Another one of life's injustices.

"You'll see soon enough." He yawns, not bothering to cover his mouth. "Mom wants me to drive you home. She needs Uncle Chow for Dad's airport pickup tonight."

Uncle Chow isn't our biological uncle. He's actually our family driver, but he's been driving us for years, since as long as I can remember, so he's more family to me than my real uncle. Than my real dad, even.

"Wait." I perk up. "Dad's coming home?"

Osprei presses his lips together, dismayed at my excitement. "He's staying at a hotel tonight. He said he'll stop by for dinner tomorrow."

"Dad's in Hong Kong and he's staying at a hotel?" I shriek. Two pigeons and a football player turn their heads my way; I lower my voice. "Why doesn't he just stay at home like normal? He can stay in the guest room if Mom doesn't want..."

"Because nothing is normal, okay?" Osprei says through his teeth. "He said he doesn't want to disrupt the family schedule. He's probably heading off to New York the day after."

It's been a month since Mom and Dad filed for a divorce, and Osprei's right, nothing's been normal since. Mom's been using the fake-polite voice she usually reserves for customer service 24/7. She also spent two thousand dollars on Zen meditation crystals, but that's another story. Meanwhile, Dad's disappeared off the face of the earth. He's a businessman in the shipping industry, so although this isn't new, the complete radio silence is disconcerting. It shouldn't surprise me to learn that Osprei, the only and eldest son, has been receiving updates, while I, the middle child, have gotten nothing. Not even an obligatory "How are you" text. Not even a question re: my SAT scores. (Shitty. Don't ask.)

Osprei's phone chimes. "Let's get outta here," he says, scrolling through his texts. "Suki's meeting us out front."

I scan the schoolyard one last time to check whether Charlie's materialized. No such luck. I guess he doesn't *need* to know that I've just failed my SATs. On that matter, does Mom really need to know either? I shake my head and force myself to think of something else. "Who's Suki?" I ask as we cross the atrium. I recognize some of my classmates gossiping on the front steps, probably comparing SAT results.

"You'll see," Osprei says, an annoying lilt to his voice.

Sure enough, when we get to the curb, there's a girl waiting for us near Osprei's car, leaning against the door holding a cup carrier with three bubble teas in one hand. She has pink and blue streaks in her hair and wears no uniform; instead, she's in ripped jeans and Converse. She hands a jasmine milk tea to Osprei, who answers by kissing her on the lips, effectively answering all my questions in half a second. (At least he's efficient?) I don't bother introducing myself to her; all his girlfriends pass with the regularity of the seasons.

"Do you want one?" Suki asks in Cantonese. She offers me a taro milk tea, which I accept with bewilderment.

"You didn't have to get me anything," I say, though taro *is* my favorite flavor.

Suki shrugs. "I work at a boba store. It's free." She shows me her gap-toothed smile, which is oddly charming. "My name's Suki. I go to the University of Hong Kong but work down the street at Sharetea. Osprei offered to give me a ride to my afternoon class, if you don't mind."

"Of course not," I respond, before sipping my milk tea. Suki seems more mature than Osprei's usual sort. For one, she actually attends uni, and two, she hasn't called Osprei any pet names in front of his sister, a courtesy his previous exes didn't afford me.

Suki turns to Osprei. "Make sure you're on time tomorrow. The *Guardian* reporter said she'll meet me at Starbucks at four o'clock sharp. I can't be late."

My head shoots up. "Did you say 'the *Guardian*'?"

Suki pokes at the dregs of her boba with her straw and nods as if this is perfectly ordinary. "They're doing a story on the pro-democracy protest movement."

"But…what does that have to do with you?" I wince, and soften my tone. "I don't mean that you're not qualified—"

Suki laughs. "I get it. Why would some random first-year with pink hair be getting interviewed by the *Guardian?*"

So she is getting interviewed. I bite my lip, unable to mask my brimming curiosity.

"I'm helping organize the HKU student protest movement," she says. "You should come by. We're demonstrating this Sunday against the extradition bill. You might've heard of it?"

A few classmates have mentioned it, but truthfully, I haven't paid the news much heed, what with my SATs coming up. "I know something about a man getting tried in China and that people are annoyed," I say, flushing.

Suki gives me a wry smile. "Annoyed is an understatement." She leans in. "People are fucking furious." She tilts her head and points at me in a conspiratorial manner, and suddenly I understand why Osprei likes her. "And you should be too. Come on Sunday and learn more. It'll be… *educational.* Your brother's going."

I turn my incredulous gaze on Osprei. "You are?"

"Why not?" he says nonchalantly. "Besides—"

"Nix!" Charlie runs toward us at last, his long legs taking the stairs two at a time. His blond hair is tousled and windswept, and his uniform collar creased and turned up. Charlie is just sixteen like me, but already six foot. It's unfair, really. When we first met, we were the same height, but then I stopped growing, and he didn't. I think he leached my growth spurt from me, like a tree that saps nutrients from its neighbor's roots. (Charlie tells me my theory has no scientific basis. He's clearly in denial.) "Sorry I'm late," he pants, out of breath. "Mr. Yim held me back."

I narrow my eyes. "Why?"

"Never mind," he says in a rush, avoiding my gaze. "It doesn't matter." I'm about to press him further when he asks, "How'd your SATs go?"

"Well," I adjust the strap of my backpack. "I—"

"Nix," Osprei interrupts, jerking his head at the car. "Suki's class starts soon."

"Come with us?" I plead to Charlie. I need him as an emotional air bag for when Mom inevitably hears my test results and explodes. "I can tell you in the car."

"Where are you going?" he asks. "And nice to meet you, I don't think we've met." He offers a hand to Suki. "I'm Charlie Henderson, Phoenix's classmate."

"Kwan Suki," she replies. "To answer your question, they're dropping me off at HKU. We're also going to a rally on Sunday. You should come along."

I nudge Charlie, jumping onto this subject change like it's the last lifeboat off the *Titanic*. "Let's check it out. It sounds interesting."

Charlie looks reluctant. "I don't know," he hedges. "I'm taking my SATs soon, and there's college prep...."

I really don't want to talk, listen, or even think about college prep right now. Not when it's uncertain that I'll even get into college. "This will be good material for your personal statement," I tell Charlie. Suki snorts. "You can talk about having a life outside your grades."

"Good point," he acknowledges, though I was mostly joking. (Mostly.)

"So that's settled," Osprei says. "Let's move."

"Hey," Charlie says after getting in the car, looking around at all the half-finished drinks in the cupholders. "Where's my bubble tea?"

Suki suddenly seems not to understand English.

2

Kai

THE APARTMENT IS CLUTTERED AND BARE AT the same time. Cluttered with outdated newspapers, unrecycled beer bottles, rusted picture frames, convenience-store ramen. Bare of proper furniture, a dining table, even a lamp. It's dim inside despite the scorching Hong Kong sun. The curtains are drawn, and dust accumulates on the sill, as if my father hasn't bothered to crack a window in months. Years, even.

I set my solitary suitcase down by the front door, then remove my shoes. I dread the thought of living here alone with my father for the next day. For the next year. For the rest of my life.

So I just won't think about the future.

The past still holds Ma, and Shanghai. It is hard to believe that I boarded a plane and left behind the mainland only yesterday. It is harder to believe that only a year ago, my mother still smiled at me, still told me she would never give me up. Well, Ma lied. I don't blame her. These things run in the family.

According to my passport, I'm a Hong Kong citizen, born in Tung Wah Hospital a few blocks from this apartment. But by all other definitions, I'm Chinese. I'm reminded of this fact about every other second I spend on this island. From the traditional fanti characters stamped on the street signs, to the Mong Kok shopkeepers shouting at me in incomprehensible Cantonese. I barely understand it anymore.

I thought I could snap my fingers and go back to full fluency just like that. It was my mother tongue, after all. Strange that I grew up here when I have no memories of this place. Strange that I'm supposed to believe I'm a Hong Konger, that I belong here.

That the man in the picture frame is my father.

I glance back at the old photograph by the front door. As I stare at my father's face, searching for some ounce of familiarity, all I recognize are those eyes, deep set and wide, dark as charcoal. I realize: It's not because I recognize my father's eyes. It's because I recognize my own.

My bedroom is the size of a storage closet. I can barely fit my suitcase through the door. My few belongings—a wardrobe of monochrome shirts, a collection of sketchbooks and ink pens—are shoved in the bin under the bed. I don't have much stuff. What I did have, I left behind in Shanghai.

Like Ma. I left her behind.

I sink down onto my new bed and pull out my phone, which was an expensive gift from Ma before she got sick, before the hospital bills went into the thousands. Mindlessly, I open WeChat. I go to my most recent chat thread, which features an avatar of a hedgehog. *Ma.*

Flew to Hong Kong today and moved into Father's apartment, I write. His life looks quite lonely and sad. He's definitely still a bachelor, as you guessed. At least he has an extra bed.

My message goes out into the void. I know it will never be read, and yet, pressing send relieves the weight on my chest.

From the plane, Hong Kong looks so small. It's tiny compared to China. Now I think I get why you left. It's the size of a prison cell.

I hunt through my photo gallery and send the picture of the sketch I made on the plane. It's the first drawing I've attempted since Ma passed. The picture's rough, with loose, sloppy lines, but Ma always liked my panoramic drawings. "You need to think bigger," she would say, studying each piece with narrowed eyes. "Don't get too bogged down in the details."

Ma was always the real artist, the one with vision. I just like to copy things, to capture on the page what I see in real life. That way I don't have to let it go. That way it will last forever.

But nothing ever does.

The hedges outside the police academy are perfectly coiffed, like the wigs of rich ladies. I hesitate before the glass doors, but they slide open for me easily, soundless in their judgment.

Inside, I wait for the elevator. My ears are hypervigilant; so are my eyes. At any moment, I could run into my father—for the first time in twelve years. He was too busy to pick me up from the airport, too busy to give me the key code to his apartment, which Neighbor Tao gave me instead. Work is his life; his life is work. So I guess it's only natural he expects the same from me.

The elevator arrives and I wipe my sweaty palms on my trousers before pushing the button for the third floor. Seconds before the doors close, a hand shoots through the crack. I straighten, wondering if I will see my father at last.

Instead, a stocky, moon-faced boy with a silver earring shoulders in. "Sorry, in a hurry," he pants in Cantonese. He presses floor three, never mind that the button is already lit. "You heading to the recruitment office too?"

I nod.

"Don't be nervous, bud," he says. "Oral interview's a joke. The physical exam is where they weed out the losers." He gives me a blatant once-over, appraising me like a car salesman. "Something tells me you won't have trouble in that department, though."

I tip my head but don't respond.

"You don't speak Canto?" he asks in Cantonese.

I shrug, still not facing him. "I prefer Mandarin," I say in Cantonese.

"But your accent's perfect! You must be a natural." He grins and thumps me on the back. "Where'd you move from? Macau?"

"Shanghai."

His grin fades. He removes his hand. "The mainland."

The elevator chimes; I'm the first out.

In the recruitment office, there are two dozen other

candidates sitting in neat rows like passive chess pieces. I've barely taken my seat to fill out the paperwork when an officer appears in the doorway.

"Marco Tsun Hei Wong?"

"That's me," the moon-faced boy says, tugging at his earring. The officer frowns at it before ushering him down the hall.

I look down at my application, filling in the appropriate boxes. *Secondary School Graduation Date: 2019. Age: 17. Height: 1.83 meters.* I hesitate before *Name,* the easiest of questions. Do I spell my name in traditional or simplified? Do I pronounce my name in Mandarin or Cantonese? Do I claim to be a native, or do I tell the truth about where I'm from?

"Zhang Kai En?"

A female training officer smiles at me, motioning for me to follow. I match her quick strides down the carpeted corridor, passing several rooms with interviews in progress. We cross through a common area, where I hear hushed voices issuing from the kitchen. One voice gives me pause.

I see him as we round the corner. His face is cast in shadow, but I can make out a defined jaw, salt-and-pepper hair. He's tall, and there's something about the way he carries himself, a slight tilt to his stance....

My heart drops. I feel a swooping sensation in my stomach and remember I haven't eaten anything today.

"We're planning to send some of the trainees undercover," the man drinking coffee next to him says. "The ones who can pass for uni students."

My father says something so low I don't catch it. His voice, a gravelly rumble, sounds like it does in my dreams.

"It'll get worse before it gets better," his companion responds. "Those protesters are like spoiled kids. They don't know how to take no for an answer."

My father turns toward the watercooler, toward me. He is a handsome man, there's no doubt about it. Strong brow, deep-set eyes, high nose bridge. My hands itch to draw his profile on paper, render it with acrylics, or maybe oils if I could afford them. I want to use color for his lips, which are thin and curved and dark, so dark they're almost purple. His skin is tan, weathered and darkened from sun. There's a scar on his neck, and his veins are greenish blue. *Yes*, I think, *I would use color for this portrait.*

Then I recall my mother's face, the memory trailed by a stab of guilt. I always thought Ma was beautiful, in the way every child admires their mother, like sprouts turning toward the sun. She was called homely by most, even my grandmother, but she never minded much. She thought looks were only useful in what they got you, never of any value in themselves. I remember a nosy shopkeeper who kept eyeing us together, who claimed Ma was lucky for having such a handsome son.

"Where did he come from?" the shopkeeper asked. "He looks nothing like you."

Ma didn't answer. But now I know: I look like my father.

The interviewer taps me on my shoulder. "Zhang Kai En?"

Father hears my name and turns. I watch the cool appraisal in his face, the lowering of his brows. It's an expression I can't place until I've walked into the interview room. That's when I realize what it is. Indifference.

He doesn't give a fuck about me.

Numbly, I sit in the lone folding chair before a panel of four officers. I can barely see their faces through the blur of their matching caps and uniforms. In my clouded vision, they all look the same. They all look like my father.

"Let's start with an easy one. Why do you want to become a police officer?"

Heat creeps up my neck. Why do I want to become a police officer? It's a stable income, I guess, solid health insurance, a way to pass the days. It's also what my father asked me to do. "Asked" is a misnomer. He didn't exactly leave me a choice, did he?

"My father is an inspector with the Police Tactical Unit," I say, my voice hoarse.

The man on the left leans forward. "Who's your father?"

"Isn't it obvious?" the woman says. "Look at him. He's the spitting image of Officer Cheung."

Murmurs go around the panel. I can tell by their eager expressions that Father is respected here, revered even. Oddly, I envy them. I wish I could respect my father too. But I don't know him. "He's always impressed upon me the importance of the police force." My father and I have never had a real conversation. "So I've always wanted to become a police officer, like him."

The lies feel like sandpaper on my tongue, rough and abrasive. I wanted to be an artist, like my ma. But Ma wasn't an artist, not really. She was a public restroom cleaner, a sanitation worker, a waitress when times were good. She worked three jobs to put me through art classes. After she passed, Grandma admitted that Ma used her medical stipend for my art supplies. So I guess she died so I could make a stupid surrealist oil painting that explores the nuances between adolescence and the uncanny. And I was naive enough to think that stuff actually mattered.

So I grit my teeth and lie. I lie and I lie and I lie.

Marco finds me after the interview. "Kai, is it?" he asks. His silver earring has disappeared. "How'd your interview go?"

I start for the exit; he follows me. "How do you know my name?"

"Everyone's talking about you. Your dad's one of the big shots, right? Officer Cheung." He grins. "He's a celebrity around here, but of course you already know all about that."

The elevator's stuck on floor two. "We're not close."

"Hmph," Marco says. "Well, he took down a human trafficking ring a decade back. It's practically legend. That's how he got the—" He motions to his neck. "One of the triad bosses tried to strangle him with a chain. They say he doesn't back down, ever."

I decide to take the stairs. Of course, Marco follows.

"Maybe with your dad's connections, you could even get us the undercover gig," he continues, panting as he keeps pace with me. "Apparently, they're selecting the top trainees to go undercover as uni students. How fun would that be?"

I shove open the exit door at the base of the stairs, squinting against the afternoon light. Even the sun feels brighter here than in Shanghai, though maybe that's only due to the lack of smog. It's a beautiful day, and I resent Hong Kong for its beauty. I wonder—would Ma have lived if she'd stayed here? She would've had health insurance at least.

"I took acting classes back in primary school, you know." Marco is still rattling on next to me, but I find my irritation subsiding. As we leave the police academy, the tension in my shoulders dissipates. "We could pretend to be intellectuals, studious nerd types," he says, laughing. He clearly sees himself as the opposite.

"You could start by running your mouth less," I tell him.

He snickers. "Touché. Maybe you'll be the nerd on your own. I'll be the jock, what do you think?" He flexes his bicep. "All the ladies will come running."

"I'm pretty sure that's illegal."

"You're right," he sighs, sounding rueful. "Rule number one about undercover: no getting involved with your marks."

Phoenix

"NIX!" I WAKE TO AN EARTHQUAKE, WHICH I realize blearily is Robin pounding on the door. "Are you awake yet?"

"Now I am!" The door crashes open and I groan. Recently, my younger sister, Robin, has learned to pick the locks on all our bedroom doors using only a bent paper clip. She's also an International Math Olympiad medalist, but that's a less crucial detail. I throw a pillow at her as I bury my face back under the covers, hiding from the noonday sun.

She jumps on my bed. "I think you'll want to get ready."

"Why?" I didn't sleep until three AM because I was watching *Friends* reruns and avoiding life's responsibilities. Mom's signed me up for a retributive SAT boot camp, which starts tomorrow, in order to get me into ninetieth percentile scores by the time college apps roll around.

"Charlie's downstairs, and Mom's asking him about his SAT study tips." Robin pauses. "She also asked him if he's dating now."

I throw off the covers so violently I nearly take Robin with them. "Mom needs to mind her own business!"

"You know she wants the two of you to end up together. She thinks he'll help you get into Yale, and then you guys can keep each other company in America." Robin pouts, following me to my bathroom. "You're all leaving me behind."

"Don't worry," I say, splashing water on my face. "With Osprei's grades, he's not leaving anytime soon."

I tie up my hair in a messy bun. My eyes are droopy from lack of sleep, and my left eye's developed a triple crease, giving me a raccoon-chic look. I remember we're going to the demonstration today in Wan Chai and smear on some sunscreen.

"You should wear makeup," Robin advises me. "Charlie's wearing a button-down. No tie, though."

I sigh. That'll make Mom happy—too happy, as if we're getting ready to go to afternoon tea, when the reality is far less glamorous. If Suki shows up here with her dyed hair and ripped jeans…

The doorbell rings downstairs.

Robin squeals with excitement and rushes out of my room. I hear her light footsteps tripping down the stairs like an off-kilter drumbeat, but it's just Uncle Chow delivering more of Mom's meditation crystals.

I open my closet. Today's Sunday, and I don't have to wear my school uniform. I pick out a sunflower dress because it's unseasonably warm for April. Then I grab my camera from my desk and run downstairs, very, very late.

"Morning," I call through the kitchen archway. Charlie's sitting at the island countertop, eating sliced dragon fruit. Mom's washing her smoothie machine. (She's been on some sort of juice cleanse since forever.) Robin is digging into her congee with her left hand and spilling it all over the table. Lately, she's been trying to teach herself to be ambidextrous; she keeps saying it's just a matter of mindset.

Charlie grins at me. "You look nice."

Mom swerves to catch my reaction, her eyes widening as if her favorite movie star, Tony Leung, just walked through the front door. Ignoring her, I pull Charlie up by the arm and haul him toward the door.

"Where are you going?" Mom calls, trailing behind us.

"We're studying!"

"Really?" Robin asks, like she's the next Detective Conan. "Where's your backpack, then? And why are you bringing your new camera with you?"

I look skyward as Charlie covers for me: "We're trying out my study materials today. I told Mrs. Lam we'd try Princeton Review instead of Kaplan." He pauses. "As for the camera, I asked Nix if I could see it. Neat birthday gift, Mrs. Lam."

Mom smiles so big her eyes practically disappear. "Do you want to bring oranges with you?" she asks quickly. "I can pack some for you."

"No, it's fine—"

"What about grapes—"

"We're fine, Mom. Bye! Aan di gin!" I slam the door before she can argue.

"It's like she thinks your place is some barren wasteland," I complain to Charlie as we walk down the driveway.

He wrinkles his brows. "Does she not like it when you come over?"

I shrug. "It's not just your place. She suspects I'll starve every time I leave the house. I wonder how she'll survive me going off to the States."

Charlie laughs. "Maybe she'll sabotage your SAT results."

I frown. "At this rate, she doesn't have to. I'm doing that myself."

"Hey." He takes me by my shoulder. "You can retake the exam." He eyes me. "Do you know what happened last time?"

I try to swallow the lump in my throat. Mom asked me the same question; so did Robin. "I don't know," I say, my voice small. "Well, that morning Osprei did let slip that Mom and Dad were filing for a divorce."

Charlie swears. "Sorry, Nix," he says. "I'm sure it was kind of a shock."

I snort. "I wasn't surprised. No one was. That would be like being surprised that your hundred-and-twenty-year-old grandma just croaked."

"Hey," Charlie says. "My grandma's only in her seventies."

"Hypothetical grandma." I scuff my sneaker against the concrete. In truth, it wasn't the shock that got to me but the apathy. I felt a little sick then, sick with myself. I just thought, *What's the point?* I wasn't doing any of this for *me*. I don't care about getting into an American university; I care about pleasing my parents. I care about keeping my family together.

But no matter what I do, everything falls apart.

"Mom expected me to go abroad this summer for the

Yale merit program," I say. "Now I won't qualify with these fiftieth percentile scores. I'll be stuck here in the city."

"Will that be so bad? I'll be here too."

"Interning with your godmother."

"Yeah, but we'll hang out weekends." He squeezes my arm. "Don't take it so hard. You'll improve with practice. And if you don't, there are other ways...."

I sense he's about to tell me why Mr. Yim held him back after class the other day. "C," I cut him off. "I'm not interested in cheating."

"It's not cheating!" he exclaims. "It's gaming the system and using the resources we've been given—"

"Are we interrupting something?"

We spin around. Osprei and Suki emerge from the hedges, both covered with leaves and dirt. Osprei is grinning like *he* caught *us* red-handed.

"Did you just roll out of a bush?" I ask, in the rude voice I reserve for my brother.

"Sort of," Suki smirks. "I slept over."

"You what?" Mom was so oblivious this morning. "How did you get out?"

"We took the window," Osprei explains, dusting leaves off Suki.

Charlie looks impressed as he eyes the distance from the lawn to the second-story window.

Suki yawns. "Honestly, your house is a mansion. I don't think your mom would hear a thing even if we conducted a taiko drumming ceremony."

"You'd be surprised," I tell her. "I don't think my mom sleeps at night."

"She did seem a bit...tense," Charlie admits. "The divorce must be hard on her."

"Where's the protest happening?" Osprei asks, changing the subject with the bluntness of a dull ax.

"Wan Chai." Suki checks her phone. "We better head over now."

As we head down the block toward the MTR station, Charlie keeps pace with me. Flashing Suki a suspicious look, he asks me, "Are you sure about this?"

I tilt my head at him. "Aren't you curious, at least?"

"About what?" He looks miffed. "We should be following the law, Nix. We don't want to screw things up *now*, during college apps. You know how admissions looks carefully at your whole record. Your criminal record too."

I roll my eyes. Protesting isn't illegal. Only rioting is. "Chill, C. We're not getting arrested. We're just taking a look. It's Southorn Playground. It's not illegal to take a walk in the park, is it?"

He sighs, uneasy but acquiescing. The truth is, I know if Mom heard about this, she would *not* be happy, but Mom wouldn't be happy with a lot of things. A little civil action should be the least of her worries.

When we get off the train at Wan Chai, the atmosphere feels charged. There are more people than usual milling about, which says a lot because Hennessy Road is famous for its epic crowds. Charlie latches on to my wrist as we fold into the throngs of people gathering at Southorn Playground, our little group merging with many. I feel bodies press in from all sides and cling closer to Charlie as we thread our way through the park, Suki taking the lead.

Within the crowd, the temperature rises several degrees, all our bodies pressed together like folded paper-doll chains. Most people are young, like us—students mainly, by the looks of them. They're dressed in black T-shirts and black jeans, with black baseball caps to match. I feel awkward in my sunflower dress, as if I'm a guest who missed the dress code, crashed the wrong party.

Suki spots a tall boy waving a green Hong Kong University flag like a tour guide and waves at him. She hurries forward, quickening her strides, and it feels like Charlie's going to dislocate my arm in his efforts to keep pace. The HKUers have guarded their own coveted spot beneath the shade of an oak tree, just off the football field.

"Ming-lai." Suki nods at the boy with the HKU flag. "Haa lo."

Ming-lai greets her quickly, handing her a rolled-up poster. We all lean in as she unfurls it.

光復香港, 時代革命.
LIBERATE HK—REVOLUTION OF OUR TIME.

"What does it mean?" Charlie asks in English.

Ming-lai scowls at him. "Who are you?"

Suki raises her hands in a conciliatory manner. "You've met Osprei already, and this is Phoenix, and Charlie," she says, introducing us to Ming-lai in Cantonese. "All students. They're here to...learn." She gives us her fiercest grin, which leaves me both relieved and uneasy.

Ming-lai studies us, scrunching his mouth to one side as he thinks. He has a sincere face, and I can tell Osprei feels amicably toward him by the way his posture relaxes. (Osprei is easy to read, like a puppy.)

Meanwhile, Suki digs around in the boxes by the tree, and I'm expecting her to pull out sticks or rocks to throw, but instead she passes around a few plastic water bottles. (Maybe I watch too many movies.) "So here's the deal," she says. "I hope most of you have at least heard of the extradition bill, right?"

Charlie raises his hand as if he's still in the classroom. "The bill was proposed a couple months ago. Because that Hong Konger murdered his girlfriend in Taiwan, but got arrested for it here, so he couldn't be sent back to Taiwan for trial. Then the government came up with the bill so our city doesn't become some sort of criminal haven."

"That makes it sound all fine and dandy, but it's a lot more complicated in reality." Suki crosses her arms over her chest. "If this law gets passed, it allows *anyone* who pisses off China to be extradited out of Hong Kong and tried on the mainland. Think of what happens to political organizers and activists."

"People like you," Charlie says.

"People like all of us!" Ming-lai interjects. "Everyone should be an activist."

Charlie bristles. This conversation is rubbing him the wrong way. "Some people just want to live normal lives... and get a real job, you know?"

I nudge Charlie's shoe, but he doesn't get the memo.

"A normal life?" Ming-lai narrows his eyes like an attack dog. "This is the new normal, kid. Look at what's happening around us. China is taking over. And if you want to just 'get a real job' and ignore the writing on the wall, soon there will be no Hong Kong. There will only be China."

"I get it, that sucks." Charlie presses on. "But we're just a little island compared to a huge nation that's been around since, well, since the Qin Dynasty. There's not really any hope that we'll...." He falters, sensing Suki's dark glower.

Osprei steps in. "Charlie," he says, in a friendly tone only I can tell is false. "No one's forcing you to be here. If you want to head home, no hard feelings."

Charlie looks from Osprei to me. I step closer to him, but before I can speak, Suki leans forward.

"Look, I know how you feel. I was there once," she says in a gentler voice. "You're thinking short term—what to eat tomorrow, how you'll score on your exams. I was that same four-point-oh kid. The one who only cared about studying and surviving." She glances at Osprei, eyes solemn. "But there comes a time when you realize there's more to life than this. And if you want a future, an actual future, then you have to stop keeping your head down.

"They want you looking at the ground, focused on putting one foot in front of the other, so focused you don't notice you're near the edge of a cliff. That's what it is. That's what Ming-lai means by the writing on the wall. That's what he means by no more Hong Kong." Her voice strengthens with conviction. "So, yes, you can head home now, if you want. But pretty soon you won't have a home to return to."

My heart is thudding in my chest. Her words have a magnetism to them, brought alive by the resonance of her voice. I'm caught in the magnitude and *urgency* of her ask, so much so that I barely hear the whistle blowing overhead and the rally speaker shouting through the megaphone.

When I think of my own future, I think of what Mom and Dad want for me. I think of what would disappoint them and what would make them proud. But that kind of thinking has never given me anything more than a brief, momentary relief—the sense that I've put off an inevitable anxiety for a little while longer. I don't know what I'm hoping for, what I'm moving toward. All this time, I've just been... *moving.*

The others have turned their backs to listen to some famous barrister giving a speech. I tug at Charlie's sleeve. "Just stay and watch," I whisper. "Please?"

Around us, the crowd cheers and picks up a chant. "No China rendition! No China rendition!" Suki starts jumping up and down, waving her poster, until Osprei boosts her up on his shoulders, locking his arms around her legs.

Slowly, we march down Hennessy Road, cars honking from the highway above us. I can't see an end to the sea of people ahead of or behind me. Though we move at an ant's pace, sweat trickles down my back. The air is sticky and wet for spring, and the crush of bodies traps all heat. Still, I don't mind. Inside the crowd, I feel... safe. Protected.

I wonder how many people are here. It feels like thousands, even tens of thousands, mostly students but working professionals and old folks too. Hong Kong, famous for its apolitical, indifferent citizens, is actually coming together, uniting in a common front. I uncap my camera lens and start shooting.

"Nix, stay with us!" Charlie calls.

I nearly get whacked in the face by a grandma flapping her fan as I try to push through the crowd. "Nei mou si aa maa?" she asks me. I give her a thumbs-up. "Be careful," she adds. She points at the cops, all stoic as statues, standing guard near the restaurants and shops bordering the road.

I wrinkle my nose. "It's not illegal to protest."

The grandma gives me a cynical look. "For now."

I catch up to Charlie as someone starts unfurling a giant white banner. Ming-lai grabs on to one edge and motions for me to do the same. I take hold of the cloth, along with a dozen others, all hanging on to keep the banner from crumpling to the ground. The characters are so big I can hardly read them.

"Tung sam zat sau," Ming-lai explains, seeing my expression. Tung sam zat sau is a singyu, a traditional four-character idiom. It translates directly to "heartbroken." But it also implies betrayal, devastation. It implies a self at war. He points at the drone overhead. "So they can read it from up there."

I follow his gaze. There are cameras everywhere, I realize. Photographers taking pictures from the skybridge, journalists interviewing protesters inside the mall, even cameras zooming overhead, suspended on drones. All this is for media attention. Because Hong Kong doesn't have a chance of standing on its own. Its only hope lies in getting other people around the world to care. But it doesn't matter if there are a thousand people out here today, ten thousand, a million—it's still not enough. Because China is so much bigger.

Against all the fanfare, Charlie edges closer to me, so that his voice is in my ear. "They have an agenda, Nix."

So he's just put it together too.

"Everyone has an agenda," I say. "You study politics. You know that."

He sighs. "It's not that I don't agree with them," he says. "It's valid, what they're saying. But also impractical. What are they going to do? Pick up Hong Kong and move the whole island like a chess piece?"

I try to smile. "If it were a chess game, we'd win."

"But it's not," he says darkly. "It's real life, and we're on the losing side."

Phoenix

OUT OF POLITICAL PURPOSE OR OBLIGATION TO his girlfriend, Osprei volunteers all of us to help move and store the leftover rally materials. Cleanup duty takes us almost four hours, so we're all equally starving and comparing stomach growls by the time we're finished. It's around ten thirty PM when we finally drag the last boxes to Ming-lai's uncle's van.

Mom hasn't texted yet, which is both a relief and a worry, but at least she thinks I'm still at Charlie's, memorizing English verb conjugations.

"I'll treat you to a siu je meal," Ming-lai tells us, decidedly more agreeable now that the demonstration was a success. "As thanks for all your help."

Suki laughs, wiping her dusty hands on her jeans. "Don't bother. They're all filthy rich. They should treat us as apology for tax evasion."

Charlie looks up from his phone. "Are you accusing our families of embezzlement?"

I shove Charlie. "C'mon, C, you know she's joking!" He's not normally this sensitive, but something about Suki and Ming-lai sets him off. It's like he's asking for a fight.

Thankfully, Suki looks amused. To Ming-lai, she explains, "They go to Whitney American School."

"Ah. International school kids," he says. "You're expats?"

I shrug begrudgingly. I hate it when people find out I wasn't raised here; it immediately makes them treat me differently. Like I'm a representative of the entire North American continent. We moved back to Hong Kong only six years ago, but I barely remember North Carolina anymore. Initially, the reason we came back was school, and then "to work on the family"—but look how well that turned out. Six years later and Mom and Dad are divorced. Now it's like Dad's moved out of Hong Kong because we've moved back here. Like we're playing some eternal game of duck, duck, goose.

"I grew up in the States, but I came back for middle school." Then I add: "And my parents are from Hong Kong."

"That explains the flawless accent," Ming-lai says, making me blush.

Osprei groans as he sets the final box of supplies in the crowded van. "Christ, let that be the last one."

"Your prayers are answered," Suki replies. "Siu je calls."

We all cheer at that. Osprei wants lobster, but Suki claims she's craving claypot rice and really, absolutely needs it because it's that time of the month for her....

We get claypot rice.

The restaurant is near the site of the demonstration, so

it's overflowing with people, even at this late hour. Siu je is a Hong Kong thing—midnight meal—for when you have that late-night craving and want to eat a second dinner. That's why restaurants stay open as late as three or four in the morning. Mom always threatens to flay us when we miss curfew, but it's worth it for the food: crispy glistening Chinese sausage and cured pork belly cooked in a traditional pot made of clay over a charcoal stove with rice and soy sauce and green onions, so that the rice comes out slightly charred on the edges and just delicious.

We pack into the steamy-hot restaurant, then secure a corner of a long, narrow table already crowded with strangers. There's no such thing as personal space here. Ming-lai goes to hunt for more chairs as I plunk down beside a group of university students.

Osprei, sitting across from me, jabs me in the shoulder. "Hey," he says, monkeying for my attention. "Isn't that your friend from school over there? Melanie, was it?"

I look over my shoulder at the table behind us. She's sitting with other classmates of ours, and they're all wearing shirts from the rally. "Melody," I correct him, "the girl you dated for less than a week. She liked you for years, you know."

Osprei looks mildly regretful, secretly pleased. I have a theory he's an overgrown peacock masquerading as a human boy. (I like that theory because it means we have no genetic overlap.)

"Melody's here?" Charlie exclaims, craning his neck to find her in the crowd.

I wave. Melody waves back, though she looks comforted by the distance between our group and hers. Osprei gives her a bashful smile that she doesn't return. "Orchid and Jiahui are with her," I say. "Looks like a group of them went to the rally together."

Charlie's face is surprised and a little relieved. "I can't believe even our classmates came."

Osprei chuckles, but I get what Charlie means. Our snobby international school is not exactly known for being radical.

"There must've been thousands of people there with us today." Ming-lai is back with more chairs. Our group spreads out to make space, and as I move my chair back to open up room for Suki, I knock elbows with the boy to my right. He's left-handed, and his chopsticks clatter to the floor.

"Aiya! I'm so sorry," I exclaim, crouching to retrieve them. He leans over at the exact same moment, and our heads bump together just like the chopsticks. Briefly, I see stars.

"Are you all right?" he asks, and his low, raspy voice makes my stomach dip.

I nod, my vision clearing. Beneath the table, I can see that his shoes are scuffed and the soles worn thin. There are Sharpie drawings along the rims, drawn and shaded with remarkable detail. I squint at the melting clocks at the toe of his left shoe, which look three-dimensional and lifelike and somehow also sad.

"Did you draw that yourself?" I ask, impressed.

He shrugs. The lighting is dim, but I can just make out his large, dark eyes, framed by an open brow.

Why is my heart pounding all of a sudden? "You're—talented."

"It's just a copy," he says bluntly. "The artist..."

"Salvador Dalí," I fill in, gratified to have taken AP Art History last semester, if only for the grade inflation. "But my copy would look nothing like that."

His eyes flash briefly, but his expression remains unreadable. "You're an artist too?"

"No." I shake my head, before thinking of my photography. My cheeks grow warm. "At least, I don't think so."

His answering smile is rueful. "I tell myself the same thing." He pauses, which lends weight to his words. "But maybe you are."

With that, he reaches for one chopstick; I remember myself and pick up the other. When he gets to his feet, I'm flustered by how tall he is. He's nearly the same height as Charlie, with lean muscles evident through his thin black T-shirt. He wears black trousers and black shoes, and on his broad-shouldered frame, the choice doesn't look lazy but instead artistic, aesthetic even.

"Here," I say, rising. "I can get you another pair." I start toward the waiter, but he stops me.

"It's fine," he says. "I'm done eating anyway."

He returns the chopsticks to his bowl, grabs his phone from the table, and heads for the door. I catch his face in the lamplight as he's paying at the cashier stand. God, he's so good-looking. Too good-looking for me, but I'm content to watch from afar. His complexion is dark, and so are his features: black hair, black eyes, dark lips. He looks like someone you'd see in an old film, with a reel turning and a grand piano playing in the background.

I'm not the only one noticing. Melody whispers to her friend as he pockets his change and steps through the plastic curtains, turning the corner almost immediately so that I lose sight of him. Was he eating by himself? I thought he was with the group of uni students beside us, but they're still in the middle of their siu je. Maybe he came alone.

"Earth to Nix." Charlie snaps his fingers in front of my face. "We're ordering. What do you want?"

I glance at the remains of the boy's bowl before it's swept away by the waiter. He got chicken and mushroom, and all of a sudden that sounds delicious. "Chicken and mushroom, please," I say to the waiter.

Charlie eyes me with suspicion. "But you always get pork belly and sausage."

"Is it a crime to try something new?" I smile. "I'm a curious person, okay?"

"What's piquing your curiosity?" Suki teases. "Something tells me it's not claypot rice."

Charlie scowls. Thankfully, Osprei, with his usual self-absorbedness, is not following the conversation and interrupts to announce: "The numbers are out!" He reads the news from his phone. "Civil Human Rights Front reported upwards of a hundred thousand people participated in the march today."

Suki lets out an emphatic cheer, earning her a dirty look from the waiter. "We're living it." She turns to us, that elusive magnetic quality growing in her voice. "We're living in history."

"Human Rights Front always overestimates the numbers," Charlie says. "I just read the police only counted twenty thousand."

Before he can dampen the mood, I cut him off to ask

Osprei, "Aa Go, since when have you started following the news?" The Osprei I know exclusively watches ESPN.

"Suki made me," he answers without a hint of shame.

"A prerequisite for dating." Suki smirks. "Take notes, Phoenix."

"They're calling for Carrie Lam to resign from her position as chief executive," Ming-lai reads aloud.

Suki sniffs. "She's just a convenient scapegoat for the ones actually in charge."

Ming-lai keeps scrolling through his phone. "At least the reporters are taking it seriously."

"Media always makes a fuss," Charlie mutters.

"You know—" Osprei leans forward on his forearms, setting his phone down. "It's not just the usual rabble-rousing this time. Things are changing around here."

For Osprei to be saying that, skirt-chasing, class-cutting, lazy Osprei, who has a list of cares shorter than you can count on one hand and the attention span of a baby squirrel... "So you're all in, then," I say carefully, because everyone else is listening. "This is *your* thing now too."

He slings a casual arm around Suki. Everything is always easy with him, easy as pie. "Sure, it was Suki's thing first. And I went along for fun. But I'm starting to get it too. On my own. I mean, like Suki said, it's fucking history. If we do nothing now, just blink and Hong Kong's gone."

"You don't think Beijing will wait?" I ask, my voice uncertain. "At least until 2047?" The "one-country, two-systems" principle expires in 2047. Until then, China is supposed to leave Hong Kong alone.

Osprei snorts. "Of course not," he says, without missing

a beat. "If we don't fight this bill, there'll be new laws by this time next year, each one worse than the last. Aa Mui, mark my words. Imagine getting your face scanned every time you walked into a convenience store. Or getting your phone calls recorded. Or Dad not being able to do business unless he joins the Communist Party."

Charlie laughs. "If that happens, we move to London."

"Only cowards run," Osprei says cockily.

To my surprise, Suki glares at him. "Are you calling my uncle a coward?"

Osprei pauses, blinking. "I forgot...."

"Then don't generalize," she says coldly, though I notice her ears are red.

"Your uncle's leaving?" I ask in the lull.

She nods curtly. "He's moving to Taiwan, but keep it on the down-low. China isn't a big fan of his." At my look of confusion, she adds, "He runs New Pages, the independent bookstore over by Admiralty."

Osprei glances at Suki as if for permission to speak; she just shrugs. "It has all the political publications the government refuses to publish on the mainland," Osprei explains. "People fly over from Beijing just to access those books. They're banned everywhere else."

Suki's brows dip. "I'm worried for him. He's all alone, and if the police decide to..." She trails off, hunching into herself.

Osprei squeezes her shoulder. "He has us," he says. "We'll help him."

Suki kisses him on the lips, and apparently all is forgiven. Thankfully, our dishes arrive before they can devolve into further PDA. The fragrant steam wafts up around us. I can see the crispy rice, singed at the edges, sprinkled with green onions and sesame seeds on top.

"I can die happy now," Suki says, her mouth full before the rest of us can even lift our chopsticks.

I reach for my phone to Instagram the food. As they say, *Camera eats first.* Charlie rolls his eyes next to me; he hates sharing food with me for this exact reason.

"You should download Telegram." Suki nods at my phone. "It's how we student organizers get the word out. It hides your identity so the dogs can't track you."

"Dogs?" I ask.

"Ging caat."

A shiver runs down my spine. *Police.* I tap my phone on, then blink. The phone I'm holding is the same model as my own, with the same transparent case, but there's a scuff beneath the camera and two parallel scratches at the bottom. And when the screen lights up, the wallpaper staring back at me isn't one I recognize, some foreign city colored with shades of gray.

This isn't my phone.

I set it back on the table and slide it to my right, next to the empty stool. I start patting my pockets, then remember I'm wearing a dress. I bend to look beneath the table, wondering if it fell in the commotion. All I see is Osprei and Suki playing footsy. Ugh.

Then I remember the boy, how quickly he grabbed his phone off the table. *My* phone.

I yelp as the realization hits me and pick up the other phone again. When I turn it back on, I realize he has no lock screen. What kind of person doesn't use a password? I can't help myself; I swipe in. WeChat is already running; the first thing I see on the screen is a text conversation between him and a...hedgehog avatar. Name: *Ma.* I smile, reading his most recent text. 10:04 PM. This is the street I now live on. I think you would like it. It's very noisy no matter the time of day, and there are people outside constantly. The ladies selling herbs downstairs always heckle me when I come home. They like to flirt and laugh at their own jokes. I think you would find them amusing.

I scroll up to see the photo he sent. When I click on it, I realize it's not a photo but a drawing, or a photo of a drawing. It looks quick, slapdash, but his talent is obvious. He must be some sort of art student. Which school would he be attending? CUHK? Or PolyU? It seems like he just moved here recently. A university freshman, then? And his mom is still back in Shanghai? His Cantonese did seem to have a slight accent.

I turn back to the sketch. Laundry lines swoop from apartment balconies, drying jeans and underwear waving like flags in the invisible wind. I see the ginseng herb stalls and a lackluster 7-Eleven sandwiched between them. It's a busy side street, and by the looks of how old everything is, probably Mong Kok or Sheung Wan.

"Nix," Charlie is saying. "Did you hear what I just said?"

I raise my head as if surfacing from underwater. My bowl is in front of me, untouched. I make a decision the way I usually do—in a split second. I want to see that boy and his melting clocks again. I take a few hasty bites, then jump to my feet. "I'm heading out. It's late and I have SAT prep tomorrow." I know if I tell the truth, Charlie will tell me it's dangerous or Osprei will try to tag along, which would be an instant mood killer.

Charlie stands. "I'll take you back."

I shake my head. "C, it's fine, honestly. You live on the opposite end of the island, and you should finish your food."

"You should too!"

I ignore this. "Osprei, can you cover me?" He gives me a perfunctory nod; I know I didn't have to ask. "Thanks again, Suki, Ming-lai."

"We'll see each other again soon," Suki says, raising one hand in farewell.

Charlie looks like he wants to protest, but I'm already halfway across the room.

Kai

AS I EXIT THE MONG KOK MTR STATION, A LIGHT rain speckles the streets, coating the cement with a sheen like gossamer silk. The clouds above are plump and bulging, ready to burst at the seams. I don't need to be a weatherman to know there'll be a downpour tonight.

I reach for my phone to take a photo; I can sketch it later using ink pens, or maybe watercolor. It's a beautiful image: *Hong Kong Wakes to Rain.*

Something in me stirs. I haven't traveled, ever—unless you count the middle-of-the-night escape from Hong Kong to Shanghai. Once we moved, we never left again. As if Ma was afraid we'd lose more than we'd already lost, bits and pieces of ourselves scattered in different cities around the world.

But Ma wanted me to travel, to make fine art, to be

inspired and to inspire. She wanted for me what she once wanted for herself, before she met my father.

Her story goes downhill from there.

Here in Hong Kong, there's so much I haven't seen. But it's strange, knowing I can never show her. How can I even draw anymore without her feedback and critique? How can I distinguish between good and bad?

My phone chimes. It makes a weird bell noise it's never made before. I turn it on and see who the message is from: Mom. My heart stops in my chest.

The text is simple, short: When are you coming home?

Then the phone chimes once more. Is Osprei with you?

Osprei...the name sounds familiar, but I struggle to place it. Then I remember: the students sitting next to me at the restaurant. Protesters, clearly.

I try to swipe open the phone, but it's locked with a password. I try a random combination. Incorrect entry. Please try again.

It hits me all at once. The girl who knocked into me. The one who recognized Salvador Dalí's work. Who said she wasn't an artist, or at least, didn't think so.

I saw the uncertainty on her face, and I understood.

Even after years of art school, the doubt never leaves you.

Her phone buzzes again. It's Suki. Got your number from Osprei. There's a planning session at HKU this Friday. Wanna come by?

Planning session for what?

And download Telegram ASAP. We don't want to leave a trail for the dogs.

I raise my head to look around, as if I'm in a simulation,

but I'm not, and there's no one watching me. Pedestrians hurry past into the MTR station, eager to escape the impending storm. For an impossible second, I want to merge with the crowd and ignore my responsibilities, my future, my life that doesn't feel like my own.

Do I report this to Sergeant Leung or…my father? Would that impress him, that I'd gotten a lead so quickly? Or would he dismiss it as nothing? I shake my head. They could be planning a birthday party for all I know.

A birthday party that requires Telegram?

I turn the phone over in my hands. So the protesters call us dogs. Animals who answer at Beijing's beck and call. They think they're better than us, don't they? They think everyone from the mainland is a brainwashed puppet, that the only thing we care about is money.

The resentment curdles in my stomach. I don't *want* to care about money. I want to be like those rich kids, the ones who can switch easily from Mandarin to English to Cantonese, like rivers diverging and merging without pause. The ones who know their families have their backs, who know their future is guaranteed.

But who am I kidding? That's never been me.

The phone rings, jolting me from my thoughts. I look carefully at the digits. It's *my* number. Hesitantly, I answer. "Wei?"

There's a quick exhale on the other end. "Hey, you picked up. This—this is Phoenix. I think we switched phones accidentally. You didn't have a lock on your phone so I…called you."

Damn it! I'm trying to remember if I have anything

incriminating on there when she asks, "Do you want to meet now? To trade?" She's switched to Mandarin, as if she thinks I didn't understand her before. Her Mandarin has no accent. But at the restaurant, I recall her group throwing around English words mixed with Cantonese. So where is she from?

I realize she's expecting a response. "Yes," I blurt out in Mandarin. "Where are you?"

"Still in Wan Chai," she says. "But I'm heading back to Repulse Bay. Is Ocean Park Station convenient for you? We should meet in a public place...somewhere safe....How about the park on Wong Chuk Hang Road?"

"Sure," I say, with no idea where that is. I'll figure it out.

"Don't worry, a lot of people are usually there at night," she says, as if I'm concerned for *my* safety. I almost laugh.

"Okay. Zai jian."

It takes over half an hour to navigate there without a GPS and in the dark. Ma would tell me to ask for directions, but there's nothing I hate more than bothering strangers for help. I make it to Ocean Park using the MTR map, then proceed to get horribly lost on the surface streets. A few late-night shopkeepers throw me confused glances when I circle down the same alley again, but thank the skies no one actually stops me to ask what the hell I'm doing.

When I finally locate the park gate, there's a girl standing on the pitch, her arms clasped around herself as she hops from foot to foot to stay warm. I recognize her dress with loud sunflowers printed all over the skirt. Her complexion is pale as porcelain and her hair shiny like a shampoo ad. She practically smells of money. For a delusional second, I wonder if I could walk up to her and pass through her like mist, as if we exist on such different planes that we could never cross paths.

"Hey!" She waves with her entire arm, as if calling from across the ocean.

I jog over, trying to ignore my rising trepidation. It's eerily quiet out here, away from Central.

"Did you get lost?" she asks. I notice that she's shivering.

"A little," I admit. "Sorry. Did you wait long?"

She shakes her head, more out of politeness than honesty, I can tell. "But I'm worried if you can get back now. You don't live on Repulse Bay, right?"

Because I don't look rich like her. "I live in Mong Kok."

"Tian ah, I knew it! The MTR just closed. I can ask my driver to—"

"It's fine." She has a *driver*? "I can find my way back on my own."

She tugs on her earlobe. "You're not…from here, are you?" I realize we've been speaking in Mandarin. As if she took one look at my face, read me, and knew immediately where I'm from.

I shift on my heels. "No," I say. "I'm from…"

"Shanghai."

I glare at her. "How did you know that? Did you go through my phone?"

"It was on your home screen!"

A fat water droplet plinks on my forehead. I look up.

"I thought it was my phone," she says. "So I—"

The rain falls without warning. One second the mist is quiet, light, the next it's a downpour. I scan the park for shelter; there's barely anything here, only open basketball courts and playgrounds. It's an hour past midnight, and all the stores are closed.

The girl moves to cover her giant camera as best she can. "Over there!" she yells, pointing at the stone archway at the end of the pitch. I nod and we bolt for cover.

By the time we reach the overhang, we're both drenched through. The park encircles us; it'll be a long walk back to the MTR station. Which is closed now, apparently. It'll be a long walk back to Mong Kok.

"It's just a spring shower," she says, shaking out her long hair. "It should pass soon." She wipes at her camera viewfinder with the end of her skirt, then slides down against the wall to sit. "My poor Nikon DSLR," she says, holding it as if cuddling a puppy.

I almost laugh. She's soaked and shivering but worried for her camera. I sit down beside her, looking out at the fields surrounding us. The composition is lovely. The youcai canola wildflowers in the foreground, the purple-blue sky blurred in the distance, all the colors bleeding together in the rain. Toward the east, the pale moon looks as if it's shivering in the storm. It feels like we're keeping vigil in the rain. For what, though, I have no idea.

I hear a click. The girl has taken off her lens cap and started snapping photos. She gets down on the ground, crouching with no inhibition; her dress rides up her thighs and I drop my eyes.

She pores through the photos on her display panel. "Hmm," she says, her lips pursing. "Too wide."

I can't help glancing over her shoulder at the photos. The

camera quality is good, really good. It probably costs more than my first month's paycheck as a trainee. But I have to admit she is talented. "That's an interesting shot," I say, more curtly than I intend.

"I think the caption is: *Hong Kong Wakes to Rain*," she says, almost as if to herself.

I pause. I wonder for a moment if she can riffle through my mind, reveal each thought one by one. There's something about her that makes me feel too exposed, vulnerable.

She raises her head. "I'm not a real photographer. I just like taking pictures. And posting them on Instagram." Then she smiles at me. Fuck, she's pretty. Fuck, fuck, fuck.

My next thought: She most definitely has a boyfriend because this Charlie guy has been texting her nonstop. Then: Her world couldn't be more removed from mine.

The thought gives me comfort. I can study her like a portrait, like watching someone from behind a one-way mirror. Her features are striking and unusual, her eyes sharp and curved at the inner corners like a cat's. She's no traditional beauty, and her taste in clothing is questionable, but there's something about her that is incredibly alluring.

Her eyes flit upward and her gaze locks against mine; I realize I'm caught staring and turn away abruptly. I can feel my neck turning red.

"What's your name?" she asks. "I'm Phoenix."

"Kai," I answer. I hesitate, then add, "You're a good photographer."

Her smile opens up her whole face. She has a dimple on one side and an extra eye crease on the other. I want to draw her so badly I nearly admit it aloud.

"Thanks. I got some good ones from today that I might post. I run a photography account on Instagram," she explains. "It's not a big deal or anything. I just started it last year to keep my dad in the loop. He travels a lot so I don't really see him. Our only interaction is when he likes my photos online." She gives me an embarrassed smile. "Sorry, I'm rambling."

When she leans forward to show me her camera display, I smell the fruity scent of her, from her perfume or shampoo or something. I'm having a hard time paying attention to her photos until she clicks to the end of the gallery, and I catch the striking neon sign:

光復香港, 時代革命.
LIBERATE HK—REVOLUTION OF OUR TIME.

A chanting crowd, mouths open and eyes blazing. Neon posters and multicolored flags. NO CHINA RENDITION. I try to school my face into a neutral expression. "I—"

She sucks in and then sneezes, violently.

"Here," I say, shrugging out of my jacket. "You can take this."

She tries to protest before sneezing again, and I cautiously place the jacket around her shoulders, careful not to touch her bare skin.

"What about—" Another sneeze interrupts her.

"Just take it," I say harshly. "I'll survive if you don't infect me first."

"But your jacket—"

"You can give it back to me later," I say, knowing I'll never get it back.

Out of the blue, she asks, "Are you an art student?"

A bolt of annoyance runs through me. "So you did look through my phone."

"It was just one photo." Her whole face crinkles with guilt: her eyes scrunching, her nose wrinkling, her cheeks coloring despite the cold. I don't think I've ever known someone with such an expressive face. "And it was open on your screen! You really should get a password." She turns up her nose. "Plus, you stole my phone first."

"I didn't steal it!" I realize we haven't traded phones yet. "Here," I say, digging hers out of my pocket.

She hands me mine. I tap on the screen. No messages, of course. Who would text me? My father, who barely acknowledges my existence? Marco, maybe, but only to harass me. And certainly not Ma, who I text every day, as if she's still waiting for me.

"My mom is going to kill me," Phoenix says with a groan as she scrolls through her messages.

I don't say anything, trying to ignore the swell of rising resentment in my throat.

"Looks like the rain is dying down."

I raise my head. Sure enough, the spring shower fades as quickly as it arrived, leaving only the rich scent of wet, clean earth in its wake. I get to my feet.

"You never answered my question," she says, standing too. "Are you an art student?"

"No."

"Do you take art classes?"

"No." I pause. My jaw ticks. "Not anymore."

She crosses her arms over her chest. "Well, you could, if

you wanted to. Any uni student can audit other classes. It's open campus policy. PolyU Design is in Hung Hom, about fifteen minutes from Mong Kok by train. Which uni are you at again?"

Tian ah. She thinks I'm a university student. All my knowledge of Hong Kong escapes me, and I pause too long before I say the first name that comes to my head. "HKU."

"HKU!" Her eyes widen with excitement. "I have friends who go there. Actually, there's an organizer meeting on campus, this Friday. For the…the extradition bill protests." She peeks up at me through her curtain of wet hair. "Do you want to come?"

Here it is, a shimmering opportunity presented to me on a platter. This must be the kind of lead the police are looking for. Marco would tell me to say yes. Father would tell me to say yes. Ma would…what would she do? Ma would tell me to forget the mission and go after the girl. She hated practical solutions; she loved romance.

But I don't want to spend a second longer with this girl. I don't want to watch her mouth, her eyes, her hands. Watch how she moves and watch how the rain plasters her long hair against the pale column of her neck. I don't want to look away and then look back, to play these stupid games of hide-and-seek, of pretending to be someone you're not.

"It's okay if you're busy," she says, turning away. "You probably have plans Friday night…."

The second she leaves, I will never see her again. And this, more than the thought of the undercover gig, more than the thought of anyone's approval, is what makes me act. I reach out and grab her wrist before I can change my mind.

"No," I say, my mouth moving. I have no idea what I'm saying. "I mean, yes. I'll come. No, I'm not busy."

Skies, I sound like an imbecile. But her expression is so unabashedly happy, I can't help giving her a small smile in return.

Xingxing zhi huo, Ma used to say. A single spark can start a blaze.

And my words just struck the match.

Phoenix

I REACH HOME JUST BEFORE TWO IN THE MORN-
ing. I take off my shoes outside the door to tiptoe across
the wood floorboards, but my caution is all for naught
because as soon as I cross the threshold the upstairs light
switches on.

There's no point in delaying the inevitable. I gulp and
climb the stairs to find Mom waiting for me in her room.

She sits perched on the *very* edge of her perfectly made
bed, as if there are people sleeping in it and she doesn't want
to disturb them. Her hair is done up in a shiny chignon, and
her eyes are lined with mascara and pale eye shadow. Usually,
she takes off her makeup as soon as she gets home. She only
forgets if she's been drinking.

"Hi...Mom," I hedge. "You're still up."

"I'm still up?" she repeats, her voice dull. "Of course I'm

still up. I'm still up because I'm waiting for you." She pauses, her eagle eyes narrowing. "Whose jacket is that?"

"You didn't have to wait for me," I say, evading the topic.

"I called Sally," she goes on. "She said you and Charlie haven't been home all day."

Extremely unfortunately, our moms run in the same social circles. "We studied outside."

"She also said Charlie left his laptop at home."

I rub my neck. "We used our textbooks—"

"Phoenix, please." Her voice is taut. "I thought you'd learned your lesson after your SAT results. Do you think Yale will just let you in because of your dad's alumni status?"

"Mom," I bite out. "I'm *trying*."

"If you don't try harder," she says quietly, "you'll end up like Osprei. Do you want that?"

I wince. Normally she tries not to compare us kids, at least not to our faces.

Her balance is precarious as she rises. "You're both smart kids," she says, as if this is an olive branch, "but you lack drive. It's because you don't know what it's like to suffer."

I resist the urge to roll my eyes. She's about to go off on the story of our family's inspiring history overcoming poverty and moving up in the world through a combination of hard work and discipline. And maybe a little nepotism. "I'll go to SAT prep early tomorrow," I say quickly, cutting her off. "Is that all?"

"Not quite," she says, in a tone that makes me wary. "You went to the protests today."

"Did Osprei tell you?" I demand, my heart rate spiking at the betrayal.

"No," she says.

It was a guess, and I confirmed it. I release a sharp, frustrated breath.

"Those protests are dangerous," she says. "Remember what happened during the Umbrella Movement five years ago? Kids got tear-gassed and jailed! Some of them are *still* serving their sentences. They're no place for a young person, much less a girl—"

"Oh, so Osprei can go but I can't?"

"Osprei is forbidden as well. I will not have you two joining those rabble-rousers and getting yourselves arrested. Imagine the news, what they'll say about our family—"

"That's all you care about—our family image?"

She clenches the doorframe to steady herself. "I am holding this family together by a thread," she says in a tremulous voice. A blue-green vein pulses below her jaw. "Your father is coming over for dinner tomorrow. I hope you can get rid of this…attitude by then."

Tears prick the back of my eyes, which I blink back angrily. "It doesn't matter," I hiss. "You know he never even looks at me anyway. He only comes for his precious *son*, and none of us will admit it—we're just the shitty leftovers."

Mom flinches. "Phoenix!" She takes a deep breath. "Your father cares for all of you—"

Without saying another word, I flee down the hall. I catch Robin's door snapping shut at my approach—eavesdropping, again. With a sigh, I head into my own room and resist the urge to collapse on my bed and cry. Instead, I wash my face and apply my bajillion-step skin-care routine: toner, essence, ampoule, mask, cream. Each step is meditative. By the time my face is gleaming with snail mucin and hyaluronic acid, my heart rate has settled and I no longer feel like crying my eyes out. Instead, my mind turns to more pleasant thoughts. "Zhang Kai En," I whisper into the dark as I burrow under my sheets. I should've snooped through his phone while I had the chance. Well, no good deed goes unpunished, as they say in the States. I recall the way he placed his jacket around my shoulders and a smile comes to my lips. I can't wait to see him again.

Never mind that our "date" is an HKU student protest meeting, and I don't even go to HKU. Never mind that Mom just banned all demonstrations—technically, although she said I can't go to a protest, she said nothing about a protest *planning* session. It's a small loophole, one that won't hold up in the Court-of-Mom, but that's for another day.

Besides, I've already posted a photo from the demonstration and gotten more likes than ever before. My photography account had only 300 followers, but it's climbed to 350 now. Who knows where it'll be tomorrow?

I hear Mom switching off the lights down the hall. I should've just said I was sorry. Her country-club friends gossip about her behind her back; they say Dad has a mistress in New York, and that's why we fled to Hong Kong. Even Po Po says Mom should've held on to him better, should've forced him not to leave her. The double standard makes me sick. Now she has me to deal with on top of all her other worries. Her invisible middle child who's never put up much of a fuss before. Osprei is the trouble kid, the one who needs remedial classes, private tutoring, even a 24/7 chaperone. (That was during his deejaying phase.) Meanwhile, Robin is the family genius, the one who was forming complex compound sentences by age two. If Dad wasn't so bent on having his son inherit the business, maybe he'd see Robin's potential.

Where does that leave me? Caught in between, meant not to fail, but not to exceed expectations either. Maybe that's why Mom wants me to end up with Charlie: He's smart, he's from a good family, and he'll stay the path reliably. Like a packhorse.

I turn over in bed. Charlie's mom posted his SAT results on Facebook yesterday. Apparently, he scored in the 99th percentile. She captioned the photo with a praying hands emoji and some prosperity gospel Bible verse. And I saw that my mom liked the post.

I logged off after that.

I'll study tomorrow, I decide. Tomorrow, and the next day, and the day after that. So that when Friday comes around, I'll see Kai, and if I miss curfew by a few minutes, or even an hour, will Mom care after I show her my new and improved scores?

She'll be pleasantly surprised, and even Dad might be pleased, especially if I can get into the 90th percentile. Then, if I'm accepted into his alma mater, maybe he'll finally remember he has more than one child. Maybe he'll even spend a few extra weeks in the city, and Mom and Dad can reconcile, and things can go back to normal around here.

And yet, as I imagine myself getting into Yale and flying off to America, Suki's words come to mind, unprompted. *There comes a time when you realize there's more to life than this.*

The next evening, all of us stand in the foyer, uncomfortable in our lace and frills. Robin wears a velvet dress with bows cascading down the front, which she hates more than spiders. She's sulking, hunched against the stair bannister. I'm in an ivory blouse with a stiff collar and my usual pearl earrings. I feel like a doll playing dress-up, but I know the sight makes Mom, who is already planning our inevitable Christmas card in April, happy. Mom wears a skintight yet elegant pencil skirt; I can tell she's lost weight, and I know that pleases her, but it worries me.

Uncle Chow left to pick up Dad thirty minutes ago. I feel jitters running beneath my skin, which is dumb, because it's just my dad. No normal kid is nervous to see their dad.

Four minutes past six, Osprei slouches down the stairs in a half-hearted button-down and slacks. Mom fusses over him, straightening his tie. The doorbell rings. Mom squares her shoulders, her lips moving soundlessly—probably reciting her mantra for inner peace.

Uncle Chow steps inside first, greeting us with warmth and affection. The contrast is stark, because Dad follows next. He looks at Mom, giving her a slight nod and reaching for, of all things, a handshake. It's professional, courteous, wrong in every way. Then Dad turns to Osprei, of course, his eldest and only son, and they too shake hands. Dad claps him on the back, and gives Robin and me a cold, fleeting smile.

I'm left chilled, as if I just swallowed ice.

We follow Mom into the dining room. "How was your flight?" Mom asks in her high-pitched voice she usually reserves for telemarketers. She uncovers the dishes on the glass turntable, and the warm fragrance unfurls in the air like dancers of smoke.

Mom really outdid herself tonight, or more accurately,

our housekeeper, Auntie Mok, did. There's a steamed sea bass on a giant oval plate longer than my forearm, steeped in soy sauce and sprinkled with green onions. Next to it is Peking duck, which is Dad's favorite: thin slivers of meat covered with browned, crispy skin, served with sweet, tangy plum sauce, shallots, cucumbers, mashed garlic, and paper-thin pancakes.

Robin reaches for the Peking duck, and Mom frowns at her because she's supposed to wait for Dad to serve himself first. But Dad doesn't seem to mind. "Easy flight," he responds, his voice huskier than I remember. "You know how it's always easier flying west. Easier to leave America than to come back."

"Then you should stay for longer," Robin chirps, her mouth stained dark with plum sauce.

Dad gives her a fake smile. "I wish I could, honey. Work gets busy in the spring. That's how Dad makes the money that keeps you in school."

"But I don't want to go to school," she says, genuinely perplexed. "I'm already smarter than the rest of my classmates."

"Robin was just named an International Math Olympiad gold medalist," Mom says levelly.

Instead of congratulating Robin, Dad looks pointedly at Osprei, as if to ask him where *his* Math Olympiad medal is. Osprei seizes the moment to shovel rice into his mouth, chewing vigorously. Dad raises a brow, a silent reproach.

I glare down at the tablecloth.

"Traffic wasn't bad, I hope?" Mom asks, her words just as bland as her plate, which consists of plain carrots, bok choy, and a few slices of lean fish. (Because heaven forbid she eat something with actual carbs.)

"Traffic was light this evening. Yesterday, God, it was horrendous. That idiotic protest blocked off all of Hennessy Road."

"Your son and daughter were a part of that *idiotic protest*."

Osprei and I exchange looks. If this were a war operation, we'd be radioing each other to abort mission right about now.

But Dad only chuckles. "They'll grow up eventually," he says in a patronizing voice that makes Osprei stiffen, his shoulders bunching toward his ears.

"I forbid them both from going," Mom says. Now I see her next move: She plans to use Dad as extra law enforcement.

"I'm twenty-one, Mom." Osprei scowls. "You can't just *forbid* me—"

"While you live under my roof—"

"Let them go." Dad makes a dismissive gesture. "They can learn how useless it is. Kids throw tantrums all the time." He levels a cool stare at Osprei. "It accomplishes nothing."

Osprei looks like he wants to punch something. I kick his foot under the table. He glowers at me but returns to his plate, affecting sudden interest in his plain white rice.

"So how is school going, son?" Dad asks.

Osprei takes a long time to swallow. In the silence, we all turn to watch him, but after a full ten seconds of chewing, he only rewards our wait with a short "Good."

Dad glances at Mom. "Has he still been seeing Dr. Kuang?"

Mom bites her lip, then nods. Dr. Kuang is Osprei's psychologist. Dad made those visits mandatory ever since Osprei failed his exams twice in a row, but Mom's against it. She thinks therapy is only for "crazy" people.

Osprei sets down his chopsticks. "He says I have ADHD."

We all still. I speak first. "Since when?"

He shrugs as if it's no big deal. "Since forever, I think. I mean, it's not like I haven't taken Adderall before."

"Osprei," Mom says tightly. She's going to get TMJ from clenching her jaw like that.

"You don't need to study anyway," Dad says, considering his son with lidded eyes. He seems entirely unfazed by this news. "You're good with people as it is."

It's true; Osprei can charm a fish out of water. He once even dated a Hong Kong TV star before she found out he was still in high school. (I still get visceral secondhand embarrassment when I remember their paparazzi photos.)

"I'm thinking of having you take over the operations leg of the business," Dad continues. "The experience may do you some good. And you'd be working with Mr. Fu, who could mentor you."

"I don't need another mentor," Osprei snaps. Dad is always foisting his contacts onto Osprei, as if one of them will finally convert him into an adult who cares about assets and revenue streams.

"It could be a good opportunity," Mom chimes in, recovered and determined to play the part of neutral parent. "Think about the scale of operations. Probably thousands of dollars."

"Millions," Dad corrects her, and Mom looks away. My own cheeks burn. Dad can do that to you—make you feel like nothing in seconds.

"And how are your college applications coming?" Dad turns to me at last as dessert is brought out.

I stab my fruit salad, skewering an innocent slice of honeydew. "They're fine."

"She's not applying this year," Mom clarifies. "She's still a junior, but she'll be retaking her SATs over the summer."

Does Dad even know how old I am? He seems to guess what I'm thinking because he reddens, twin splotches of color high on his cheeks. He's gained weight, and the bags around his eyes are puffy and swollen. I don't think he was telling the truth when he said the flight was easy. It looks like he hasn't slept for days.

For that matter, neither has Mom, but she knows how to wear concealer better.

None of us know how to tell the truth in this family.

"Let me know when you apply, and I can put in a word with Dean Schmidt, if he's still around," Dad says. "Yale calls me all the time demanding donations; they might as well give something back in return."

"I don't want to be a legacy admit," I say to my plate.

"Phoenix," Mom warns me.

But Dad only laughs. "Then study harder."

I stab at a grape; my fork misses and screeches against the porcelain plate instead. Osprei winces; Robin gawks; Mom shoots me a stern glare. I don't know how Dad reacts because I don't look at him again.

On some level, it thrills me to disobey Mom and Dad because, every time, I'm surprised I can actually do it. *What would happen*, I wonder, *if I didn't go to Yale?* What would happen if I refused to leave Hong Kong? America has always been their dream for me, especially after they worked so hard to make me fluent in English. They don't even like the

States; they just like what it represents. Privilege. Status. Bigger dreams and bigger bank accounts. I understand that my success reflects on them and that, in the same way, my failure becomes their fault. Like a many-headed beast, a family is one body. One loud, cranky, infighting body.

Sometimes I feel indifferent, some days I feel scared, and sometimes, in the middle of the night, I feel plain furious. Why do Chinese parents feel like they can dictate your whole life for you? In North Carolina, my friends were shocked when they heard I didn't get free time after school. I had tennis practice, then piano practice, and now in Hong Kong, SAT practice. "It's because they want me to do well," I would tell friends, missing their sleepovers for the second or third time.

The invitations usually stopped after that.

"Thank you for dinner, Michelle," Dad says at the end of our trial. He gets to his feet; we get to our feet. He walks down the hall; we walk down the hall. He puts on his coat; we wait, as vigilant as guards standing sentry.

I don't know when I'll see him next, next week or next month or next year. He says he'll stop by soon, that he has business keeping him on the island, but we don't know what that means, and nobody cares to ask. You don't ask to be disappointed.

"Well." Mom dusts her hands after he leaves, as if we're in elementary school again and she wants to get rid of Dad's cooties. "That went fine."

"Did it?" Robin asks, after Mom floats away to the kitchen.

Osprei looks like he wants to take a long, scorching-hot

shower. "As fine as it ever does with Dad." He ruffles Robin's hair; she looks aggrieved but also secretly pleased. He lowers his voice: "At least no one screamed and threw things."

"An improvement from last time," I agree. The three of us climb the stairs together, each heading to our respective rooms. "Do you think you're going to do it?" I ask Osprei. "Take on the business duties?"

He grimaces. "He's not actually giving me any responsibility. He knows if he did I'd just screw things up. That's why he put Mr. Fu in charge, to clean up my messes."

"It sounds fun," Robin pipes up.

"No, it sounds shitty and boring."

"Osprei!" We're not supposed to swear in front of Robin.

"I'm sick of trying to earn his approval. Aren't we just supposed to...I don't know, get it? Isn't that what it means to be someone's kid?"

I don't say anything. It's the question we're all trying to answer and all failing to.

"I guess it depends on whose kid you are, and who that someone is," Robin says sagely. Then she adds: "Like Pokémon. Some Pokémon are given to you, and some you have to catch for yourself. You know?"

Kai

I'M WALKING UP TO THE POLICE ACADEMY WHEN Marco barrels into me. "You got one too?" he demands, waving his offer letter in the air.

I hide a smirk. "Try not to look so surprised."

"We're in!" He whoops. "We're officers now."

"Not quite. We still have to pass the training program."

His face is dreamy and far away. "Officer Wong," he says. "It sounds regal, doesn't it?"

But when we enter our dormitory, where we'll live for the next twenty-seven weeks, there's nothing regal about it. The mattress is about as thick as a tissue. And the bed frame looks like it was made during the colonial era.

"Sir, I live close by in Tin Wan. Can I stay there instead?" one of the trainees asks.

Sergeant Leung acts like he didn't hear him. "You have

five days of training per week," he announces. "And two days off—unless you're on call that weekend. You're expected to stay in the dorms if you have work the next day."

Unsurprised, I claim a spot by the window, then shove my backpack's worth of supplies under the bed. I left most of my belongings in the Mong Kok apartment.

"Report to roll call at nine o'clock."

"But that's in ten minutes!" Marco, who has multiple suitcases, says. "Sir."

"Get on with it, then." Sergeant Leung turns away. "We don't tolerate tardiness here."

In the gymnasium, we're joined by the head course instructor, the assistant course instructor, and the lead training officer. We file into orderly rows before them, identical in our matching uniforms.

"Each of you was given an identity number in your welcome packet," Lieutenant Chan explains. "This is your name from now on, do you understand?"

I shift, and his eyes immediately fall on me. "Twenty-Four, where is your trainee badge?"

"I left it in my dorm. Sir."

"Never come to class without it again. Retrieve your badge, then run ten laps around the track."

I narrow my eyes at him. He waits.

"Yes, sir." I swallow my resentment and run back to the dorm, then run the ten laps around the track. I consider stopping at eight, but there are police officers everywhere, as well as security cameras. I'm sweating and out of breath by the time I rejoin the class.

"We're learning defensive maneuvers," Marco whispers

to me when I return to the training ring. Everyone has paired off, but Marco and Tommy let me join their group. Marco grabs Tommy by the wrist from behind and wrestles him face-first to the ground, pinning his elbow into his shoulder. Then Marco uses his knee to keep Tommy's arm wrenched up.

I wince. That looks uncomfortable.

"Wanna try?" Marco asks.

I nod and move behind him uncertainly. I copy his movements, grabbing his wrist and shoving. Marco staggers forward and I kneel on top of him. His face slams into my shoe with too much force and he yells. I'm trying to hold his arm when he raises his head. His cheek is bleeding.

"Shit." I release him.

"Your shoe, bud," Marco says, sitting upright. A thin line of blood trickles down his cheek. I look at my shoe. There's a pebble caught between the laces, just above the melting clocks.

Tommy peers into his face. "Lucky it missed your eye. Do you need a Band-Aid?"

I put a hand on Marco's shoulder before he rises. "I'll get it," I say quickly.

"Thanks, bud. I mean, Twenty-Four."

I jog toward the exit and am almost to the door when Lieutenant Chan shouts, "Did I give you permission to leave, Twenty-Four?"

It takes me a second to realize he's addressing me. I stop. "Marco—I mean"—I try to recall his badge number— "Eighteen is bleeding, sir. I was going to get him a bandage."

Lieutenant Chan makes a tsking sound. "Eighteen, go to

the infirmary yourself. Twenty-Four, if you're so inclined to leave, then demonstrate what you've learned."

I glance at Tommy, who nods. He joins me in the center of the training ring, and I wrestle him to the ground easily, pinning him using the same technique Marco showed me.

Lieutenant Chan chuckles. "You'll find most criminals are not so eager to please. Why don't you try again with one of us?" He looks at the other course instructors before spotting someone behind me. "Officer Cheung," he says. "Care to provide a demonstration?"

Blood rushes to my face. Of course it's him.

I haven't seen my father since the day of my interview. He must take night shifts, because he's never in his apartment. The few times we've both been home, his door was closed, and I could barely hear his low, rasping snores. It's like living with a specter.

Now he's very much awake. He wears his full police uniform, and his face looks flushed from the sun. I wonder if he's just returned from making an arrest, if he's been chasing a triad gang or conducting a routine patrol. I want to know more about his life—if he eats breakfast, if he watches TV. Does he have a girlfriend? A second family? Is that why he doesn't care about me, because he has another son, a better one?

Father's face is inscrutable as he advances. All the students instinctively move to let him pass. "Why not," he says, entering the training ring.

I'm reminded of the sheer physicality of his presence. He's more than twice my age, but we're almost the same height, the same build. When he was younger, he must have been bigger than me, stronger than me. But then again, he was trained to be a fighter. I was trained to be an artist.

And he knows this, I realize. He thinks I'm as incompetent and weak as the five-year-old child who left him. But that was years ago.

He looks at me with a hard expression. "Try it."

I grit my teeth and grab him; he doesn't move. It's like trying to topple a statue. I try to twist his arm behind his back but instead he knees me and flips me to the ground. I hiss in pain before scrambling back upright.

"Try again." His voice is level, indifferent. I hate his indifference.

I'm angry and can't think clearly. I lunge for him and he twists out of my grip like I'm made of putty, then feints and kicks me off my feet. I land on my back, winded.

I remember what it's like to be nothing.

There's an awed hush from the crowd, and then the students clap. He gives me an indefinable look before speaking with Lieutenant Chan and striding off. As soon as he's gone, all the students whisper about him.

"He's a living legend, man."

"Do you know that's his son?"

"No way."

"They don't seem close."

"I thought Twenty-Four's from the mainland."

"Maybe he's a bastard kid."

"Wai," Marco interrupts, having returned from the infirmary. He turns to Edwin, the loudest one. "Your nose is crooked, Eddie. Want me to adjust it for you?"

I put a hand on Marco's shoulder, steering him away from

the other trainees before he starts a fight. "Don't bother," I say. "I don't care what they think."

We have physical exercise in the morning and lectures in the afternoon. I'm not the best at anything, but I'm the most well-rounded. I stay up the latest. I rise the earliest. I work harder than anyone else.

I want to be at the top of my class. And not just my class—one day, I want to beat my father.

We don't receive our first-round evaluations until next week, but most people know my rank is up there. I can bench nearly as much as Marco and run faster than Eddie, who boasted about turning down the Olympics to come here. (Marco claims it was the speed-eating Olympics.)

So on Thursday evening, when Lieutenant Chan pulls aside Eddie and Yulei to report to the commander's office, I'm confused. When they return to the dorm that night, bragging of their new mission, I'm stunned.

"Chief wants us to go undercover," Eddie says, propping his pillow behind his back. "We're going to infiltrate the student union committees."

"Why are they getting *you* to do it?" Tommy asks, digging out his hidden snack rations from under the bed. "You're just a trainee."

Eddie smiles, gloating. "I look the part, apparently," he says, before stealing a potato chip from Tommy.

And I don't. Despite my efforts, I'm not good enough. I wonder if Father warned them not to choose me. *He's too immature,* I imagine Father telling them. *Do you know he wet the bed until he turned five?* My face grows hot. I take out my phone, spinning it between my fingers as I think. I don't care whether they give me permission or not, whether they choose me or not. I should've known—given the choice, Father would never choose me.

I'll prove myself to him regardless.

I text the girl I met in Ocean Park Station—Phoenix Lam—asking her for the coffee shop address. After all, I was the one invited to the HKU planning session tomorrow. Not Eddie. Not Yulei. Me.

Yulei returns from the restroom. There's toothpaste on his chin. "Did you hear the news?" he says, a bit overdue. "Now we'll finally get to use those mics. Apparently, we're not supposed to go anywhere without them. We need them for proof."

I recall the hidden mics they showed us when we onboarded. I guess I'll take one tomorrow, though I won't use it unless I have to.

From the next bed over, Marco leans toward me. "Are you going back to your dad's place for the weekend?"

I nod. "What about you?"

He grins. "Spending both my off days with Yee-ching. She misses me now that I'm an officer in training. I guess it's true what they say—absence really does make the heart grow fonder."

I used to think that was true too. But then I came back to Hong Kong. Twelve years later, my father still doesn't give a fuck about me.

Kai

SERGEANT LEUNG RELEASES US EARLY ON FRI-
day, since it's our first week of training.

It's only one in the afternoon, and I still have four hours
to kill before heading to HKU in Lung Fu Shan. I haven't
had lunch yet, so I walk to Flower Market and grab beef noo-
dle soup at a corner stall.

As I eat, I take out my phone and check Instagram. I
pause at a photo of a flag waving in the wind. It's Phoenix's
post. I click on her profile and scroll through, even though
I've already seen her entire feed. For a moment, I imagine
showing these photos to Ma. But Ma wouldn't humor me.
She used to complain that I was like water, reflecting back
whatever peered over its surface. *Don't ask me what I think,
Kai. You have opinions of your own. Find them.*

Phoenix's advice about art classes comes back to me.

She said *anyone* could audit those classes. I mean, I'm not an actual university student, but who would know that? I've missed drawing. I've missed creative input. So I do a quick web search and take the train to HK Polytechnic, blending easily with the uni students as I enter campus.

When I find the correct room for Form and Motion, I'm surprised by the sheer size of the lecture hall, with its many rows of tiered seating. I'm not early, but the room is only half full. I take the steps two at a time before sliding into a deserted row in the back and dumping my backpack onto the empty seat beside me, not that anyone would voluntarily sit next to me. But, you know, just in case.

The professor comes in five minutes late, sweating profusely and muttering apologies. He wears a bright floral shirt with clashing neon sneakers, as if determined to be an eyesore, but not without purpose. I'm instantly intrigued. Most of the PolyU students have the same "cool" backpack, same shoes, same boring mainstream aesthetic. I guess I shouldn't be talking, not when I wear a police uniform nine times out of ten these days. Lieutenant Chan even made me toss my "graffitied" sneakers. He thought the melting clocks looked like gang symbols.

"Today we're covering the interrelation of two-dimensional surfaces with three-dimensional forms," the professor begins, opening his laptop. "Take out your drawing utensils."

Almost everyone in the row before me whips out an electronic drawing tablet. I feel self-conscious pulling out my wrinkled notebook and stubby pencil, glad no one is sitting behind me.

"Did you get the editorial illustrator internship?" the girl in front of me whispers to her classmate. "I heard the interviews were so competitive."

"I did," the other one sighs. "But it's unpaid. All the fine arts internships are unpaid. They expect you to come just for the experience and the '*passhion*.'" She giggles, saying an English word I don't fully understand. Briefly, I wonder what that would be like, pursuing a career just because you love it, not for money but for the sake of art.

Who could live like that?

When class ends, I sneak out the door before anyone can ask unnecessary questions. I'm halfway down the lawn before I realize no one is chasing me; no one is going to sue me for sitting in an empty chair and listening to a professor talk about traditional and experimental materials when half the class is sleeping or on their phones.

What would it be like, I wonder, to actually be a student, not an impostor—attending these classes, working with these professors, paying tuition? Tuition can't be cheap, what with the state-of-the-art lecture halls, material resource centers, and photography studios. With masochistic curiosity, I take out my phone to search tuition prices.

Five figures. I swallow.

These kids will be the ones. The ones going to shiny design jobs and shiny apartment complexes and living life like they do in the movies. With *passhion*.

And me? I'll be at the Mong Kok police station, watching the days slip away like flotsam on the tide.

With that optimistic thought to buoy me forward, I head to HKU.

Phoenix texts me the address while I'm on the train. Our

meeting point isn't on the actual campus, but in a "yellow" coffee shop nearby, just off HKU West Gate. I don't ask what yellow means, but I assume it's some sort of pro-democracy label, because it clearly doesn't mean the actual paint of the store, which is brown.

I pause outside the door, my heart rate picking up. I'm acting like a little kid, I know. *Get it together, Kai. Just do your job.* Absurdly, I wish Marco were with me so I wouldn't have to walk in alone. Marco would have come along if I'd asked, though that would only have raised suspicion.

Before I can overthink it, the door swings open. A tall white boy brushes past me, barely sparing me a glance as he barks into his phone. But the door's already open, and I don't miss my chance; I walk in.

The tables are arranged haphazardly, with chairs scattered throughout, though most are overturned, and students are sitting on the ground. Boxes are bunched against the walls, overflowing with paper flags and T-shirts and other junk. The students themselves chat casually while drinking mango sago smoothies—not at all the atmosphere you'd expect for a revolution.

But what does a revolution look like anyway?

"Kai!" I hear my name with tangible relief, and turn.

Phoenix emerges from behind a towering column of boxes with another girl in tow. They both head over to me. "You came!" Phoenix says unnecessarily. Her huge black camera is still slung over one shoulder, the lens uncapped. She grins up at me, smiling so wide both her dimples show. She looks different today somehow—more polished, or put together, or confident? Her hair, long and shiny, is clipped back with a barrette, and she wears pearl earrings that catch the fluorescent lights and glimmer.

"I'm Suki. Acting president of the student union council," the other girl says. I recognize her from the restaurant. Not just because of her bright pink hair, but also because of the way she speaks. With gravity. "Phoenix tells me you're an HKU student. Which department?"

Shit. Math? But I don't remember linear algebra. Art history? But what if that's a really small department, and all the students know each other? I'm scrambling for an answer when the white boy pops in again, bounding over to Phoenix and saving me an immediate response.

"Who's this?" he asks in English.

"Kai," I say, affecting nonchalance despite my rudimentary English. If he asks me anything other than my name, I probably won't understand.

"I'm Charlie," he says, extending a hand. "Nice to meet you."

"Nice to meet you," I echo, my accented English obvious and painful even to my own ears. I can't imagine what it sounds like to them.

Charlie turns to Phoenix, gesturing to the phone in his hand. "I can't believe Mr. Yim would accuse me—" I don't catch the rest. His English is too fast and runs together, so the words merge into one long mass like a garbled magic spell.

Phoenix glances from Charlie to me. "Charlie and I both go to Whitney American School," she explains in Mandarin.

Charlie says something else in English and Suki laughs. I don't understand the joke, but I smile too, because what else is there to do? I feel like an impostor, moronic and slow. Too dumb to know if I'm the target of the joke.

Phoenix elbows Charlie in a way that makes me think they're close. I recall the Charlie name that kept flashing across her phone. This must be him. I wonder if they're dating. Then I remind myself that it doesn't matter. Who Phoenix is dating has no relevance to the job. "What major are you?" I ask in Mandarin.

"Oh, I'm not in uni," Phoenix replies, coloring. She colors easily, I note, with her complexion.

"Ah." Shit. "You seem like a university student."

"Really?" She beams again. "I—"

"Don't let it go to your head." Another boy slides into our group on a rolling chair, sitting backward so he straddles it. "She still gets height-checked on theme-park rides."

Phoenix scowls at him. "Not for years, Osprei!"

Osprei laughs, inclining his head at me. "He's handsome. Good job, Little Sis."

Phoenix's whole face turns red as she shoves her brother so hard he falls off the chair, though more from laughing than from Phoenix's efforts. They look so comfortable together, I let myself wonder for an indulgent moment what it'd be like to have a sibling—someone to joke around with, tease you, someone to always walk into a room with you.

"Sorry about him," she tells me, taking my arm and leading me away from the group. She blushes, pressing her lips together; she has very full lips, I notice. "Osprei's sole mission in life is to embarrass me. If it was up to him I wouldn't ever date at all."

"And is that your boyfriend?" I nod at Charlie, knowing it's not my place and asking anyway.

She turns back to look at him as if expecting a different person to crop up. "Who? Charlie? No way!" She shakes her head emphatically. "We're just friends. We've known each other forever. Our parents go to the same country club."

By the way Charlie keeps eyeing us, it doesn't seem like he thinks they're *just friends*. But I keep my opinions to myself.

"What did you say you study again?" She leans in as the conversations around us grow louder. I can smell her hair again, like sugar and flowers. How do rich people always manage to smell so good?

I realize she's waiting for an answer. My brain doesn't function properly around her. "Design art," I say, naming the only subject I could make an attempt at fibbing my way through.

She exclaims with delight, as if I just gave her a gift. Then she reaches for her camera and thrusts it into my hands. "Zhang Laoshi," she says solemnly, as if I'm some wise experienced teacher, "jiao wo, hao ba?" *Teach me, will you?*

She looks up at me with those wide, laughing eyes. *She's flirting with me*, I think slowly, as if I'm watching a movie of my own life. As if I'm not living in it. I can feel my neck growing hot. "I'm not any expert at photography. I'm only a freshman anyway."

"Oh, you're eighteen?" She frowns as I hand her camera back, her disappointment open and undisguised on her face.

"Well, in a month," I say, compelled by some miserable desire to be honest when I'm lying about everything else.

"Seventeen?" Her eyes light up. They're a light chestnut color speckled with gold, gold and copper.

I nod reluctantly.

"You seem older," she says, fidgeting with the lens cap of her camera. "I'm sixteen, but people usually think I'm younger." Her nose wrinkles as she says this, which makes me want to smile. "I think it's because of my height."

I shake my head. "It's because of the way you talk."

She bites her lip. "I talk too much, huh?"

"No, it's not that. You talk like…like you expect everyone to listen to you."

Phoenix raises her head suddenly and catches me looking at her. Her lips part, just a hairsbreadth. They're full and dark, the hue of summer plums. I know I shouldn't be staring, but I don't look away. A smile tugs at my mouth.

"Nix." The white boy squeezes between us, effectively extinguishing the mood. "Your brother's looking for you. I think Suki just got some bad news."

Worry lines pleat her forehead. "What happened?" she asks quickly.

"She didn't say. But they went out that way." Charlie points to the dark corridor behind the barista's counter. Phoenix shoots me an apologetic look.

"Go," I say. She nods and hurries away.

Leaving me and Charlie alone. He shifts awkwardly, planting his hands on his hips. "So," he says in Mandarin. I straighten, annoyed to find he's a few centimeters taller than me. "Er—what do you study?"

The first lie is always the hardest. Now my answer comes out without hesitation. "Design art."

Charlie hmphs. "What do art majors even do? How do you get, like, a real job after graduation?"

I shrug, unperturbed. "Some people think art actually matters. Go figure."

He sneers at this, his mouth thinning. "Can I see something you made?"

"Sure." I take my phone out and tap the screen. It's a painting of Shanghai—one of my best.

Charlie snatches my phone out of my hand and holds it up to his face as if he's trying to inhale it. Then his scowl deepens. "I guess it's true what they say. Still waters run deep."

I don't know what that means, but I'd bet my paycheck it's no compliment. He hands me back my phone and I wipe it surreptitiously against my back pocket. "I'm gonna go...use the restroom," I say, and turn away before he can respond.

The barista hands me the restroom key, pointing to the corridor behind her. "Second door on your left," she says.

I head into the hallway and spot the restroom, but farther down, the back door to the coffee shop alley is propped open by a recycling bin. I hear voices filtering in from outside.

"My uncle doesn't have a choice." I recognize the pink-haired girl's voice. Suki. "His orders are straight from the police—to funnel information back to Beijing. They want to leak the names of the bookstore customers."

"Is he going to comply?" a boy asks.

"Of course not," Suki growls. "I'm going to help him escape next week. But the ging caat are watching him as we speak."

I sink into the shadows, then edge closer to see what's happening outside.

Phoenix's brother has his arm around Suki. "We'll smuggle him out right under their noses," he promises. Phoenix nods beside him.

Marco said I would recognize it when I saw it. I do. This is much worse than graffiti and firecrackers. I was imagining a light punishment—a slap on the wrist maybe, or a night in jail to scare them back onto the straight path. But smuggling out someone on the blacklist? Going against a direct mandate from Beijing? I don't even know what the consequences would be.

I'm in way deeper than I thought.

"Is he going to Taiwan?" Phoenix asks. "They accept people like him, right?"

Political criminals, she means.

Suki nods. She's trying to finish her cigarette, but her hands are shaking.

"That's . . . good," Phoenix says uncertainly.

"It's not *good*," Suki snaps, and Phoenix flushes deeply. "It's a complete travesty. Hong Kong is his home and he's being forced to flee from it. He's never going to be able to come back, do you understand? He's going to die on foreign soil."

Luo ye gui gen. A *falling leaf returns to its roots*. Above all else, Chinese people understand how important it is to come home. I guess that's why Ma never wanted to return to Hong Kong.

"We can't have another Yuen Fat-tai," a short-haired girl mutters. "Not again."

"Did he ever turn up?" Suki asks.

"No, just disappeared off the face of the earth. Even his

wife doesn't know what's happened to him." The girl turns to stub out her cigarette. Her short, cropped hair is dyed blue, which matches her bright-colored contacts. In her satin blazer and loose-fitting trousers, she looks like some kind of K-pop idol.

I count four of them out there. All of them are young, in high school or college. And risking their lives against a force as big and wide and nameless as the government, which has the power to make someone disappear, just like that, without even a trace to follow years later.

I feel a muscle twitch in my jaw. *Don't think like that, Kai. You know better. Don't let yourself get brainwashed by these Hong Kong radicals.* Yuen Fat-tai could've gotten lost, fallen ill, had an accident. People disappear all the time. It doesn't have to be some wild conspiracy theory.

But wouldn't his wife have found him? Wouldn't she have searched across all of China and Asia too, until she tracked down his body, his corpse, to bring him home?

Your father didn't. Your father let your ma leave without saying goodbye. Your father let you go.

"It's too dangerous for you," Osprei snaps at his sister, loud enough to jolt me from my thoughts. "You'll just be a liability. Do you know what the dogs will do if they catch you?"

The dogs. Meaning the police. That's my job now, to figure out the when and where of the getaway, to earn their trust and then to break it. A dull roar grows in my ears. I remember Father's cold eyes of indifference.

"It's not your scene," Suki agrees reluctantly. "But we need another lookout. There's so few of us already. If we fail..." She looks like she's on the verge of tears.

My ears still ringing, I step out into the alleyway. "I can help."

Phoenix jumps; Osprei narrows his eyes. "How much did you overhear?" he demands.

"I can vouch for him, Ge," Phoenix says quickly. "He's safe."

Suki cocks her head at me. "I've seen you before," she says. "On PolyU campus. You said you're an art student?"

"Design," I say. I don't know why I'm so calm. It's like the calm I felt when I brought Ma to the hospital. When I don't feel like I'm living in my own body.

"We do need the help," Suki admits. "But are you sure? If the dogs catch you, you'll be blacklisted."

Father didn't think I could do it. But I'm no longer the five-year-old boy who ran from his apartment in the middle of the night, biting a blanket to keep from crying. I'm seventeen now. I'm changed.

I have to do this. I have to show him.

"I'm in."

Phoenix

THE REST OF THE STUDENT UNION IS STILL arguing about the protest route for Sunday's demonstration, but Suki makes an executive decision to head out early for dinner and karaoke. Ming-lai isn't happy about this, but as Suki says, "You can't refuse the president."

"See?" Osprei smirks at Suki. "Power corrupts." But I can tell by his expression he's dying to get out of here. (I'm allergic to pollen; Osprei's allergic to meetings.)

It's a mild spring night with a pale moon rising above the distant skyline. Our group is small, fewer than ten people, but somehow I keep getting separated from Kai. Someone's always talking to him: asking his opinion, telling him a story, pulling him aside. I track him with my eyes but he never notices, or maybe he's just avoiding me. I'm surprised he volunteered to help Suki's uncle next week. He's so reserved I can't tell what he's thinking.

"He's cute," Suki says in my ear. I yelp, nearly elbowing her. She's slowed to walk with me in the back as we head to the station, taking the train to KTV in Sai Wan. "A little too pretty for my taste, but I can see the appeal. You, though"—she sticks her finger in my face—"are being way too obvious."

"What do you mean?"

"Anyone can tell you like him from a mile away." She winks. "To win a man, you have to play hard to get."

I snort. "It's the twenty-first century, Suki, and I'm sick of playing those games. If I like someone, can't I just be open about it?"

Suki chortles. Instead of arguing with me, she surprises me by squeezing my shoulder affectionately. "I like you," she decides, as if I'd asked her a different question. "You're just like Osprei."

"That's the worst compliment I've ever received."

She falls into a fit of giggles that doesn't let up until we swipe our Octopus cards at the turnstile. "You go after what you want," she says, after recovering her breath. "And you're honest. But remember, not everyone is like you. Not everyone is as straightforward as you are."

Kai certainly isn't. His shuttered face, his long silences followed by terse yet thoughtful responses. He has an undeniable air of mystery, one as intriguing as it is frustrating.

What are you hiding? I wonder.

At KTV, we order French fries and Japanese karaage fried chicken, Taiwanese braised pork rice, and scallion pancakes.

"Only in Hong Kong," Osprei announces grandly, adopting a fake British accent. He's mocking the tour guides that cater to white tourists. "Asia's World City!"

Suki applauds as he brings out cocktails and soju for the group. Even though some of us aren't eighteen yet, no one cards at KTV. Charlie bows out after the first round of shots; I offer to take on his portion with my own as we play drinking games. It's common practice between us; Charlie's never been able to pull his own weight in alcohol. After the third round, I tell him dizzily that he owes me one. Big time.

"Wanna sing Eason Chan with me?" Charlie asks, seizing the remote.

"It's too early for sappy songs!" I practically shout, though we're sitting inches apart. "What about Jay... what's his name?"

"Aa Mui, you're gone," Osprei says, reaching over to knock on my forehead like it's a door.

"Hey!" I spring up and try to wrestle him but end up sliding onto someone else's legs and tumbling to the floor. A half-full drink gets knocked over, spilling everywhere.

Someone offers me a hand. It's Wing-chi, the handsomest girl I've ever met. She's tall and made of sharp edges; her jawline could cut glass. She wears a blazer in an androgynous style and keeps her hair cut short, dyed silver and blue. Up close she looks like a celebrity, and I'm mesmerized.

"She's taken, Nix," Osprei calls, laughing. I realize I'm staring and stumble to my feet.

"Sorry to disappoint," Wing-chi says, her smile crooked.

"How many fingers am I holding up?" Osprei asks, teasing me.

I shove his hand away and turn toward the door. "Where's the restroom?"

"It's down the hall, to your left," Osprei says. "Charlie, take her."

"No," I say, pouting. "I want Kai."

Kai is sitting in the corner of the booth, slouched back with his hands folded on his stomach and his long legs spread out. In his all-black attire, he practically fades into the shadows.

"Me?" he asks, in the cutest way.

I nod, sticking out my hand. (Alcohol makes me brave.) To my infinite surprise, he takes it and I pull him up. When we head to the door, he puts his hand on the small of my back to guide me. Maybe because I'm stumbling. Or maybe because he's been drinking too. Either way, I don't mind. Not at all.

In the hallway it's much quieter, and a salt-laced ocean breeze filters in through the open window. I try to sober up in the cool air and use the bathroom quickly. Adrenaline is coursing through me. I smile at the mirror; I imagine smiling at him.

When I come out, he's waiting for me. It's like I summoned him into being; he is so beautiful. He doesn't see me, and in his unguardedness, he looks...*sad*.

Without thinking, I touch his arm. "Do you miss home?"

He looks up. "Yeah," he says, letting out a soft sigh. The wine's made his voice warmer, raspier. "More than you know."

The most honest response I've gotten from him yet. I peek cautiously at his face, but it's closing once more, as if he regrets his answer. "Why don't you go back?" I ask.

He rubs at his brow. "There's nothing for me to go back to."

I don't know what that means and don't have the sober brainpower to process this information at the moment. "If you could go anywhere"—I sweep my arm out grandiosely—"where would it be?"

He cracks a smile. "What?"

"Oh." I cover my mouth. "Sorry, did I use the wrong language? Did I say that in English or Canto?"

He laughs out loud. It's a pleasant sound, rich and full. "Neither. You just slurred real hard."

"God, I'm drunk." I put my hand to my cheek to cool my face down. "Is my face red?"

"Like a fanqie." He grins, using the southern phrase for tomato. Then he puts the back of his hand gently to my forehead, and my heart stumbles over its next several beats. "Your temperature's high."

"Too many shots . . ." I smile weakly at him. "I usually cap at five."

"A lot of alcohol for a small girl," he says. "That was nice of you, though, to look after your friend who couldn't drink."

He noticed I did that? So he *was* watching me! "Charlie's always been a lightweight. He's all right, though." I sway, and he puts a hand on my waist to steady me. "It's probably helped his SAT scores. Meanwhile I'm out here zapping all my brain cells."

"You take care of each other."

"That's what friends do, right?" I'm so close to him I can

count the freckles on his cheekbones. "I would do the same for you."

His brows draw inward. "But we just met."

"I know." I shrug. "But I trust you."

He barely smiles, but up close, I can tell his eyes crinkle. "You're funny, Lifeng," he says, using a Mandarin variation of my name. *Feng*, phoenix. *Li*, beautiful. *Lifeng*.

I want to hear my name on his lips again and again and again.

His eyes are lidded as he leans down, a half smile playing across his mouth. Unconsciously, I rise on my tiptoes. The space between us feels like a ringing dissonance, begging to be stilled. We're so close I can smell the wine on his breath. I close my eyes—

"Nix!" Charlie grabs me by the arm, jerking me around.

"C?"

"What have you two been doing out here?" He gives me a glare worthy of Mr. Yim, as if I'm the one who's been caught cheating on an exam. "You know you shouldn't be by yourself, with *him*." He says "him" a decibel lower, as if Kai won't be able to hear him stage-whisper from two feet away. To his credit, Kai just looks amused.

"C, it's fine." I belatedly remember to switch to English. "You can go back first."

Stage-whisper voice continues. "But we don't know anything about him. He could be one of those—"

I do *not* want him to finish that sentence. "C, I can take care of myself. Go back in."

"I'm heading home now," he says. "I bet you forgot you have SAT prep tomorrow morning."

Crap—I did forget. But I won't give him the satisfaction of being right.

"You need someone to take you home. You're in no state to go by yourself."

I groan. "I'll be fine—"

"I can take you home," Kai says quietly, in Mandarin. "I mean, only if you want."

I hesitate. "Would that be too inconvenient for you?" I know Repulse Bay is in the opposite direction of Mong Kok. "You probably wanted to stay longer."

He shakes his head. "I have an early start tomorrow too."

"Classes?" I ask.

He shrugs.

"Wait a second." Charlie steps between us, not letting go of my arm. "Tomorrow's Saturday. Why would you have classes on Saturday?"

"Work," he answers, leveling his gaze on Charlie.

Charlie straightens, as if trying to use his height to intimidate him. Kai doesn't step back, but I notice his stance shifts, his shoulders squaring in response.

"Where do you work?"

"I work for my father."

"Where do you go to school?"

"Why is that your business?"

"He goes to HKU, C," I snap, tired of the unnecessary drama. The excess testosterone in the air is enough to make me puke. (Or maybe that's just the aftertaste of vodka in my mouth.)

"What year are you? What classes are you taking? And which professor is your department adviser?"

"Lay off the Spanish Inquisition, okay?" I shove Charlie, with more strength than usual, because he stumbles. He whirls, offended and angry at me now too. I remind myself that I'm still drunk and don't want to say anything I'll regret in the morning. "Kai will take me home. I'll see you tomorrow, C?"

Then I turn to Kai and ask him to wait for me downstairs. "What about the bill?" Kai asks, pulling out his wallet. "I can—"

Charlie makes a disparaging noise, which I ignore. "Don't worry about it. Osprei takes care of stuff like that. You're our guest. They would kill me if I let you pay."

"Let me at least—"

I close the wallet in his hands and return it to him. Then I run back to our KTV room before he can protest. "Where's my camera?" I ask Osprei.

Osprei hands it over. "I like the photos you took of me and Suki today," he says, slouching back in his seat. "You should post them on your Instagram. Maybe we'll get famous."

Suki yawns. "How many followers do you have now?"

"I can't remember," I say, though I could've very well answered, *Eleven thousand and twelve.* (I may have started tracking my follower count semi-obsessively.)

"Millions," Osprei supplies inaccurately. "You're even verified, aren't you?"

I nod. "Keep posting," Suki says with a grin. "Do you write your captions in English?"

"English and Chinese."

"Good," she says. "The more people who know, the better."

"What will you write about me?" Osprei asks. (Of course, the only topic he's interested in.)

"Your face won't make the cut," I tease. "Maybe I'll crop you out." I wave good night to the rest of them.

"Heading home already?" Suki winks. "And where's mystery boy?"

"You shouldn't go alone," Osprei adds, not even bothering to look at me as he scrolls through the karaoke menu. "Call Uncle Chow. He'll pick you up."

"You can call Uncle Chow," I tell Osprei, while Suki stands to give me a kiss on the cheek. Like me, she's a lot more affectionate when drunk. "Kai's taking me home."

Wing-chi whistles. I salute her with a giggle, then scramble out the door.

To my relief, Charlie's gone from the corridor; so is Kai. I head down the elevator with some trepidation, but it's only Kai waiting in the lobby downstairs, his head down as he goes through his wallet. When he sees me, he shoves his wallet back in his pocket and some black wires fall to the ground. They look like earphones.

"Ready?" he asks, opening the door for me.

I reach for the earphones and hand them to him. "You dropped this."

His expression contorts, his eyes widening in shock. He shoves the earphones back in his pocket as I step outside. "Thanks," he says stiffly.

"It's no problem." I laugh, because he looks troubled. "I'd go crazy if I lost my earphones. I can't go anywhere without music."

His jaw tightens. After a beat, he asks, "You go to KTV often?"

"Whenever there's a group of us. It's just what everyone's always down for." I glance up at him in the lamplight. "Why? You don't like karaoke?"

His smile is quick and fleeting. "I do, but only by myself."

"How come?"

"I'm a terrible singer."

"Oh c'mon. You can't be that bad."

"No, Lifeng. I'm atrocious. The worst you've ever heard."

I laugh. "That's a talent in itself, then. You'll need to prove it to me."

He raises a brow. "You'll charge me for eardrum damage."

"I have really good health insurance," I say, though I know it's more of an American joke.

He laughs anyway. Second time I made him laugh. The accomplishment thrills me, and I laugh too, rejoicing in the brisk night air and the quiet lull of the streets and the fact that it's finally just the two of us, alone.

When we get to the MTR, the overhead signs show the Island Line train is departing in thirty seconds. Kai exhales in disappointment but I shriek and tell him to hurry up, nearly jumping the turnstile as I swipe through, then fly down the escalator.

I can hear him right behind me. The train is already on the platform, beeping in warning as the doors begin to close. Kai passes me, faster than I thought possible, then slides in through the crack and holds the doors so that they open for me. "Hurry!" he shouts, breathless, and I slip in a moment later. We both collapse onto the empty seats.

The train chugs away beneath us.

The way we're sitting, Kai's shoulder brushes against mine. He notices at the same time I do, and abruptly stands, grabbing hold of the overhead handrail.

I look up at him. Kai is watching me with a subtle, quiet intensity. "You have plans tomorrow?" I ask boldly.

Instead of answering, he reaches up for the railing with his other hand, so that both his arms are raised. His shirt lifts up at the hem, exposing a strip of tan, lean muscle. My stomach flutters.

"Don't you have CAT prep tomorrow?" he asks.

I don't bother correcting him. "Yes. But only for three hours." God, I never thought I'd say the phrase "*only* three hours" about SAT prep in my life. Mom would be so proud. (*Positive mindset makes positive life, Phoenix!*) "What about you?"

He seems to remember something, something that makes his face turn hard. "Work."

"Oh." I can tell by his body language that he doesn't want me to press him on it. His answer feels like a wake-up call. I pinch my thigh, but I'm already sobering up. When I check my phone, I realize it's close to midnight. "I'll get off at the next stop to transfer, but you should ride to Admiralty."

"It's late. I can walk you home."

"No," I say, a bit too firmly. For some reason, I'm mortified by the idea of letting him see my house, with its tall hedges and iron gates. I know he wouldn't look at me better for it; he's not that kind of person. "It's a really safe neighborhood, and I don't want you to miss your transfer like last time. I'll be fine. I'm practically sober already."

He eyes me, then nods. "It's your call."

I cross the car to check the train map by the door. "Do you know how to get to Mong Kok from the Tsuen Wan Line?"

I turn. His eyes are crinkled in amusement, like twin crescent moons. "I know how to ride the MTR, if that's what you're asking."

I nod, laughing at myself. "It's a direct transfer—" The train jolts sharply and I lose my balance, pitching forward with a startled cry.

Someone grabs me, and for a moment I'm completely disoriented, clinging to him. Then I look up and remember: Kai. His chest is warm against mine. He can probably feel my heart pounding through my dress.

I straighten, blushing, and grip a pole to steady myself. "I guess I'm more drunk than I thought."

He shrugs. "The train tracks here are shitty and old. I would've lost my balance regardless of drink." As if to prove his point, the rails shriek below us. "The Shanghai subway is much steadier."

"I didn't know you were such a train snob," I say, teasing. "Are you about to tell me Shanghai is superior to Hong Kong in every possible way?"

"Not in all ways." He doesn't quite smile, but his eyes dance. "The girls are cuter here."

"Doors will open on the left," the intercom announces. On cue, the train doors slide open.

I don't have time to say goodbye. All I can do is listen to this sudden impulse that seizes me with strong arms and won't let go. My gut is screaming for me to go for it. Adrenaline races through my bloodstream, turning the world shimmering and distant. The train starts beeping, doors about to close.

I lean in and rise on my toes. Then I kiss him.

His lips are soft. They part beneath mine easily. I feel the breath of surprise that escapes him.

I draw away. His eyes are open in complete shock. I take a step back, my heart still pounding a mile a minute, then turn and jump out of the train. The doors slide shut. Through the glass, I see him standing there, blinking. His lips are still parted.

My heart sings in my chest.

I wait until the train rushes past and the station empties before heading toward the stairs. Just before I rejoin the world, I touch my fingers to my lips, breathless.

Then I let out a little shriek of joy, just because I can. No one hears me but the MTR rats, who scatter across the tracks, diving for the shadows. I hear their little pitter-patter feet and imagine they're dancing for me.

Kai

I FALL INTO THE NEAREST SEAT AND SCRUB MY hands over my face. I did what I had to do tonight. I made contacts. I hashed out details. And every time I found myself at a loss for words, I imagined what my father would say. I thought of what he'd do. And it worked.

Then why do I feel so sick to my gut?

I meet my reflection in the dark glass of the train window. *He looks like a liar.*

Light filters through the crack in the doorway when I get home around midnight. My chest tightens as I unlock the door and step inside, the creaky frame giving me away. Father sits on the solitary stool by the kitchen counter reading a newspaper, his back slouched like the curve of a fan brush, the kind used to stipple paint. His hair is rumpled in the back, as if he just woke up. There are beer cans scattered by the sink, the metal crunched for recycling.

"Hi." I stand in the doorway like a guest, unsure if I'm invited in.

He grunts and folds the newspaper. I notice he's dog-eared certain sections he wants to return to. The thought makes my throat constrict. I want to know what kinds of articles he's interested in, which stories he'll come back to for a second read.

"How's training?" He looks past me, at a point beyond my shoulder.

I guess he has trouble with eye contact. So do I. "Good," I say.

This is our first actual conversation, I realize, even though we live together.

"Open a window when you paint," he says. "The fumes make me sick."

"Yessir," I say instinctively, before biting my tongue. "I mean, sure."

He stands. "I don't know why you bother," he mutters under his breath. "You're just like your ma."

I put a hand to my temple. I remember I'm still drunk. "What?"

His eyes rove over me, and I shrink back. His gaze feels like a lash. "You look down on my line of work, don't you?" His lip curls. "It's your ma's fault, for turning you into this puk gaai dreamer boy."

"I don't," I grind out, swaying. I grab the counter to steady myself. "You just haven't been paying attention."

He arches a brow. "Really."

Blood rushes to my head. "I've sourced a lead with the HKU student union," I blurt out. "I'm a part of their operation to smuggle out a political fugitive. They're planning to send him by boat to Taiwan next Sunday."

For the first time, Father looks off guard, caught between irritation and grudging surprise. "Well," he says gruffly. "Did you report this to Lieutenant Chan?"

"I was about to," I lie. "I'll send in my report tomorrow."

Father's forehead furrows with three distinct wrinkles; his hairline shoots up. I concentrate on these minor details because it's easier to see these parts of the picture rather than the whole. And yet, I hear Ma's voice in my head, forcing me to step back. To see the wider implications.

The whole is that I'm offering myself as a spy. I'm taking Phoenix's trust and breaking it.

"Don't expect to run the sting just because you sourced the lead. That's not how it works around here. Maybe on the mainland, but not in Hong Kong."

I nod, forcing my face to remain neutral.

"Lieutenant Chan assigned a couple of trainees to the protest groups because he thought it'd be an easy gig, but so far it's not panning out that way. The riots are forecasted to get bigger when the protesters break from school." His mouth twists with disdain. "The spoiled brats."

"They're not awful," I say half-heartedly.

He cuts me a glare. "Don't get too familiar with them. Those kids are not your friends."

"I know."

He appraises me, grimaces, then heads to the door.

I breathe out a sigh of relief, but apparently it's too soon, because he turns back to add, "There was a big screwup yesterday. I arrested a crook for public destruction; he claimed to be doing it in the name of democracy. Thinks he's some noble hero for Hong Kong."

I look down at my feet, wishing I'd escaped to my room faster.

"Apparently, this kid is only twenty-four. He's barely been in handcuffs longer than five minutes when Neighbor Tao starts calling, begging me to change my mind and let him go, because apparently his daughter's engaged to this wangbadan crook." He takes his keys from the peg, his whole body wired with displeasure. "Personally, I would disown a daughter like that."

Before I can reply, he walks out the door.

In my father's wake, I start to feel nauseated again. All my exhaustion has disappeared and sleep feels far away. I try doing a series of push-ups; lifting weights—soup cans; pull-ups—hanging from the doorframe; but the jitters won't go away. Finally, I go for a run.

It's raining outside, again. The bars are still open. Party-goers head out for siu je, while late-night hawkers shout their goods. Hong Kong is always a flurry of color, sound, motion. It is easy to find people to draw, faces to recall. No one cares if you stare too long, because they're already staring back. No sense of personal space, no room for isolation. People packed together in tiny two-hundred-square-foot apartments like Lego pieces.

And I'm still here, out of my mind and fucking lonely.

I sprint through the crowds and turn to abandoned side streets.

Last week Sergeant Leung took us on a raid to gain first-hand experience. We found a few scared kids hiding in a protester fumou's basement, their hands still blackened with the spray paint they'd used to vandalize a district council office. Apparently, they'd thrown eggs and tried to start a fire, but only succeeded in giving themselves minor burns.

One of them put up a fight, throwing a punch at me. I didn't think; I just dodged and struck. I felt the blow connecting; I watched his eyes roll back in his head. And I staggered back, remembering how Ma had looked, crumpled and limp just like him.

Sergeant Leung woke him in seconds and handcuffed him. The protester spit on me, called me names. And I thought: Is he right? And I looked at myself at the end of patrol and thought, *Maybe*.

Father will probably read the report tomorrow. He will learn that I read the room wrong, that I was slow to act. Then he will have more names to call me.

No one wins at this game.

When I reach Morse Park, I slow, then drag to a stuttering halt. If Hong Kong is truly a second chance, then why does it feel like I'm failing again?

I open WeChat on my phone, my hands shaking and clammy.

I hate my father, I want to pretend he doesn't exist, but then in the same breath, I know I would do anything to make him see me. I hate him even more because of how he makes me feel. Because of what he forces me to do. But I know I can't blame him. I'm the one who's guilty.

My thoughts are bleak, but when I finally send the text and lift my head, I'm caught in the pristine, overwhelming beauty around me. The tall, leafy trees lean over me like hunched, benevolent grandmothers, their vines hanging down from the sky, glittering with raindrops. By the park gates, banyan roots wrap across and over the stone walls, their branches like gnarled mazes preserved from ancient times. The rain has stopped, but beads of water coat every surface, so that even at night the grass looks as if it's infused with light. I can smell the honeysuckle, the rich, earthy scent of turned soil, the dampness in the air. I can't believe I'm actually here, in this body: sweat dripping down my back, my lungs heady and clear, the cold night air no longer a curse but a cool caress on my skin.

I snap a picture, making plans to draw this later. I try to recall Professor Ng's lecture on specificity and flatness, and wish I hadn't been so sleep-deprived in class.

When I get home, the nausea is gone but I've developed a bad cold. I shower and change, then take out my sketching tools.

The next morning, I rise early to head to the academy. This is a drawing I made after my run yesterday, I text Ma on my way to the station. I tried Professor Ng's two-dimension technique. He's a poor communicator, but a genius artist.

I press send, then look up. A girl across the street pauses in front of an egg waffle stall. She wears a dress with flowers printed across the skirt, and her hair is jet black, glossy. My stomach flips when the girl turns; it's not her. Of course it's not her. She is safe in her Repulse Bay neighborhood, sheltered from liumang afei, from wretched, lying dogs.

My hand clenches around my phone. So what if I'm lying to her? The protests are pointless anyway. So what if I'm breaking her trust? My actions will barely cause a ripple. The protesters will lose against the insurmountable force that is China, regardless of what I do or don't do.

I focus on Father's reaction instead—his surprise when I told him. The glimmer of grudging respect in his eyes. I hold on to that moment, that sensation; it feels like a drug. A trickle of unease slides down my spine. I can see myself growing addicted, wanting more, heading further and further down this path.

And what would be so wrong with that? I ask myself angrily.

I take the MTR to the academy and type up a report for Lieutenant Chan. I'm jittery with suppressed adrenaline. I tell myself it's from my cold—that's why my head feels like it's going to split in half. After all, I can leave the lofty questions of morality and justice to the big guys at the top of the pyramid. The lawmakers and billionaires and faces you see on TV. I like following orders; I like keeping my head down. So what if the lying makes me queasy? It's in the name of the greater good. Peace and control and all that shit.

My job is just to obey orders.

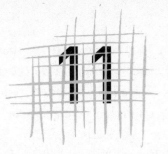

Phoenix

A WEEK BEFORE TIN-LOK'S PLANNED ESCAPE, Osprei, Suki, and I visit his bookstore. At New Pages, old newspapers cover the narrow glass door, concealing what's inside. Though there's a CLOSED sign tacked to the entrance, when Suki tries the door, it swings open, unlocked. On the inside, the shop's bigger than I expected. The bookshelves crisscross through the room like the walls of a maze, and books spill out of their cases, some even heaped in stacks on the floor. I take out my camera and unscrew the lens cap, hoping to find something interesting to capture.

There are others in the bookshop, though no one I recognize. They look to be around my parents' age or older. Some wear face masks, others baseball caps. All of them wear an air of mourning, as if it's not a shop that's closing but a dying friend.

"You're here!" An old man emerges from the back door. "I've been waiting for you. Tea is almost ready."

For all his notoriety, Tse Tin-lok is a small man, frail in stature. He wears spectacles with no rims, and a T-shirt that was clearly free, advertising some new tech company in Quarry Bay. He opens his arms wide. Suki laughs and pounces on him with a giant hug, and he stumbles back a few steps. Osprei looks like he's going in for a fist bump that devolves into an awkward handshake. I opt for a quick bow.

"Have you heard from Wes Foo?" Suki asks, leaning against the counter as she breaks a buttered pineapple bun in half. The sugary golden crust crumbles easily, and Suki licks the crumbs off her fingers.

Tin-lok sighs. "Still no word. But I was expecting as much."

Suki hisses in disappointment; Tin-lok gives her a sharp look. "Don't think too badly of him. You don't know how much pressure he's under." He looks at all of us, then takes off his glasses to wipe them on his shirt. "You don't know what those holding cells were like. In some ways, I'm luckier than him. I don't have a wife and kids trapped in the mainland. How could he refuse the police's demands? They have his family as leverage."

"So he's gonna leak the publishers' names? And the authors' too?" Suki asks.

Tin-lok doesn't answer. He tries to pour us tea, but his hands are shaking; some of the tea spills on the countertop. Osprei gently takes the teapot from him.

"Do you mind if I smoke?" Tin-lok asks. "My mind hasn't been the same since I got back. The nicotine's the only thing that calms my nerves."

He sits and motions for me to do the same. There aren't enough seats for everyone, so Suki plunks down on the countertop and Osprei leans against it.

Tin-lok takes a slow drag of his cigarette, his face troubled. "It's hard to say what will happen. But these authors know their books are controversial. They've taken precautions to ensure their names remain private." His mouth twists. "Even so, if their identities are somehow leaked...I would wish no one, not even Carrie Lam herself, what I experienced in Zhejiang."

Suki nods, looking like she understands perfectly. Osprei seems too confused to speak up. "If you don't mind me asking," I say quietly, "what happened in Zhejiang?"

He's not offended. Instead he nods, as if expecting this question. He turns away to blow out smoke, then taps his cigarette against the ashtray. "This is what I called you here for," he says. "Once I'm in Taiwan, I want you to publish my story. I want the world to know what really happened."

"Sook...," Suki starts.

"I know it's dangerous," he says firmly, peering at us over the rim of his glasses. "I'm aware of the consequences. But I'll be in Taiwan, where the extradition bill won't apply, and you know my wife has passed. I thank God we couldn't have children. I see now that it was all for a higher plan."

Suki and Osprei exchange glances. I pull a notebook out of my bag. "I'll take notes," I say. "For the story."

He smiles at me in a way that reminds me of my grandfather. "Are you a journalist, dear?"

"N-no," I say, caught off guard. "I'm not good with words. I usually just take photos."

He sips his tea, and the steam fogs his lenses. He looks so harmless, I wonder how the government could seriously view him as a threat.

Tin-lok grinds out the stub of his cigarette. "Where to begin? This banned book business has been going on for quite some time now, as you know. There's a real market for it here in Hong Kong. We're close enough to the mainland that we get plenty of customers from there—tourists, fanatics, even some Beijing politicians. The Chinese laws don't apply to us—at least, they didn't used to—so we could publish what the mainland could not. The money was pouring in.

"It wasn't the safest job, but it was what I wanted to do. I opened this shop over twenty years ago, and through the years, I learned how to minimize risk. I only shipped books through the busiest ports, where customs rarely checks your packages. I bribed inspection officers. I used fake dustcovers. I was careful."

Suki frowns, her eyes worried. "But not careful enough."

"Yes," Tin-lok agrees. "Times are changing, and I should have read the writing on the wall. A few years back, the Communist Party's Propaganda Department took control of all print media, including books. That was when things started getting worse. Last year, I got held up at a border checkpoint between Hong Kong and the mainland. I only had a few items with me, but they must have recognized me. They knew about New Pages, about all the illegal books that come through here. They arrested me on the spot, blindfolded me, then shipped me off on some train. I don't know how long the journey took. When I awoke, they put me in a cell. They gave me a change of clothes, and dinner. I had no idea where I was."

"Were you able to get in touch with anyone?" I ask, taking notes furiously.

He shakes his head. "I lost all connection to the outside world. My first night in the holding cells, they brought me to an interrogation room, where they made me sign away my rights to contact anyone or hire a lawyer. I thought if I complied, they'd let me go faster." He crosses his legs, as if trying to make himself smaller. "I'm just a bookseller, you know?"

Suki reaches over to take his frail hand.

"Several officials asked me about New Pages. They asked about my customers, my authors. They wanted their identities. Of course I told them I didn't know, that all transactions were anonymous. But they weren't satisfied. And days turned into weeks into months. In the end, I told them what I knew." He looks at us, as if expecting judgment.

But none of us knows what to say.

"You don't understand what it's like. I didn't know if seasons or years had passed. Sometimes I pretended to use the bathroom only to climb up on the toilet seat, to try to scan the window for any indication of where I was. All I saw was endless trees, mountains. I thought I would die there."

Feelings of hopelessness, I write. *Thought he would die there.*

"But they let you go?" I ask.

He lights another cigarette. The air thickens with smoke. No one dares prop open the door; this isn't the kind of conversation that can be overheard. "It was probably late winter when they decided to offer bail. I remember the barren trees, the silence in the sky. Someone met with me to sign a guilty plea as a precondition for bail. Then they put me back on a train and sent me south from Zhejiang. I thought I could finally go home. But we had to make one last stop first.

"We arrived at a luxury hotel in Shenzhen, just outside the border. I was so confused. When I came to dinner, I realized I wasn't alone. The other guests at the table—they were all banned booksellers, just like me. They'd been slowly rounding us up, one by one. China's playing a long game, you see. They're coming for all of us."

A cold tremor runs down my spine. It feels like the future's cheated and jumped ahead, as if it's determined to cannibalize the present.

"We couldn't talk candidly, with all the guards and security cameras monitoring us. But the message was clear. Foo told me, 'If you cooperate, you'll be released. Make sure you cooperate.' That was the last time I saw him."

I sketch out a timeline and map in my notes. "Did you return to Hong Kong from there?" I ask, looking up.

"Yes, but they gave me my directives first. I was to return to work at New Pages, gathering information as a mole and reporting on my customers behind their backs. They set a deadline to send them the names of customers, authors, and other publishers. This is how they take us out, you see, one by one. By turning us against each other."

"When was the deadline?" The sound of my pencil scratching against paper fills the silence.

He looks me in the face. "Next week."

I think of what would have happened to Suki if he'd gone through with his directive. I know she's frequented this shop in the past. And what about Wing-chi? Ming-lai? What about...Osprei? It hits me all at once how close I am to immediate danger. If someone were to find this interview in my notebook or learn I helped write this story...the extradition bill would apply to me. I could get shipped off to China, arrested in the middle of the night.

Would Mom think I had simply run away? Would Dad even care?

But what's the alternative? I wonder. To stop writing, to walk out the door, to remain silent? I can't do that either. People need to know what happened to Tin-lok. They need to hear, unequivocally, what's happening to Hong Kong. I see that now. When we stay silent, we take the side of those in power.

I look out the window at the busy, bustling street below. I think of Mom and Robin and even Uncle Chow, who needs his job to support his three grandkids in Guangzhou. I understand why people like Mom are still hoping for the best—it's simpler that way. They don't want to raise a fuss; they just want to go on with their lives.

"As soon as I heard news of the extradition bill, I knew what it meant," Tin-lok says. "They're coming for all of us now—anyone who dissents. It gives them the power to silence *anyone* who tries to fight back."

Suki pushes off the counter abruptly. She paces back and forth, walking the length of the counter. Osprei keeps twitching; I can tell he's feeling paranoid. I am too.

Tin-lok raises his voice. "Children, I do not tell you this for you to lose heart. I tell you this so that you will not go on blindfolded. You will not win this fight." He looks at each of our faces, as if trying to memorize them. "Today, you enjoy liberties in Hong Kong that most Chinese people do not possess. Freedom of speech, freedom of the press, freedom to protest. This will not last. China has armies and manpower beyond your comprehension. Even if every student comes out on the streets, China will still take over. Your only hope is that the world will listen to your plight and intervene. But if they do not, then you are alone."

"We have each other," Suki says fiercely.

Tin-lok looks grim. "It is a sad day when only children are willing to fight for their future."

I grip my pencil harder. "People like my dad think it's useless," I admit quietly.

Suki stops walking to stand over me. "We're not fighting to win," she says, her arms folded. "We're fighting because it's the only thing we can do. You said it yourself—our backs are pressed to the wall. But I'll be damned if I go down without a fight."

Suki resumes her pacing. There's too much frantic energy in her to stay still. "China wants to claim us, but we're not Chinese," she says. She's angry; twin splotches of red bloom on her cheeks. "We're Hong Kongers. That's our identity." She whirls toward us. "Right?"

Osprei nods, but I have a hard time meeting her sharp gaze. Am I a Hong Konger? I feel like one most of the time. These streets and sights and people are more familiar to me than North Carolina ever was. But I don't know if I have a right to be one. In the same way that I feel a visceral discomfort when someone labels me as an American, I feel a kind of shame when I claim to be a Hong Konger. I'm neither and I'm both. And if Hong Kong goes into lockdown and the city turns into a totalitarian state, my family has the funds to flee. But millions don't have that privilege; they'll be left behind.

I glance at Tin-lok, who's smoking again. "Why do you want your story told?" I ask him, my heart thudding.

He smiles at me; it is not a happy smile. "I'm a simple man, with small ambitions. I prefer books to people. I'm not trying to make a big fuss or overthrow the Beijing government." He laughs, which turns into a cough. I watch his flickering cigarette stub, the flame slowly dying. "All I want is to make sure our history isn't erased. I know there's propaganda everywhere these days. I know history gets twisted every day. But there's nothing I hate more than censorship. When people don't know what happened to their ancestors, they forget where they came from. They forget who they once were. Then everyone loses."

I look down at my hastily scrawled words, barely legible except to my own eyes. I have to transcribe this, I think, organize it, turn it into something powerful. I have to find some way to let others know what's going on here, how *all* of this is coming apart—this bookstore, this city, this way of life.

It's all happening so much faster than I thought possible.

"What was your name again?" Tin-lok asks me as he refills the teapot.

"Phoenix."

"You ask all the right questions, Phoenix," he says, in his slow, deliberate way. "You told me earlier you weren't a journalist. But I think you are."

A small, subtle warmth spreads through my chest. I smile at him and wish with all my heart that next Sunday's plan goes well. I hope he finds rest in Taiwan.

Before we leave, I take more photos of the bookstore, though I don't plan to post them until Tin-lok is out of Hong

Kong. Osprei and Suki go over the plan with him one last time while I pick up a few books. Tin-lok won't accept any money from me; he says it's the least he can do.

We leave New Pages at sunset. Suki heads off to work and Uncle Chow arrives to pick up Osprei and me. In the car, Osprei is uncharacteristically quiet, staring out the window. Then he pulls out his phone. I wonder if he's reading a news article or drafting a long text for Suki. I glance at the screen out of curiosity. It's a football game.

"I thought you were actually doing something serious!"

"This is serious," he retorts. "They're in penalty shootouts and the score is tied."

I make a noise of dismissal and slouch low in my seat. The boulevard is clogged with traffic, and our car inches forward at a crawl. I can't remember the last time Osprei and I were alone, without someplace to be, some person to meet. Our lives run parallel, but we rarely cross paths—at least we didn't until the protests brought us together. Ironic, isn't it? The movement dividing Hong Kong. Bringing us together.

"Have you been feeling okay? With the new meds?" I ask hesitantly. Talking about mental illness is basically taboo in our family. Since Dad's visit, no one's brought up Osprei's ADHD diagnosis at all.

"No change," Osprei says, engrossed in his phone. "I still hate studying." When I don't respond, he sighs. "It's not a big deal, Nix. I'm not insecure about it, if that's what you're worried about."

"You're not insecure about anything."

He flashes a grin at me. "You should try it sometime."

I scowl and turn toward the window. "Do you think we're

allowed…" I watch the traffic, instead of him. "I mean, do you think it's right for us…to be a part of this?"

"A part of what?" Osprei yawns. "The protests?"

I nod slowly. "I mean…do we even belong? Do we even have a right to fight for this place?"

"What the hell? Aa Mui, where's this coming from?" He puts down his phone. "This is our home. You believe that, don't you?"

"I do!" I tell him. "It's just, would other people believe it too? We were raised in North Carolina, of all places. Some might say we don't have a right to this."

"Fuck that," he says, and he means it too. His eyes are flashing, which only happens when he gets in a fight with Dad or loses at Fantasy Football. "We get to choose where we call home. What does it matter where we grew up?"

It feels good to hear him say this, but it also scares me. In a softer voice, I ask, "And what about the plan?"

Osprei releases an irritated sigh. We both know what I'm talking about. For the Lams, complacency has never been an option. After all, what we do in this life reflects not only on us but on our family. There's only one reason I've been cramming for the SATs: to go back to America. Hong Kong is just a seven-year pit stop. It was never meant to be my final destination.

"I mean, you can still leave," Osprei says in a dismissive tone. College is a sore subject between us, with him having flunked his classes. "But I'm staying here."

"Because of the protests?"

"I told you, because Hong Kong is my home. Because I belong here. Because I've never cared about anything bigger than myself before and this might be it. We're going to read about this shit in the history books one day, you know that, right? This might be Hong Kong's last stand. It'll be like *Les Misérables* or whatever."

"They all die in *Les Mis*," I mutter. "Besides, didn't you say you fell asleep during that movie?"

"Whatever, I got the gist of it." Osprei likes to pretend he doesn't like dramas, but he's honestly the biggest softy of us all. "The point is, who gives a damn if some hoity-toity Cantonese folks think you don't have a right to protest?" He throws me a suspicious look. "Did someone say something to you? Was it Ming-lai?"

I shake my head quickly. "No, just my own doubts. Anyway, I'm still applying to Yale. Mom and Dad would kill me otherwise."

"No one's stopping you," he grumbles, before glancing back at his phone. "Crap! They lost the game. This is because I wasn't paying attention, Nix. You jinxed me."

When we get home, I go up to my room and check Instagram. My username is @phoenixlampics—a name I chose when I'd intended it just for friends and family. But now my account's blowing up, especially with all the media coverage Hong Kong is getting internationally. I remember what Tin-lok said about the police trying to track down the names of any dissidents—customers of banned books, authors of alternate histories, publishers who advocate for free speech. If this extradition bill passes, any one of us could be next. *I* could be next.

This might be Hong Kong's last stand. My stomach hollows out at the thought.

I glance through my most recent photos—all pictures from protests—then scroll down farther. Tin-lok's warning still fresh in my mind, I go through my profile and remove any incriminating photos that might reveal my identity. I delete a bathroom selfie, a photo from a Whitney classroom. I even delete the photo of Osprei's foot at the beach with a crab clinging to his heel, though I'm sure no one could identify him by his toes.

I run through different options for display names. Finally, I decide on a popular protest chant: @hk_bewater.

Change confirmed.

Kai

MING-LAI SENDS ME HIS ADDRESS USING AN
end-to-end encrypted voice chat on Telegram, followed up
with a self-destructing message that says only "Don't be late."
The boy is more paranoid than my late grandmother, and she
lived through the Cultural Revolution.

I write down his address before I forget it. The meeting
tonight is only for the immediate team, the ones smuggling
Tin-lok out, so Phoenix won't be there. The brief relief I feel
is tailed by a twinge of disappointment.

"Are you nervous?" Marco asks as we're changing in the
gym locker room. I'm wearing black joggers and an oversized
linen tee with dropped shoulders. I can tell Marco admires
my style; he keeps checking the labels on my clothes. Never
mind that half my wardrobe comes from seedy wholesale
markets in Shanghai.

"No," I say, right before sneezing. I'm definitely sick.

"What?" he asks.

"No."

"Oh." He fiddles with his earring, which mysteriously disappears and reappears depending on whether Sergeant Leung is around. "Do you need backup for tonight?"

Marco knows about my involvement in the Tin-lok operation, though Lieutenant Chan warned me not to spread it around. It's impossible to keep secrets from Marco; the boy must've been a tabloid journalist in another lifetime.

"No need," I say, through a congested nose. "It's a smaller group of us this time. Any new outsiders would raise red flags."

"That district's pretty far out, you know," he says. "It's by the slums, and there's barely any cell service, for that matter."

"I'll be fine." I slide on my plain black sneakers, the only pair Lieutenant Chan deemed acceptable for training. "We're just finalizing the logistics. You'll be in the action soon enough."

Marco leans against the sinks. "It's not that I'm afraid of missing out." He makes a clicking sound with his teeth. "It's just not a safe area. And if you're stranded without reception..."

I snap my locker shut, then head to the door. "You said it yourself, 'They're just kids.'"

"*You're* just a kid," he protests, following me down the hall. I wait for him as he submits his paperwork and makes nice with our administrative supervisor. He turns to me after. "Don't get cocky and do anything stupid."

"No," I agree. "That's your job, remember?"

He chuckles, though he doesn't look exactly reassured. "You do know you stand out, right? That's why they didn't choose you initially for the undercover gig."

"What do you mean—why didn't they choose me?" It's a question that's bothered me for days. Our class ranking was posted this morning, and as I expected, I'm at the top. Yet Lieutenant Chan didn't even blink before passing me over.

Marco snorts. "You're a little dense sometimes, you know that? Everyone knows why." When I just stare at him, he sighs. "Kai, it's because you're too damn good-looking."

"You're joking."

He claps me on the shoulder. "I wish I was, bud."

I sputter. "But—how does that—why—"

"People remember your face. So don't get cocky tonight, got it? You weren't their first choice. You may still get caught."

I process this as we leave the academy together, stepping out into the darkening evening. It's painfully cold for early May, and my T-shirt does nothing against the wind.

"You know, I saw your dad checking your class ranking after our shift," Marco says, shooting me a sidelong glance. "Looks like he's started keeping tabs on you."

I make a scornful sound as if the idea annoys me. It's messed up, like a dog adoring its master when he feeds it scraps from the trash. But still I imagine my father going through my reports, caring about what I'm up to, proud of what I've managed to accomplish.

It thrills me, but it also terrifies me. Because I know his trust is precarious.

Marco scans the horizon, Shenshui Bay glimmering in the distance. "Looks like rain's coming," he says morosely.

"Again. I was supposed to take Yee-ching out dancing tonight."

"You can still go," I say, barely listening as I check my phone for directions. I sigh; Ming-lai's apartment is really far, beyond the outskirts of the city.

"She hates the cold. And she thinks some deadly flu is going around."

Right then, I sneeze. Loudly. Marco looks at me as if I'm the reincarnation of SARS. He literally skirts back two steps. I try to roll my eyes but end up sneezing again.

Marco clears out faster than I've ever seen him. "Ngo zau laa!" he shouts. "Good luck tonight."

I'm halfway to the MTR when the drizzle turns into a torrent. In seconds, I'm soaked down to the insides of my ears. I sprint the rest of the way to the station, then get promptly blasted by the air-conditioning, which is still on despite the freezing temperatures outside. I shiver my way down the platform, trying to cover my coughing with my sleeve. When I catch my reflection in the train window, I groan. I look like a drowned dog.

My vain boy, Ma used to say, in her teasing voice. *Tounao jiandan sizhi fada*. Beauty on the outside, airhead on the inside.

I used to be quite frivolous, didn't I? I used to care about more than money and sleep, duty and responsibility. I used to chase after beautiful things and dream a better dream, hai shi shen lou, castles in the air, all mirages, all empty. The light refracts, you cross the desert, and you realize you hold nothing. There is nothing at the top of the mountain.

After another sneeze, someone nudges me from behind.

It's an old lady, offering me a tissue. I thank her and take it, wondering how pitiful I must look.

"Aiya, you're wearing so little," the lady mutters, the disapproval clear on her face. "How could your ma let you leave the house like that?"

I shrug, turning away.

After a bus transfer and an uphill slog on foot, I make it to Ming-lai's apartment over an hour late. In the lobby, there's no security guard on duty to question me, just a shabby bulletin board with community announcements and depressing "Hire me" ads. I hit the elevator button for the twenty-third floor. The even-numbers elevator is already here, but I have to wait for the odds elevator to chug down from floor 31. I remind myself to stop grinding my teeth.

The twenty-third floor is coated in a thin layer of grime, with stained concrete walls, naked pipes, wheezing fluorescent lights, and something that might have been, a very long time ago, a striped wool rug. I make out Ming-lai's apartment number and knock gingerly. Inside, the hum of voices falls silent.

The door swings open. Suki stands on the other side, her hair now purple instead of pink. "You showed up," she says, not bothering to hide her disbelief. "We thought you'd been eaten by the dogs."

"That or your mother," someone calls. It's Wing-chi, who I met briefly at the last meeting. The handsome one with short hair and colored contacts. Ming-lai's second cousin studying biomedical engineering, or an equivalent major with just as many syllables.

I follow Suki inside. The apartment is cramped and

cluttered, exactly as you'd imagine the hideout of a brilliant mad scientist. There are yellow hard hats and gas masks stacked haphazardly on the kitchen counter, along with corrosive acid and bottles of spray paint, most half empty. I won't ask about that. A few students sit cross-legged on the carpet sorting glass bottles and cutting cloth wicks, crafting what look suspiciously like the beginnings of Molotov cocktails. I won't ask about that either.

The group I recognize sits around the dining table, which is outfitted with a Sailor Moon–patterned tablecloth. I recognize Ming-lai at the head of the table, Wing-chi, Osprei, and...Phoenix.

Her shock mirrors mine. "What are you doing here?" I ask, taking the farthest possible seat from her across the table.

Suki grimaces. "She wanted to help, and we needed some feminine distraction."

I look at Suki with a blank expression.

She rolls her eyes. "Distraction other than me. I'm needed in the Chaus' apartment; they trust only me. So Phoenix gets to play the part of leading actress instead."

Ming-lai huffs in annoyance. "Suki, catch him up on the details, will you? The rest of you, pay attention. Let's get through the remaining action items before we break tonight."

Suki slides her chair closer to mine and lowers her voice. From down the table, I can feel Phoenix's eyes on me.

"Don't worry, you didn't miss much," Suki says. "Tin-lok's getting smuggled out on a speedboat to Taiwan. Don't ask which one; we don't know. No one knows more than necessary, in case one of us gets caught." She eyes me for a second, long enough to make me wonder if she has xianjian zhiming, if she can read my mind. But then she goes on. "Our half of the plan is getting him to the meeting checkpoint on Lantau Island. Tin-lok's friends will handle the rest." She reaches for a loose sheet of paper, which Osprei slides toward her. It's a blueprint detailing the positions of Tin-lok's guards, with tiny numbers scratched into the sides for patrol times. It's not a high number of guards, but still absurd for a bookshop owner. What's he going to do? Throw books out his window? Read aloud from a controversial passage?

"So what is *her* role, exactly?" I ask, jerking my head at Phoenix.

Suki grins. "She's a distraction. She'll target the patrol guard."

"How?" I can feel a splitting headache coming on.

"She'll be a drunk party girl, reeling from a breakup. Think: big tears, plenty of blubbering, and of course, a sexy clubbing dress."

"We never agreed on the dress," Osprei interjects, causing Ming-lai to shush us.

My skin feels stretched too tight across my body. Fear seizes my chest and for a moment I'm so scared that I'm furious. She's too inexperienced for a job like this. She has no idea what she's getting herself into.

"The minute it's not safe, run, okay?" Osprei tells Phoenix. "And don't wear anything revealing."

Phoenix tucks her hair behind her ears, revealing her stupid-expensive pearl earrings. "It's not against the law to get drunk."

That's debatable, I think to myself, but now's not the time to reveal my extensive studies of HK law from police training.

"You can cry or whatever," I tell Phoenix, my face carefully neutral. "But don't provoke the officer. Don't do anything to get yourself arrested."

Her eyes meet mine, and there's a glimmer of something there, an ask of recognition, or just acknowledgment. I can't give it to her. What stake does she have in this night anyway? She's a rich kid from Repulse Bay. Can't she mind her own business and stay out of it?

Sweat pools down my back. I can feel my forehead heating up too, and the tips of my ears. I don't know why I'm so hot when I was freezing only minutes earlier. There are too many voices in my head telling me what to do. For a second, I can't remember why I'm here in the first place. I remember painting Ma's portrait, winning first place in my middle school art exhibit. That was the first time I really knew what I wanted. How did I get here? To this stifling apartment, this city, trying to satisfy everyone and no one. How did I get so far from what I wanted?

You're like water, Kai. You go with the flow.

I think about walking out of here. I think about doing something flimsy, something fun, something with *passhion* like the other art kids. But my thoughts, as always, lead me back to Ma. I remember her cheap gravestone on the outskirts of Shanghai. Grandma claimed it was fate, it had to be, that Ma passed at forty-four. After all, the characters for *four* and *death* sound almost the same. *Sì* and *sǐ*. Forty-four had too much death in it, Grandma claimed. The year arrived and the hungry ghosts were waiting. There was nothing anyone could do.

I don't believe that. She didn't *want* to die. She was too

young to die. But if there's one thing I've learned, it's that people like us don't get what we want. People without power, without money. We do things out of duty, out of debt, out of obligation. Duty to your country, or just your shitty father.

"Are you okay, dude?" Suki is peering into my face, her brows drawn in puzzlement. I blink; my mouth is dry like cigarette ashes. The fever turns my vision hazy at the edges, like those vignette watercolors with blurry borders. *The negative space manifests as a symbol of the design*, Professor Ng said. My field of vision narrows; I only see Phoenix, and Phoenix, and Phoenix. Her eyes are wide, searching. Anger or maybe just heat fills my insides. She has no right to look at me like that. Like I'm vulnerable, like I'm stripped bare, like something intimate has passed between us. I lurch to my feet, then grab on to the table for balance.

"Whoa, man," Wing-chi says distantly. Her voice sounds like it's coming from far away, from underwater. "What's wrong with you?"

"It's getting late anyway," someone who might be Ming-lai says. I hear chairs scraping back against the floor, the sound of chatter and commotion. I feel her presence before I see her.

"Hey," she says softly. "Are you okay?"

I'm trying not to look at her. Trying, and failing. How is her hair always so shiny? She looks perfectly kempt, like before, despite the rain and wind outside. Money, I remind myself. It's just money. Youqian neng shi gui tuimo. *Money can make even a ghost your slave.* Only when she catches my arm do I realize I'm swaying.

"You don't look well."

I shake my head. "I'm sorry," I tell her. "I'm sorry for what I did."

"What you did?" she asks. "But you didn't do anything."

The group bursts into laughter behind us. Suki is telling some Cantonese joke that is impossible for me to follow.

I feel her hand against my cheek, and I let my eyes fall shut. "You've got a high fever," she says. "Let me take you to the hospital."

Why did I have a bad feeling about this again? I can't remember why I didn't want to see her, why I was supposed to avoid her like SARS reincarnated or, wait, that was supposed to be me. I stumble back, confused. I don't want to give her my fever. I don't want to infect her.

I don't want to betray her.

Barely clinging to consciousness, I move toward the door and manage to unlock the safety latch with palpable effort. Prying open the door leaves me short of breath, so I'm winded as I cross the hallway toward the elevator. I hear her call out behind me. "Kai?" She's coming after me. *Cao!* I curse under my breath and look wildly around the hall. Phoenix's foot-steps sound louder and louder in my ears, echoing as if we're in a tunnel.

I spot the emergency staircase to my left and make a break for it. The hinges are rusted with disuse and wheeze like a smoker as I shove the door open. The world is shadowy, black and gray. The vignette has narrowed to a mere sliver, so that all I can see is the immediate step before me. Just make it down this step. Then the next one. Then the next.

Distantly, I hear the door open above. "Kai!"

I think it's Ma's voice. The thought doesn't surprise me, and I feel only a pleasant sort of delight, a mundane delight, as if she's back home early when I was expecting her an hour later. *She came back after all*, I think to myself, slumping against the wall. *That's nice of her.*

Then the world burns to black.

Phoenix

THE STAIRWELL DOOR SLAMS SHUT BEHIND ME with a vicious bang, sending centuries-old dust and spider corpses flying at me. "Kai?" I cough, spooked by the darkness. Something crunches under my feet. I check my shoe; it's a very old, very dead cockroach. I shudder. I think no one's touched this stairwell since the Qing Dynasty.

From down below, I hear a thudding noise. "Kai!" I run down the stairs, nearly tripping over my own feet. In the landing between floors, I see a figure slumped against the wall, sitting with his head between his knees. "Oh God, oh God, oh God." I crouch beside him, wishing I'd paid more attention in eighth-grade health class. I never learned how to administer CPR, unless you count watching that episode of *The Office* when Michael brings in a training dummy.

But Kai is breathing, his chest rising and falling visibly through his sweaty T-shirt.

He tries to sit up with some effort, tilting his head back against the wall so that his Adam's apple protrudes sharply against his exposed throat. "Li-Lifeng?" he rasps, saying my name in Mandarin. My heart squeezes. He sounds like a little kid.

"It's me," I say, taking his hand. "You'll be fine. I'm going to call 999."

"No!" He tries to sit up straighter and only succeeds in practically wringing my hand into pulp. I pull back and he loosens his grip on my fingers. "No," he says again. "I...I can't afford it."

"Don't be ridiculous."

"My father, he's done...enough...for me...."

I take in his face, covered in a faint sheen of sweat, his hair damp, his eyes half closed. I don't know how serious his fever is, but as they say in America, better safe than sorry. "I'm calling an ambulance. They're free here."

I take my phone out. No signal.

"Crap. There's no service here." I get to my feet. "I can go out to—"

"Wait. I—I feel better," he rasps, clearly lying through his teeth. "I'll head back now."

"To a hospital?"

He shakes his head a fraction. "I'll go...home."

"Where is home for you?"

His eyes fall shut. "Shanghai."

I exhale. I meant his Mong Kok apartment, but it feels cruel to clarify this now. "Here," I say instead, offering him a hand. He takes it with some effort, then staggers upright, causing both of us to stumble. Even though he's lean, he's shockingly heavy, so much so that we both nearly lose our footing.

"Baoqian," he says, catching his breath. *Sorry.*

"This is my fault," I say, because the guilt is plaguing me. "If I hadn't forgotten to return your jacket, you could've worn it today against the rain." I look ruefully at my boots. Actually, I didn't forget it; I just didn't want to give it back yet. "And now you're sick."

He laughs, which quickly derails into a cough. "I have more than one jacket, Lifeng." He pauses to catch his breath. "This isn't the first time. I'm bad at taking care of myself, that's why I got sick, last time...."

He breaks off. He seems to take in my presence as if for the first time, registering me and the stairwell and the concrete walls around us. Taking a step back, he starts coughing, then turns away from me, leaning into the wall.

"We have to get out of here," I say, putting my hand on his arm. "The dust—"

"Get away from me," he says, shrinking back. "I don't want to get you sick."

He looks so earnest as he says it, as if it's a matter of life and death. "Kai—"

When I reach out, he stumbles back, genuinely afraid. I've never seen him like this before. He looks like an animal caught in a trap, eyes ringed white. Breaking away from me, he starts climbing the stairs, breathing hard as he tries to put distance between us. But when he gets to the door and tries to pry open the rusted hinge, nothing happens.

He pulls again. Nothing.

I climb up beside him; this time he lets me. I tug hard on the door, not daring to believe.... It doesn't budge.

He swears under his breath. (He knows a lot more Chinese curse words than I do.)

"We're not locked in," I say firmly. "This door is just broken. Let's go to the next floor. I'm sure that one's fine."

I steel myself and march down the stairs to the twenty-second floor, my heart pounding. I refuse to accept our current predicament. There are thirty-one floors in this apartment building. Surely there's a 99 percent chance that one of the thirty floors we haven't checked yet will have an unlocked door. (If Charlie were here, he'd be complaining about my sloppy math skills right about now.)

The door on the twenty-second floor doesn't budge. Neither does the twenty-first floor, nor the twentieth. I pound on that one extra hard, shouting at the top of my lungs. "Help! Anyone! Can you hear me?"

Kai just rests wearily against the wall beside me, his eyes half closed. "We're locked in," he says tonelessly.

Tian ah, Mom is going to kill me.

That is, if I'm still alive when she finds me.

"Wait!" I cry out, struck with sudden inspiration. "Your phone! Maybe you have service."

He withdraws his phone from his pocket with a resigned air. "No bars."

I exhale, trying not to panic. My knuckles are raw from knocking, but I beat at the door one last time, just in case someone's passing by. "Hello? Anyone?"

"Save your breath," he mutters. "We don't have any water."

The thought drops my stomach to my knees. We could die in here. It could be another dynasty by the time they find us! I turn toward Kai, fully despairing, until I remember how sick he is and shut my mouth. I'm really not the one who should be complaining right now.

"I'm sorry," he says, rubbing his eyes. "I dragged you into this."

"It was my decision to follow you," I say. "I'll get us out of here. I promise."

I decide to try the next floor. And the next. By the sixteenth floor, Kai can't keep up anymore. He slumps down on the steps, his elbows on his knees, his face in his hands. I can't even be upset with him. I'm just scared.

I check one more floor on my own, but my echoing footsteps in the face of the enveloping silence intimidates me, and the possibility of being abandoned here, all alone, unnerves me so badly I race back to the sixteenth floor, terrified that Kai has disappeared, died, teleported into another dimension. But he's still there, right where I left him, his posture unchanged.

I take a seat beside him. He doesn't move.

"Kai?" Slowly, he raises his head an inch, so that I can see his profile. His cheeks are red, his hair mussed. I sigh. "I thought you were dead!"

"Takes more than a flu to kill me," he says, before biting his lip. Now he only looks more wretched. He turns his face away. "Rubbish collection will probably come by in the morning. We're lucky tomorrow's Wednesday." He swallows, and I track the knot at his throat. "You shouldn't sit with me."

"Where else would I sit?" (Well, I guess there *are* thirty other floors.)

"I don't want you to get sick."

"Why do you care so much about that? I'll be fine." I try to smile. "Takes more than a flu to kill me."

He looks up sharply at this, almost angry. To my surprise, his eyes are wet. "What is it?" I ask softly, even though we're alone. "Tell me."

For a moment, I think this time will be like all the others. He'll refuse again, and we'll fall into silence.

Instead, he clears his throat. "My ma," he says hoarsely. I still, afraid to even blink, as if any sudden motion might disturb his admission. "I killed my ma."

"What?" Now I sit up. "Kai, you're not feeling well—"

"No. Listen to me." His voice is low and rasping. "I was stupid. I—I told you, I'm not good at taking care of myself."

"What does that have to do with—"

"I went out with a girl. She was sick, and she told me, but I said I didn't care. It was hailing in Shanghai. We stayed out all night. By daybreak, we'd both caught the flu." His voice is thick with anger, and it radiates off him. It makes me want to back away, but I can't. I can't move.

"Ma was a smoker. She tried not to do it in front of me, but I always knew. You can't hide these things from family." He pulls at a loose thread in the rip at his knee. "She had COPD. Lung disease. She'd get these coughing spells, but I thought they were normal. Everyone knew the smog in Shanghai was bad." He laughs, a raw, scornful sound. "I didn't think about anyone but myself. I was in my head all the time. I came home sick and she took care of me. I let her. I even asked her for things."

"Kai, it's normal for a mother to care—"

He shakes his head; he's talking now and I can tell he can't stop, not when he's held it in for so long. "You know, she got the flu a few days later. By the following week, she could barely walk from being short of breath. At night she couldn't even lie down. She had to sleep sitting upright on the sofa. But I was gone most of the time, recovered already and dating a new girl. I thought she would get better too."

I regret wanting to know what's in his head. It's nothing like what's in mine. We're only a year apart, but our lives are poles apart. Maybe I could try to reach across the space, to bridge the gap, but right now it feels impossible, like trying to grasp at smoke.

"I got home one night around eleven. I found her on the sofa, her face turning blue. She was put on a ventilator. By then, it was too late. She died within the week."

"It's not your fault, Kai. You didn't know."

"But I could've known." His eyes fall shut. "If I'd cared enough."

His expression is far away. I imagine his thoughts tracing familiar lines of self-loathing and regret—well-beaten circles, like the rings of an ancient tree.

"Kai." I grab him by the shoulders and force him to look at me. "Your mother isn't the one blaming you. You're just blaming yourself."

He inhales shakily and I can tell he's holding back tears. I could let him go, walk away, give him space and pretend we never had this conversation. That's what Mom would do.

The thought stings. Instead, I press my arms around him, so that we're both trembling now. To my surprise, he burrows his head in my shoulder, and I can feel his breath against my neck, hot and fast, his bitter tears wet against my skin.

When he speaks, his voice is slurred. "Bai shanxiao..." He hiccups and doesn't finish the sentence. But even I recognize Confucius's famous words: *Of all virtues, filial piety is highest.*

I think of my own mom, what she expects of me. To be a filial child is to obey. To obey and serve. Filial piety is supposed to be the bedrock of Chinese culture. It's why Chinese people are successful, why we're resilient. Because we stick together; we do what's right not for ourselves but for the family.

It's a blessing, I suppose. But sometimes, I think, looking down at Kai, it feels more like a curse.

I brush his hair out of his eyes. He doesn't notice; he's fallen asleep, entirely spent.

I wake to the sound of a screeching door in the distance. My first thought is that the lower half of my body is freezing cold, but my head and neck are warm. Then I realize that my head is on someone's thigh; that someone is Kai, and he's wide awake, looking at me. His eyes are soft.

I shoot upright, flushing. "I didn't mean to—"

"We both fell asleep," he says coldly. His tone jolts me

awake. Last night feels like a vague half dream. I stare at Kai, at his shuttered face. We're back to being strangers.

"Are you feeling better?" I ask, almost timidly.

He gives me a clipped nod.

Two little girls in school uniforms run down the stairs past us. "How'd you get in here?" I ask, hoping they're not stuck with us too, for the rest of time.

"The lift's down," the taller girl chirps. "They told us to take the stairs."

"Who?"

She shrugs, then tugs on the hand of her friend, giggling. They skip past us, pigtails flying behind.

I feel like we just heard we won the lottery, but Kai's face is unsurprised. "Let's check," he says.

Sure enough, the door is pinned open by an orange traffic cone. I nearly cheer aloud, before I see Kai's glance. His eyes are dark, narrowed; he looks angry.

Angry at who? I wonder. *At me? Or at himself?*

I keep quiet as we trek back to the bus stop, then the MTR station. When we reach the turnstiles, I know it's time to part ways. We live on opposite ends of the island. We run in different circles, different lives. That's what's expected of me now—to accept the status quo. To pretend I don't care.

But I'm sick of this. No matter what he wants, I can't erase last night from my memory. I can't go back to treating him like we're barely acquaintances.

"Kai." I step forward; he jerks back, surprised. Frustration and something else flashes across his face before he forces control over his expression again. "Are we just going to pretend last night never happened? And that time at KTV? And on the train..."

A muscle feathers along his jaw, but his face remains inscrutable. Somewhere beyond us, a fire alarm is ringing. "Yes," he says, his voice hoarse.

My stomach twists. "But...why?"

He avoids my eyes as if I have the face of a jiu gwaai. "I can't talk about this," he says tightly, emanating coldness. "I just—we can't see each other."

He takes a step back like he's preparing to go, and for a second I see our future flash before us—Kai disappearing into the Hong Kong streets, anonymous in a sea of seven million. I search for him every day, but never find him again. And why would I? Our paths weren't meant to cross. We live different lives, separate as yin and yang. But even yin and yang touch. Isn't that the whole point? I glare at him, willing him to meet my gaze.

"Just tell me this," I say, my ears ringing so loudly I can barely hear my own voice. I remember waking up in his lap, his eyes warm as he watched me. I remember kissing him on the train, his breath soft on my lips. I can't have imagined it all—he must remember too. "Do you care about me at all?"

His answer costs him; he hisses through his teeth. "Of course."

This should please me; instead, it infuriates me to no end. "Then why?" I demand. Warring expressions cross his face. Buoyed, I take his hand. "Why can't you give this—us—a chance?" Suki would shake her head at me. *This isn't how you play the game, girlfriend.* I know I'm going against the advice of a hundred rom-coms and self-help books. All I know is that this pull between us is undeniable, and if I let him go now, I'll regret it. Today, tomorrow, the day after tomorrow. That's as far as I can think right now.

"You don't understand."

"Tell me," I press. "Tell me what I don't understand."

He shakes his head. "I just...*Lifeng*..." As soon as he says my name, I know I've won. His body relaxes, he wraps his arms around me, and I press my cheek to his chest.

Too soon, he pulls back. "Lifeng," he says seriously. "You can't tell the others."

I try to read his expression, but it's like picking at an unbreakable lock. "Why?"

"You just...can't." He looks down, his face hardening. "If the others found out, they'd think I'm only involved because of you. It'd be a...conflict of interest."

I don't fully get it, but it makes sense he would want secrecy, being the mystery boy that he is. Besides, this arrangement works for me too. It'd be a real pain to tell Charlie, who's decided he has a massive grudge against "the emo artist boi."

"Okay."

"I'll text you tonight," he says, in a voice that makes me think he won't. I know he has to go, and so do I, but I'm a gambler and I don't like to hedge my bets. Impulsively, I stand on my tiptoes and press my lips against his. His mouth is soft, eager, open like he never is.

This time, I'm the first to draw away. "See you soon," I whisper, and I know now I have a winning hand.

Kai

GODDAMN IT, KAI, I THINK, OVER AND OVER. *Why are you such a baichi fool?* I was supposed to hold fast to my resolutions, stubborn as stone. Instead, I'm water. Ma used to say I was water.

I stop by the pharmacy to pick up medication, but I can tell my fever's already down. That's the way I've always been, burning hot then cold. I get sick fast but recover faster. I never thought much about it, not until Ma's death.

In high school, I read an article about a cook named Typhoid Mary. People thought she was cursed because wherever she worked, the families always got sick and died. Turns out she was an asymptomatic carrier. What really caught my attention was Mary's forced quarantine—imprisonment for twenty-six years. She said she just wanted to be a plain old cook, to live free. But did you deserve to live a normal life when you lived it at the cost of others? What if everything you did was destructive, and you couldn't stop, and you couldn't go on? Then what?

The silence in my head is answer enough. *Ma*, I want to say, *give me the answer*. But she will never speak again.

That night, I take out my phone. I can't believe I'm doing this.

Hey. Did you make it home okay?

A text bubble pops up almost immediately. Mom flayed me alive for missing curfew, but yes, other than that, I'm good. Before I can think of what to say in response, another text bubble appears. I'm not sick, by the way.

I exhale. Good.

I fall back in bed and hold my phone out at arm's length, as if it's a ticking grenade. Without thinking it through, I type: Want to meet Friday night?

She sends back a grinning smiley face. What does that mean? Yes or no?

I can't wait, she adds. And now my smile matches that dorky emoji.

We meet in private, after dark. We go to Repulse Bay on both Friday and Saturday, because my father would never venture down there, and the police are scarce; as a general rule, we leave rich folk to their own devices. Phoenix has the best ideas, because of course she does. It's her idea to meet at a movie theater in Cityplaza, to come in from different ends. I find her in the back row, wearing just a sliver of a tank top with jean shorts.

After, we both can't recall the movie.

She says she likes the mystery, the sneaking around, like we're in some elaborate spy conspiracy. I don't know if I believe her. We can't meet each other's friends like a normal couple; we can't wear matching couples' shirts like they do in the movies. (Not that I would be caught dead doing that.)

Father notices my change in mood but doesn't say anything about it, though I do catch him eyeing me at inopportune moments. Marco also notices—and won't shut up on the subject.

"Who's the girl?" he keeps nagging me. "I know there's a girl. Just tell me her name. One character in her name. I'll look her up online."

That's the last thing I need him to do. I pretend I can't hear him and keep walking through the grocery aisles, grabbing a few bananas and tossing them in my basket. It's Sunday morning, and Marco is heading back to the academy after this without me. Meanwhile, I'm participating in my first real operation. Tonight's the night of the New Pages sting.

"Yee-ching is mad at me for flirting with the barista at Starbucks. How was I supposed to know she was eavesdropping?" Marco sulks. "I'm as pious as a monk now. I need to live vicariously through you, pal."

"Hold this, will you?" I dump my basket in his arms so I can grab a jug of soy milk.

Marco is scowling when I return. "Why do you keep buying groceries lately? Getting domesticated? Who's the lucky gal?"

"My father," I say, suppressing a laugh. "I've been cooking for both of us on weekends."

Marco raises a brow, impressed. "Filial son," he says, in an offhand way that shows how little this means to him. "My parents might want to swap kids. But alas, they're stuck with me." He nabs a packet of barbecue cha siu pork buns from the frozen foods aisle. "I visit them at New Year. Once in a blue moon, I get a spike of guilt and consider visiting more often. Then I call my mom and remember why I avoid the place like a funeral parlor. All she asks about is when I'm getting married and how many kids are on the way." He snickers. "You're lucky your dad isn't a busybody."

It's true my father isn't a busybody, but only because he couldn't care less about anyone besides himself.

"I bet she's a real stunner, huh?" Marco continues. The boy has a skill for holding up one-sided conversations. "Given your height and dark looks." His lip curls in irritation. "You know, girls really need to start caring about inner personality. I mean, look at you. Handsome, but with the character of a Styrofoam box. No offense. At least a Styrofoam box makes some noise. Especially when recycled."

"Hmm," I say blithely, unbothered. "Can you even recycle Styrofoam?"

"And then there's me. A bit short, you know, could be taller—I blame my dad; he wouldn't let me drink milk as a kid—thought it was a white people conspiracy thing."

I snort.

Marco grins, pleased he got me to laugh for once. "But my personality, on the other hand, you have to admit, Kai, I'm a real crowd-pleaser. If any girl would just give me a shot, they'd fall head over heels. Even your lady pal. Introduce us, will you?"

"Not a chance," I say.

Marco pounces. "So there *is* a girl! I knew it! I told you so!"

"*You* told *me* so?" I repeat as we get in line.

"Secret's out, bud." He sticks out both hands as if begging for money. "Cough up. Pictures, immediately. It's not fair. You've been in Hong Kong less than a month, with trash Cantonese, no offense, and already the girls are falling in line. Meanwhile, me, more fluent than Sun Yat-sen himself—"

"I highly doubt that."

"—and I still can't keep a girlfriend even though I'm practically out on a date per week. If you doubt me, ask my wallet. It's hurting."

"Stop eating out so much, then," I say, loading lettuce onto the checkout belt. "Buy groceries and cook for yourself."

Marco pouts like a lost puppy. "What am I gonna do? Invite a girl over for a home-cooked meal in our coffin-sized dormitory? No, thank you, sir." He props an elbow on the conveyor belt, which promptly shoots forward and propels him off. "Though I don't need to be telling *you* how expensive dating is, am I right? Where have you taken her to? Dinner at Robuchon? Fireworks at Disneyland? Tell me so I can run into you, accidentally, of course."

I look down. We haven't done any of those things. We can't. Not for the first time, shame ties knots in my stomach. Phoenix deserves someone better, someone who can actually be there for her. I keep telling myself I'll end things with her next time. And then next time comes around. And she smiles at me. And I say nothing.

"Eighty-nine fifty man is your total," the cashier tells me.

I pay at the register as Marco eyes me. I can practically hear his brain plotting how to get me to spill Phoenix's name. If only he tackled our classwork with as much dedication as he does dating gossip.

"Shouldn't you be heading back to the academy?" I ask as he starts tailing me to my apartment. "I'm just dropping these groceries off."

"You *are* just going back to your apartment, then heading to the sting later tonight, huh? Not meeting your girlfriend in between?"

A morbid part of me wants to laugh, because if he knew the truth—that Phoenix will be at the operation tonight— he'd probably combust from shock. Then promptly report me to management, and get me fired, then disowned.

Some things are better left unshared.

Father is awake when I get home and in a peculiarly good mood. He's made himself a cup of coffee for once and sips it by the window, looking out at the Mong Kok market below us. I busy myself with washing lettuce. Still, I can feel his presence behind me like an empty oil drum, silent yet full of vapor, ready to burst into flames. I finish breading the pork katsu, then transfer the pieces to a skillet to fry. Just as I crank up the fire and turn on the vent, he speaks.

"You've been remiss lately," he says over the crackle of the stove.

"What?" I shout, switching off the vent. I'm surprised he's speaking to me, even if it's just to berate me.

"Sergeant Leung mentioned Trainee Hai was sick

yesterday, and they needed backup for Hennessy Road crowd control. They called you, but you didn't pick up."

"I was off duty," I say, flipping the katsu. One side is burned, so the meat is charred black at the edges. The katsu remind me of ink drawings when the pen blots and smudges the wrong way.

"An officer is never off duty."

"I'm not an officer yet."

"What?"

I bite back my retort and turn the fire off. "I understand."

"Look at me."

My stomach twists but I do it, I obey. His face is stern yet intent; he genuinely believes the police force is the most important job in the world. "Don't show that attitude tonight," he says. "There is no room for error, understand?"

I swallow. *His trust is precarious.* "Yes."

"Make sure you're on time. Go along with their plan, so the gaat zaat don't figure out who you are," he says, using the derogatory name, cockroaches, for protesters. "Give the signal when the bookseller's out in the open. Not too early so he can claim plausible deniability. Not too late so he actually gets away. You know the rest. The unit will respond to your signal. They'll arrest the cockroaches while you run. If you do your job right, the protesters won't suspect you. Then you can stay on the op."

"I thought I was the one making the arrests."

"You're too green for that," he says. "The senior cops will handle the dirty work. Your job is to keep your head down."

I transfer the katsu to a plate. I don't know if I should feel better or worse. I guess I'm relieved not to have that responsibility. But it doesn't change the fact that the secret's out; the police know about the operation and Phoenix is not safe. None of them are. Tonight, they'll all go to jail, or worse. I feel sick to my stomach imagining myself standing by, doing nothing. But I feel just as sick imagining my father's face as he learns the truth.

"Don't tell me you're getting cold feet," Father spits out. The animosity in his voice is sharp enough to spill blood. "You can't even handle this much?"

"No!" My voice shakes. I sound childish to my own ears. "I—I can handle myself." *Why can't I speak properly?* "You don't need to keep drilling me through the plan. I already know my orders."

"Then act like you know them."

"I do."

He glares at me. I leave the steaming katsu on the kitchen counter and go to my room, no longer hungry. The door closed, I drag out my sketchbook and flip through the pages, filled with a red-hot urge to rip them all to pieces. I flip through faster and faster, unsatisfied, wanting. The wanting is always there. It leaves me empty inside.

My hand freezes at a familiar face. It's a drawing of Phoenix, finished last night. The truth is, I was with Phoenix yesterday when Trainee Hai got sick, and my phone was very, very off. When I left her and saw the three missed calls, my heart nearly fell out of my chest; I was sure they were firing me for misconduct or arresting Phoenix for skies knows what. Instead, when I listened to the voice mail, I learned they were only asking for backfill. I didn't call back. I knew the academy could find someone else to cover. As for me, I went home, taking the stairs two at a time because I was in a hurry. I wanted my charcoals so I could draw Phoenix. I wanted to try a multidisciplinary approach for a study of her profile. Graphite for her eyes, charcoal for her silhouette. I drew the way her profile looks when she's concentrating: Her nose turned up, her lips turned down. Her big eyes narrowed and slightly off focus.

Ma, I wish you could meet her. You always liked the girls I brought home. But Lifeng's different. I know you would like her best.

Kai

TSE TIN-LOK LIVES IN KOWLOON, IN A QUIET middle-class suburb. By the time midnight rolls around, the streets are deserted, the lights off in the apartment windows and balconies. An eerie wind flutters across the streets, scattering candy wrappers and dried leaves into the gutters. I feel deceptively alone. As if I could shout and no one would hear me.

I know it's a lie. The officers wait somewhere in the car park. They could be that extra-long shadow beneath the truck, or the blur by the rosebush. Every shadow feels potent, weighted, hiding a human or perhaps a hungry ghost.

Sergeant Lai has brought a team of half a dozen officers, all seasoned. I'm the youngest, the weak link in the chain. I'm the one I don't trust.

From the nineteenth floor, a flashlight blinks on and off three times. That's the signal from Suki. She's waiting in the apartment of her uncle's upstairs neighbors. Their balconies sit parallel, so Tin-lok only needs to climb up to their balcony to avoid detection, then take the stairs to the roof. From there, he'll cross over to the adjacent building, Sing Yuet Villa, to skirt the patrol officers. The best break point will be by the getaway car, if I can time it correctly.

I cross the street, affecting ease though every muscle in my body is wound tight, a metronome set to full speed. I slink around the back to take the villa service entrance; the door is propped open just as Suki promised. From there, I take the stairs to the third floor, with the broken security camera in the corridor, and wait for the elevator to take me to the roof. A tired graveyard-shift worker is already in the elevator when it arrives, but his eyes are glued to his phone, which plays a clip of a scantily clad dancing girl on repeat. He won't remember my face.

Up on the roof, the wind is stronger, less a breeze and more like the opening act of a gale. A half-hearted fence stands guard over the straggly community garden, with unused wood planks scattered on the ground. I choose a few of the longer boards and try stepping on one to test its strength. Safe enough. These will clear the distance.

From up high, the streets look foreign and unnatural. I use the car park to orient myself; I recognize the blue sedan I was hiding behind, and the curved alleyway perpendicular. A lone figure walks at a leisurely pace down Sing Yuet Street; this could be the aforementioned patrol officer. The figure glances at his phone, then starts dancing to an unknown beat, breaking out into 360-degree spins and jump kicks. Never mind.

Another figure catches my eye: a girl walking in the middle of the road, unafraid of potential passing cars. Even from this distance, I recognize her long hair and small frame. Phoenix. She looks cold.

Go home, I want to tell her. *Don't come any closer.*

Instead, I turn away. Ming-lai will be with Tin-lok now, guiding him up the stairs. Osprei will be holding up the even-numbers elevator, moving furniture and making enough noise to distract the apartment complex security.

My job is simple: set up the bridge.

I drag the boards over to the edge, then secure one end with duct tape. The boards teeter in the wind as I gauge the distance. If you're not afraid of heights, it's an easy step over. If you are, then that's another story. Tin-lok is a bookseller. I'm sure he never signed up for this. But like Ma always said, in this life, there's a lot of things we never signed up for.

With a quick exhale, I cross over the makeshift bridge to the other side. Then I secure the bridge with duct tape and take the stairs down to the ground floor. The stairwell reminds me of Ming-lai's, which reminds me of other things, unbidden.

Your mother isn't the one blaming you, Phoenix said. *You're just blaming yourself.*

I confessed awful things to her, and yet she stayed with me, even comforted me. Does she know how nice it is to hear those words, words you've been trying to convince yourself of for countless sleepless nights, replaying moments in your head, wondering how you could've done things differently, said no, walked away, come home early, went to your ma and kissed her good night? There are so many things I would do over, if I could.

Let tonight not be one of them.

Emboldened, I steal over to the garbage area and catch

Wing-chi in the driver's seat of a green minivan. She's smoking a cigarette with the blacked-out windows rolled down. I consider alerting her to my presence, so they know that I showed up, that I played my part. Marco told me to make friends with these people, to garner their trust.

I stay away.

Time passes with the lethargy of a sleepless night, when your bedsheets feel claustrophobic, and every sound seems like a scream. I crouch beside the recycling bin, wondering if I should pretend to patrol. It's hard to remember who I'm betraying. The lines cross over each other a dozen times, a spiderweb.

I leave Wing-chi to her chain-smoking, then skirt around the villa lobby, past the car park. When I catch wind of voices, I slow, turning toward the side street.

Phoenix stands in the middle of the road, chatting with the patrol officer. It takes me a moment to ID him; he's one of the auxiliary police who only recently graduated, in his early twenties. They look friendly, unperturbed by the hour or Phoenix's fancy getup. He smirks, amused, then slips a hand onto her bare shoulder.

My blood turns hot.

I take a step forward, then stop. I can't run out there and blow my cover. I scan the dark streets, the sleeping apartment complexes, all quiet but for the blustering wind.

I think of my father, the scars encircling his neck, the man who never backs down. I think of my mother: all the sights she will never see, the stories she will never hear. She wouldn't say it aloud, but I know she didn't want me to end up like him. Maybe that's why we left.

I think of Phoenix, who says she trusts me. That trust was a gift.

Shaking, I take out my phone. You know those moments that define you? This is one of them; I can already tell. Abort mission: the dogs are onto us. We can try again another day.

I press send before I can second-guess myself. In seconds, Suki likes my message, then Wing-chi, Osprei. Phoenix is still chatting with the officer. His hand has slid lower; it's on her back now. I hiss in frustration, too loud, and both of them turn, startled. I duck behind the corner hastily.

Moments later, Phoenix likes my message. I exhale in relief and head toward the car park. Sergeant Lai will be expecting me there. It's crucial he thinks I'm waiting for them, as planned. Nothing's gone wrong; I know nothing.

Too late, I realize the only one I haven't heard back from is Ming-lai, the one with Tin-lok himself. Just as Wing-chi starts the engine and prepares to back out of the loading zone, two figures shuffle out of the apartment building, one hooded, the other unmistakably Ming-lai.

I swear under my breath. No one needs a signal from me; Sergeant Lai jumps out of his cover by the trees and shouts something into the night. In seconds, a swarm of officers follows him, ordering Ming-lai and Tin-lok to raise their hands in the air. I enter the clearing too, but Sergeant Lai looks over Ming-lai's shoulder, directly into my eyes, jerking his head in a very clear signal to run. I remember the plan: I'm supposed to maintain my cover, pretend I'm one of the gaat zaat. I'm supposed to run from the cops now. But unlike the rest of them, I'm supposed to get away.

Instead, I remain frozen, my heart tripping in my chest. It

wasn't supposed to be like this. I just wanted to draw, to draw and dream. I just wanted to live freely. But Typhoid Mary wanted to live freely too. Look where that got her.

Don't you remember? Forget hai shi shen lou. You will be paying for the rest of your life.

Behind me, there are the sounds of a scuffle. I hear cursing, then a yelp of surprise. "Who are you?" an officer demands. "Where's..." I don't catch the rest. Drawing on the last dregs of self-preservation, I turn on my heels and stumble away.

That's when I hear the second engine start. Beyond the lobby, I spot a weathered Mini Cooper with a familiar purple-haired girl sitting in the driver's seat. She catches my eye and winks. Then I register the old man staggering toward her. He moves painstakingly slow as he hobbles down the steps toward the car. The moment crystallizes in my mind. I could cry out, grab him, arrest them both. I could make my father proud. He would see me—he would know I'm no puk gaai dreamer boy.

But maybe I am. Because as the bookseller opens the passenger door, then falls inside, I just watch. I stand there, frozen, judging them, judging myself. The door slams shut. Suki guns the engine. Tin-lok braces himself against the seat.

I am the worst kind of liar. The one who betrays both sides, and in the end, betrays himself.

The car disappears into the night.

I run. It's the one thing I know how to do.

Phoenix

I HEAR THE SHOUTING BEFORE I SEE THE COPS. One minute I'm hurrying back to our rendezvous point, trying to shake off the greasy feeling of that officer's hand on my back, the next I'm running. The sounds are coming from the car park. I spot Osprei and Ming-lai, surrounded by what feels like an army of police officers. They're all huge, and tall, with heavy black things strapped to their belts, and batons in their hands. There's Wing-chi, stepping out of the car with her hands raised in the air. Where's Suki? And Kai?

"You there!" It takes me a full second to realize the officer is speaking to me. He peers through the bamboo leaves dividing the loading zone from the lobby as if trying to see if there's someone beside me. Then I realize: Tin-lok isn't here. Did he escape?

"What are you doing here?" the officer barks.

"She must be a cockroach," someone says.

Osprei jerks his head in a clear order to run. The officer steps toward me, but I take off first.

My heel snaps and I nearly lose my balance as I kick off my shoes in a hurry. Something sharp digs into my toe; I wince as hot blood wells on my foot. I turn down Sing Yuet Street, avoiding the wide boulevards with no places to hide. I can hear footsteps thundering behind me, harsh breaths, muffled by wind. Should I climb a tree? Beg a neighbor for help? I can barely think as I run, my lungs burning, my foot bleeding, my vision tunneling.

I spot an alley branching off the main road and veer sharply left, tripping over the sloped curb and catching myself an inch before sprawling headfirst. I stumble toward the light at the end of the alley, my steps lagging, trying to think through the pain, begging my feet to just keep moving, one step in front of the other—

Someone grabs me by the shoulder. I nearly pitch forward in shock. We both lurch clumsily before he steadies himself against the brick wall.

"Why are you running?" he demands in Cantonese. His silver badge glints in the dark. *Officer Ho Yi-tung.*

I try to pull out of his manacle-like hands, but his grip tightens. "Because you're chasing me!"

He doesn't answer right away. Instead, his eyes rove down my body. I squirm, which only makes him laugh. "What are you doing here?" he asks again. "Are you a runaway? A druggie?" He pauses. "Or part of the terrorist group?"

"What terrorist group?" My voice turns shrill despite my best efforts. "I'm not a runaway and I'm not on drugs! Let me go!"

He leans back and cocks his head like a bird inspecting a bread crumb. "You're a gaat zaat, aren't you?" *Cockroach.*

I glare at him, our heaving breaths filling the silence. He smiles like he's figured me all out, like he knows the exact day I was born and the exact day I'll die. Like he's God himself.

"It's quite late, don't you think?" he asks. "Odd time to be out and about."

"It's not like we have a national curfew," I snap. "It's not a crime to walk around."

"No," he agrees, "but something tells me you weren't just walking."

My stomach clenches, but I remind myself to remain calm; he doesn't have any evidence.

He smiles. "You're a pretty one."

"Is that a crime too?" I jut out my chin, trying not to show how scared I am.

He chuckles. "It can be, if you're not careful." Then he pushes me back against the wall, imprisoning me between his arms.

Every bone in my body goes cold. I've never interacted with a cop before, but I know, I just know, this isn't proper police protocol.

I should've stayed with Osprei. I should've woken the neighbors. I should've run down the busiest street into the 24/7 stores—

"Which school do you go to, little miss?" His eyes are on

my chest. "Let me guess, HKU? All the gaat zaat come from there."

I shake my head but can't speak.

"It's okay, sweetheart, don't be scared," he croons. "I won't arrest you for your illegal political inclinations. We'll keep it a secret between you and me." He fingers the strap on my dress. "But I can arrest you for drug possession."

"What?" I try to shout. It comes out like a squeak. He presses closer, his gun riding into my thigh. I squeeze my eyes shut; those things can't go off randomly, can they?

"Drug possession." He's speaking. I should be listening. I should really be listening right now. "It's penalty by death, you know. And you're too young to die."

"But—I have no drugs. Check me!"

"Oh, I will. Only if we can prove your innocence, then I'll let you go." He steps back, giving me maybe a foot of personal space. "Go on."

"What do you mean?"

"I need to search you." He places his hands on his belt. "Undress."

I feel like I've just swallowed a lit match. I choke out: "But—"

"Or do you want me to arrest you? Take you to jail? No bail, no food, no water, not to mention the potential death penalty..."

I know he's bluffing. I know this is against the law, and that he's betting on my ignorance, the fact that I'm just a naive schoolgirl. But I am just a schoolgirl. And I can't think. His gun is right there, and his eyes are black holes, sucking all oxygen out of the air.

"Go on! Don't make me lose my patience with you. I'm being nice. I won't be nice for long."

I pull my dress up over my head. It's made of thin fabric, not substantial by any standards, but without it, I feel like even the wind could knock me over. I can see the goose bumps lining my arms. I bunch up the dress and hold it over my chest, crossing my legs tightly, trying to disappear into the wall behind me.

"Stand up straight," he says. "I need to make sure you're not lying." He pushes me toward the center of the alley, toward the light, then walks around me in a circle. "Little girls are often liars."

I'm shivering so hard I can hear my teeth chattering.

I hate you, I think. *I hate you, ging caat, more than anything in the world.*

Around the corner, I hear an old man calling his grandson back inside. I try to shrink back into the shadows, as if I *am* a criminal. The officer turns toward the noise, then faces me, frowning. "All clear this time. But don't tempt me again." Then, just as I think he's about to leave, he gives my butt a quick pat before walking away.

I've never felt so humiliated in my life.

It takes me four tries to put my dress on straight, and even then, it's inside out. I don't care. I can't care. I stomp toward the street, toward the boulevard with the passing cars and flashing convenience-store lights. All I want right now, more urgently than ever before, is to be with people, surrounded by people, invisible in a crowd. I knew cops were scary; I always knew not to get on their bad side. But something in me always believed that when it really mattered, they would protect me.

That protection doesn't extend to "cockroaches," apparently. Cockroaches, who would be arrested at the slightest provocation, tried for hearsay charges, convicted for pennies.

I'm a cockroach now.

I don't dare call Uncle Chow in my current state. Not when I know he'll report everything back to Mom, who would have an aneurysm and die if she heard the news, and then Dad would be forced to take care of us kids, and he might just ship us off to an orphanage to save himself the trouble. Instead, I call a taxi and cover my face as best I can, though the driver still notices something's wrong and tries repeatedly to offer me tissues and packets of chewing gum. When we reach Repulse Bay, I shove a wad of cash into his hand and scramble out of the car. "Wait, miss! Your change!"

I don't respond.

The house is dark when I get in. Thank God for small mercies—Mom is visiting Po Po tonight. I take in the familiar silhouette of our dark foyer and breathe in the ordinary scent of roses and varnish. Then, safe at home, the tears fall.

I muffle my cries, stuffing my knuckle in my mouth as I climb the stairs so as not to wake Robin. I'm crying so hard I can barely see the staircase, but I know each step by heart. When I get in the shower, I turn the heat on full blast, then scald myself from every possible direction, trying to incinerate the memory from my mind. I can't tell anyone. Osprei would commit murder if he knew. Suki would make me go to court, and I never want to see that officer again. And poor Robin, who still believes in the system, who is so smart and good; she of all people can never know.

Phoenix

WHEN I GET OUT OF THE SHOWER, IT'S ALMOST six in the morning. The sky is a pale cerulean. A single wispy cloud floats across the horizon like a streak of chalk against a blank slate. It's almost cruel to know the world still goes on, the orbit of Earth hasn't stopped, or even skipped a beat, though my life is irrevocably changed.

I know now why Suki is willing to risk her grades, even her life, for the protest movement, even though she's the crowning achievement of her family and the first one to go to college. I understand why Ming-lai spends every cent he has on the demonstrations, on supplies for his crew, despite having no savings to fall back on. I even understand why Wing-chi chose to drive for Tin-lok's escape in spite of her probationary status. Because none of us can live like this anymore. And we can't keep quiet a second longer.

I open my window, lean my head out, and *scream*.

It feels good, so good my throat is rasping and completely parched by the time I'm done. I shake out my wet hair and make my way downstairs to grab a glass of water. Too late, I remember Robin.

She's awake in her pink Cooky pajamas, standing on the landing. "Nix?"

"Go to sleep, Robin, it's still early."

"What was that sound?" she asks, rubbing her eyes.

"Oh." I try to laugh. "I was just stressed."

"Over SATs?" Robin asks. "Do you want me to study with you?"

My chest tightens. I go to her and hug her small shoulders, which makes her wriggle out from under my too-tight grasp. "You just want to show off," I tease, poking her nose.

"I don't need to," she replies pertly. "Everyone already knows I'm smarter than you."

"Robin!"

She giggles and runs down the stairs before me. With Mom gone, today feels like a sleepover morning, even though it's a Monday. It's hard to believe that for other people, yesterday was just a normal night, when for me, it feels like I've aged a year.

"Do you want breakfast?" I ask after a long gulp of water. "I can make congee."

"Your congee's always too thick," Robin says, wrinkling her nose as if she's Marie Antoinette herself. "I want Osprei's."

"Well, Osprei isn't home right now," I say, setting the kettle on the stove. It's been over four hours and he's still not back. What if he's been arrested? What if he's in jail?

"Hmph. When's he coming home?"

"How would I know?" I snap, before wishing I could take it back. Robin looks like she doesn't know what she's done wrong. *Nothing,* I want to tell her. *You've done nothing wrong.* It's the ging caat who's wronged us.

While the water's boiling, I check my phone. Osprei hasn't texted me. But Kai has.

Are you okay? he says. Did you make it home?

I hesitate, then thumbs-up the message. But am I really okay?

Texting dots appear on the screen. He starts, stops, then starts again. What happened? he finally asks. Three characters. That did not warrant the thirteen seconds of typing time it took him.

I hate the police, I write back impulsively.

A long pause. Are you all right? he asks again.

I'm about to text back when I hear heavy footsteps in the hall. There's a muttered curse followed by the slam of the door. Osprei.

Robin and I run toward the foyer at the same time. Osprei's dressed in full black with his hood pulled up. "You missed curfew by eight hours and twenty-four minutes," Robin announces, the benevolent angel that she is.

Osprei would usually throw back some witty remark in English, but instead, he ignores us, stomping to the kitchen and trailing dirt across Mom's polished herringbone floors.

"Where were you?" I ask, trying to stay out of Robin's earshot. "Did they arrest you?"

"They tried to," Osprei grunts, taking out leftover food containers at random from the refrigerator. He looks like he's about to empty the entire contents of the fridge into his stomach. "I hate those motherfucking dogs. They're corrupt as hell—" I glance sideways at Robin, but she's clamped her mouth shut, hoping we'll forget about her so she can eavesdrop longer. Osprei's obviously too riled up to care. "Fucking abusive, violent—"

"Osprei," I say in warning. We're walking a fine line here. I turn off the kettle and brew jasmine tea for us. Osprei barely drinks it, opting for a gallon of tap water instead.

"What happened?" I ask, lowering my voice as Robin heads to the closet to grab her school backpack.

He throws off his hood, revealing a giant black eye. I suck in my breath; meanwhile, Robin looks delighted by the drama. "They brought us in for questioning but had to release us when there was no basis found for arrest. Obviously, Tin-lok wasn't with us."

I exhale through my nose. *Thank God.* "So he got away."

Osprei nods. "Suki said he made it to the boat. Now it's just a matter of not being caught by the coast guard," he says, before cramming a piece of bread topped with an entire pack of deli ham into his mouth.

"That's not a sandwich," Robin remarks from the kitchen archway. "You're like a gong zyu."

Osprei and I both freeze at the mention of Hong Kong pigs. "Where'd you learn that phrase?" I demand at the same time Osprei says, "Be careful when you say that."

Robin can tell something's amiss. "The protesters used that word...."

Osprei tries to bite down on a frozen dumpling and winces, rubbing his jaw. I cut him a glare before taking out a wok. I'm no Iron Chef but I *can* reheat some dumplings. "Robin," I say as I pour the plastic bag of dumplings into the pan, "you shouldn't go near those people."

"I didn't go near them, I just passed *by* them. They were hosting a demonstration next to my gymnastics center. I overheard them. They were calling the chief executive some big names. They said Carrie Lam was a Communist cog. Is that true?"

"Mrs. Tsui let you stop by the protests?" Osprei asks, astonished. We've all had Mrs. Tsui as our babysitter at one point or another, and all suffered under her plastic ruler. To call her strict is like calling a fish wet.

"Well," Robin hedges. "I kind of lost her at one point. It was a big crowd."

I groan, imagining Mrs. Tsui's reaction. Robin has always been a slippery kid. Why Mom agreed to her gymnastics lessons is beyond me.

Osprei starts eating the dumplings off the pan, never mind that they're still sizzling. I slap his fingers away before he burns himself. "Listen to me, Robin," I say in my serious tone. (Robin calls this *my* Mom tone.) "Those protests are dangerous, okay? You shouldn't go near them." I think of the police officer from last night, his long, leering looks. *You're a gaat zaat, aren't you?* I shudder at the idea of that man anywhere near Robin. "In fact, you should stay far, far away."

"But you go to the protests. You both do."

"We—" I turn to Osprei, caught in a blatant lie.

"That's different," Osprei says, his mouth full. Already his mood is recovering with his appetite. He's been sneaking dumplings in my inattention. I turn off the stove before he accidentally sets himself on fire. "Phoenix and I are old enough to make our own decisions now. We can take care of ourselves."

Her lower lip starts quivering. That's never a good sign. "That's what you said in America! You said when we came to Hong Kong, things would be different. You said everyone here would be just like me! I wouldn't have to worry about being Asian anymore. I'd get to be my own person here. You said I'd get to be myself."

Robin, unlike the rest of us, has an American passport. She's the only one born in the States, and yet she was the one happiest to immigrate. I remember how excited she was to try out a new house, a new neighborhood, a new life. Osprei was sulky yet resigned; he was the oldest, with the most to leave behind.

And me? I was devastated, crying every night, refusing to venture out into the Hong Kong streets despite the fact that our new house was ten times smaller than the one in Cary, North Carolina. I was convinced I would never fit in; I couldn't keep up with the fast, slurred way everyone spoke, the dark humor, the long idioms and poetic turns of phrase. When I was finally forced into school (and I mean physically forced), I thought I would get bullied like a protagonist in a TV show. Turns out, I was thinking too highly of myself. The reality was that no one paid me any attention at all. I was disoriented by everything: the uniforms, the textbooks, even the way girls applied makeup. If Charlie hadn't found me by the end of the week, I think I might've tried to book my own ticket straight back to America.

Even now, there's a cultural gap, though most days I don't

notice it. It's in the small things, a different pronunciation of a single phrase, or a childhood TV show that everyone's seen, everyone except me. Hong Kong is my home, more than Cary now, more than the entire US. But it's been hard for me to admit this. In the back of my head, I feel like if I try to claim Hong Kong as my home, it will push me out. And then where would I belong? Neither here nor there. Just drifting somewhere indefinable, between East and West maybe.

"You are your own person," I say, but I know my words aren't enough. I wonder, is this how Mom feels, when genuine words meant to comfort and protect come out flimsy and cheap instead?

"It's not fair," she says. "You guys do everything together. Without me."

I exchange another look with Osprei. Actually, we've never done anything together before these protests started. But now we talk almost every day. I study him silently: his mussed hair, his black eye, his pursed lips. I don't know if it's him who's changed, or me. But it's true—everything's different between us now. I used to see Osprei as a failure; I used to think ending up like him was the worst possible outcome. But now I recognize there are different kinds of metrics for measuring success. *Actually,* I think, glancing between Robin and Osprei, *I lucked out in the sibling lottery.*

"You know that's not true, Robin," Osprei says distractedly. He's already scrolling on his phone. Probably waiting for Suki to text him back. "We're just looking out for you. Since our parents are too fucked up to do their jobs at the moment."

I cough. On the plus side, this tactic seems to work on Robin, who, at the very least, understands to back down and try Osprei again when he's in a better mood. (She's read *The Art of War* and borrows Sun Tzu's tactics for getting her way.)

My phone chimes. I'm about to check it when Robin asks, "Is that from your boyfriend?"

My face warms. "What? Robin!"

Osprei looks up. His brow lifts as he catches my expression. "You have a boyfriend?"

When I don't reply, he smiles archly and returns to his phone. "Charlie must be a happy man."

"It's not Charlie," I say. I jut my chin out like I'm arguing, like I have to prove my point. "It's Kai."

Now both his brows go up. He appraises me, then whistles. "Zhang Kai, the HKU kid?"

I nod. Kai did make me promise not to tell anyone, but Osprei's my brother. He doesn't count. Besides, Robin already knew. She probably broke into my phone while I was sleeping. Passcodes don't work on her.

"Color me impressed." He grins, stretching. "Guess the charm runs in our family, eh? You must've picked up some of my swag."

Robin giggles. I roll my eyes. "You are so full of it. The only thing we have in common is some unfortunate DNA."

Osprei's grin widens; he reaches over and rumples my hair. I slap his hand away; he probably got dumpling oil in my hair. Yawning, he heads toward the stairs to wash up. Robin runs after him. "Aa Mui, good for you!" he calls. "He's a ten."

"Is he ten foot tall?" I hear Robin asking from upstairs.

I grab my backpack from the closet. I remind myself that I still have to go to school and SAT practice and sit down with college counselors and talk about why Yale represents success to me. And yet, I remember the heat of that officer's eyes on my bare skin; I remember Tin-lok's face as he surveyed his bookstore of the past twenty years for one last time. I remember his warning: *They're coming for all of us.* And I know that I've changed. I know that my dreams have changed.

Every day that goes by, the police continue to arrest and silence the people who dissent. The government continues to criminalize protesters and label them as terrorists. Beijing slowly strips away our freedom of speech, our freedom of protest, so insidiously we don't even notice, like a poisonous fog that robs us of breath. And because we're afraid, because we're weary, because we're disillusioned, we stand by and watch. We let them take our memorials, our history, our homes, and our sense of self.

Uncle Chow honks his horn when he's outside. I call Robin and yell at her not to be late for our last week of school. When I run out the door, the sun is shining bright-eyed and cheery overhead.

It feels like an omen.

I open Instagram and return to my latest draft, typing out a lengthy caption for my next post. I look out the car window as the Repulse Bay streets blur into muddled colors.

I guess I did make up my mind a while ago. I made up my mind when I decided to transcribe the notes for Tin-lok's interview. I made up my mind when I started documenting the protests on social media. And I made up my mind when Officer Ho Yi-tung looked me over with his burning eyes and decided he could use my body however he wanted, just because I was a gaat zaat to him.

Hoeng Gong, I write, ***it's time to take a stance.***

PART TWO

In the midst of chaos, there is also opportunity.

—Sun Tzu, *THE ART OF WAR*

Kai

MARCO CALLS ME AT FIVE IN THE EVENING, jolting me out of a restless sleep. I stayed up late last night: mixing oils and recreating old Shanghai, Puxi, with its winding cobblestone streets and leaning sycamore branches. I must've fallen asleep sometime in the wee hours of the morning, lost to the world.

Only to wake to this: "Where the hell have you been?" Marco shouts over the din in the background.

"It's Sunday," I say, rubbing my eyes. "I'm not on call this weekend."

"Check your phone, man. They need all the backup they can get right now."

I groan. "What's going on?"

"There's over a million people on the streets protesting Carrie Lam's response to the extradition bill. They think it means we're going to start shipping people off to Beijing for no reason." In the background, the chanting grows louder. "*No China rendition!*"

I sit up in bed. "One million people?"

Marco sighs into the phone. "Sergeant Leung told us to report to Admiralty; they need crowd control ASAP."

Twenty minutes later, when I step out of my apartment, the streets are empty, hushed with the strange, preternatural quality of an impending natural disaster. There are people shut inside their stores, gossiping and whispering on the phone, but no one goes out in the open.

I hurry to the MTR, ignoring the prickling feeling at the back of my neck. When I get to the station, I realize certain train lines are shut down. This is an emergency, then. Marco told me: Hong Kong *never* shuts down public transit.

I take the train to the closest stop at Central. The station is swarming with people; even just getting through the turnstile involves waiting in line. It takes me over thirty minutes to ride one stop when it usually takes five minutes. We're packed against each other in the car, bodies crammed together as if trying to force a jigsaw puzzle.

And when we pour out of the station onto the surface streets: It's a different world out there. For a moment, I lose my breath, like I'm viewing the original masterpieces, Van Gogh or Durer. This feels like art, like motion and color that needs to be captured, remembered. This feels like witnessing something you'd see only in a museum.

But I'm here, right now, alive. *Ma*, I think, *if only you could witness this.*

Marco said one million, but this feels like one billion.

People from all sides and directions flooding into the massive thoroughfare, old and young and tall and short and rich and poor. Nearly impossible to categorize. Chanting, holding signs, sweating, laughing, smiling, glaring, yelling, provoking. I never understood what a sea of people meant, but now I see it in front of me. Yes, this is a *sea*.

A giant red sign whooshes past me, nearly bonking me on the head. RETRACT EXTRADITION BILL. Beneath the block-letter words, there's a graffitied picture of Hong Kong's chief executive, Carrie Lam, her smile twisted into a devil's grin.

While making breakfast the other day, I heard the news of Carrie Lam's decision to send the bill directly to the full legislature for a second reading. Something about wanting to pass the bill as quickly as possible. She must've been trying to outrun the protesters, get it done before they had time to organize. *Too bad*, I thought, scrambling my eggs. *Too bad for people who don't get along with China.*

I didn't realize that meant one million people. I didn't realize this many people, this sea of white T-shirts and red banners, cared enough about autonomy from China. I mean, aren't we all Chinese? Don't we all look the same, dress the same, speak the same language, share the same values? Don't we even share the same history?

Sure, Hong Kongers get special privileges. I always knew this. Better internet, more complaining, more money. I thought that was it. And I believed the posts I read on WeChat, the ones that said the protesters numbered less than a hundred.

But there are thousands out here. *Millions.*

Don't you know? Phoenix said. *The media lies.*

"Hoeng Gong jan gaa jau!" A cry of encouragement goes out. "Hong Kong people, add oil!"

The chanting rises in unison, one full, coherent voice made of thousands, tens of thousands. Despite all my cynicism, I feel shivers down my spine. These people…they're *furious*.

I don't get it.

I've always considered myself apolitical, uninterested in following things outside of my control. Why read the news if it makes you feel powerless? Why vote if it doesn't make a difference? The only people I know who bother with that sort of thing are rich. They actually have time on their hands.

Marco agrees with me. Last week, he told me shutting down the protests would be an easy gig. "After all," he said, "us Hong Kongers are famous for being gong zyu pigs. We're lazy as fuck. And it's near impossible to get us mobilized to do anything political. We'd rather eat pork chops than get out and vote."

The writing is on the wall. Marco, Sergeant Leung, my father, even me, humoring the student protest groups: We're all dead wrong. Despite the fierce sun, refracting against the glass walls of towering skyscrapers, despite the slow crawl of the march and the heavy traffic, more and more people keep showing up, at every street, at every station, even from the docks. I recognize some of the signs from Ming-lai's apartment. He must've printed them from unified templates, organized and coordinated across schools.

"Hong Kong is burning!"

"Stop killing us!"

"We know you are lying!"

I'm so lost in the details of the crowd that I don't notice the glares directed at me, not until someone nearly jabs my head off with a neon-yellow umbrella. "Go home!" the man shouts at me. Then, at my blank look, he spits at my feet. "China dog."

And that jolts me back to reality. That's what I am to them, a China dog. *Is Phoenix here?* I wonder. Is that what she thinks of the police? And if she knew the truth about who I am, would she think the same of me too?

"Get into riot gear. Now!" Sergeant Leung barks orders at us trainees, directing us like a traffic controller at an intersection. Despite the madness, there's a structure to the chaos. Marco and I are paired off and rushed with a unit toward Gloucester Road, where protesters have descended on a Chinese-owned restaurant chain.

We race into the shopping mall and hear the screams immediately. The banquet hall is on the ground floor, and diners are stampeding out the doors in droves. A little boy trips in the commotion and falls on his hands and knees. Someone shoves him and his head goes down. I barrel through the crowd and grab him out of the fray. "You all right?" I shout.

He's crying, his eyes squeezed shut. I used to play this game too—close my eyes and imagine I'm somewhere else far away. There's no blood, but he could have an internal injury....

"Get your hands off him!" A gray-haired woman whacks me in the side with her massive purse. I gape at her in surprise as she wrenches the boy out of my arms. He's still bawling, but the sound is barely audible above the din.

"Come on!" Marco yells, and I turn my head his way. When I look back, the woman and her child are gone.

We enter the banquet hall. Protesters dressed in black stand on the tables and chairs, unscrewing chandeliers, smashing windows, spray-painting the walls. They wear yellow hard hats with surgical masks covering their faces. Only their glittering eyes are exposed, hard and furious as they glare down at us.

Across the room, the floor-to-ceiling window shatters; people scream as shards of glass fly everywhere. There are civilians still in the restaurant; some look like they were in the midst of eating dinner when the protesters barged in. One girl cowering against the staircase still holds her chopsticks in one hand, as if that will save her.

"Get down!" I shout to the kid nearest me, standing on the table. He's trying to unhook the chandelier from the vaulted ceiling.

He whirls toward me and trips on the folds of the tablecloth. I try to catch him but he throws a punch at me. Instinct kicks in and I wrestle him to the floor. He goes in for my face, trying to jam his thumbs into my eye sockets. I rear back and headbutt him. In moments, he goes limp. I'm shaking, hard; the adrenaline leaves me like a cut wire, crackling with electricity. Then someone throws a Molotov cocktail through the open window.

The explosion throws us all back. I can feel the heat on my face, oppressive, crackling. Marco swears behind me and I turn toward him. He's okay; I'm okay. The fire is catching on the linen tablecloth. The girl with the chopsticks is crying, transfixed by the flames.

"Get out of here!" I shout at her. "Run!"

She only looks at me in horror. I curse and drag her to her feet, then shove her toward the exit. To my relief, she stumbles forward, then starts sprinting, recovering from her stupor.

"Dirty cop!"

I swing around, which is my first mistake. There's a tall protester standing in front of me, holding a bottle of spray paint in the air. His eyes are glazed with malice.

"Wait—" My second mistake. He sprays the paint in my face. I choke. He kicks me in the gut and I fall, disoriented.

"Hak ging sei cyun gaa!" *You and your family should die.*

"Kai!" Marco is somewhere by my side. "Get up!"

I force myself to my feet, numbly. Is this what my father hears? Is this the kind of vitriol he gets thrown at him daily?

"There's too many cops!" I hear a protester shout in the distance. "Jat cai zau!"

"After them!" Sergeant Lai orders us, pressing onward toward the street. I follow, breathing hard.

Outside, it's chaos. Protesters have taken over the highway overpass and set up roadblocks in the street. They use steel pedestrian barriers, traffic cones, even ripped-up stadium seats from who knows where. The sheer number of protesters is overwhelming. It feels like all of Hong Kong is out here tonight—out here and determined to kill us.

Something wet splatters against my cheek. I put a hand to my face: raw egg. Then something much more lethal whizzes past me and I duck instinctively, my heart stuttering. The brick shatters against the garage service door behind me with a resounding crash.

"Put your gas mask on!" Marco shouts, jabbing me with his baton to get my attention. He points at the black flag behind me, held up by a helmeted officer. WARNING. TEAR SMOKE.

"But—" The hair on the back of my neck rises as I read the printed characters. My brain can't compute this. "There are civilians everywhere!"

"Do these people look like civilians to you?" Marco demands.

Not twenty meters away from us, protesters are tearing bricks from the streets and hurling them at the front line of riot police. Some have taken sticks of bamboo from the construction scaffolding; they point these at the front line like javelins.

"Twenty-Four!" Sergeant Lai has spotted me. "Gas mask. Now!"

I jam it on. Not a second later, I hear the crack and pop of tear-gas shells striking the cement, strange and out of place, like firecrackers at New Year. Eerie clouds of smoke drift and billow over the crowd, hanging in the humid air like floating ghosts.

"Hak kei! Hak kei!" the protesters call in warning. A few are ready with wet cloths covering their noses and mouths. Others wear heavy-duty gas masks like ours. But most are vulnerable, unprepared. They look younger than me. They look terrified.

The effect of the tear gas is horrifying in its immediacy. The mob collapses upon itself, writhing like a many-headed beast. I watch a group of teenagers crawl blindly toward the alleyway, coughing. "Help!" a boy cries; his high-pitched voice has not yet reached puberty. "He has asthma! He needs an inhaler and—"

Before he can finish his sentence, another round of tear gas shoots into the air. A smoking canister lands directly beside the boy. His eyes widen with terror just before it explodes, and I lose sight of them all in the white haze.

I whirl around and shove through the rows of ging caat. "What are you doing?" I demand, pushing toward Sergeant Lai. "They're just kids!"

He ignores me until I grab the tear-gas gun and jerk it downward. I try to wrestle it from his hand, but his grip is firm. "Stand down, Twenty-Four," he orders, his voice lethal.

Someone throws a flaming rubbish bin toward us; it arcs over our heads.

"There must be another way—"

"Are you disobeying a direct order, Twenty-Four?"

Someone seizes me from behind, and I recoil in surprise. It's Marco.

"No, sir!" Marco answers for me, before grabbing me in a chokehold and dragging me away. He's stronger than me, and the way his arm is wrapped around my throat, I can't speak, much less fight back.

He finally releases me once we're near the front line, far from Sergeant Lai. "Do you want to die?" he yells.

It's hard to hear him over the roar of the crowd. The protesters have reorganized, beating their makeshift shields and umbrellas against the ground, sounding like a death rattle.

"It's us or them, Kai," Marco continues. "Get used to it."

I shout in warning as a protester attempts to skewer Marco with his bamboo javelin. Then my baton is out and I'm in the mob, fighting.

They hate us. They hate us and they hunt us, so we hate them and we hunt them. I see it now. An escalating cycle of violence, one that only ends with death.

I read once that athletes see black before their games, and that, after, they barely remember what happened. All I know is the haixiao wave of bodies pressed against one another, screaming, hurling bricks, petrol bombs, umbrellas. I dodge most of the lethal ones but get a water bottle smack in the back of my head. I don't know if it's a concussion or the suffocating heat; ripples of dizziness wash over me.

All around, riot police press on. Beanbag rounds, tear gas, pepper spray, sponge grenades. Someone's on the ground, clutching her eye. It's a girl, I realize with a start. She's wearing a thin T-shirt, no helmet, no gas mask. I'm stopping to help her up when another kid tackles me. We both go down in the gravel, a blur of sweat and grunts and shouts. Then the boy screams.

"My eyes!" he cries out. "I can't see!"

I disentangle myself from him. On the side of his helmet, I make out neat characters written in black Sharpie. *Do NOT resuscitate if wounded and unresponsive. Will in back pocket.*

I go still, reading those words over and over again. He's written a *will*?

Marco pulls me up just in time; a fresh line of protesters has grabbed part of a barricade and is using it as a battering ram. The edge of the barricade slams into me, nearly throwing me off my feet. I pull out my baton. I hit. I hit again. And again.

After a while, even the screams start to sound like silence.

"Get in the van!" Sergeant Lai orders us after nightfall, as the crowd begins to disperse. "Now!"

I'm herded in behind Marco before the van doors slam shut. It's dark outside, but I can still hear screams in the distance. The man next to me keeps twitching, his knee jerking against mine. Outside, the roar grows. It feels like driving into the mouth of a beast.

"They need backup at the Legislative Council Complex," Sergeant Lai explains, voice hoarse from shouting. "The rioters have broken into the building. Arrest anyone on sight. Use full force if necessary. We need to teach the gaat zaat never to try something like this again."

Full force if necessary. My stomach dips. *Phoenix.*

I'm on duty, but I pull out my phone anyway, hoping Sergeant Lai won't notice. Don't go to LegCo tonight, I text her, my pulse skittering. *Please, please, please,* I pray.

She starts texting back immediately. Are you there already? she writes. I'll look for you ☺

My heart leaps into my throat. Phoenix. Don't go.

Too late, she answers. On my way.

Phoenix

A METAL TROLLEY RAMS INTO THE GLASS AGAIN and again as the crowd cheers. It's not going to work, I think, but then it does. The glass shatters, and suddenly protesters swarm into the Legislative Council like water sluicing down-hill. I almost drop my camera in shock.

"Phoenix! C'mon!" Suki shouts, grabbing my hand and tugging me inside. I've never been inside LegCo before, the official headquarters of the Hong Kong government. The high, vaulted ceilings and glass walls are sleek and imposing, almost otherworldly at night, and it feels impossible that *I* am standing here, in my ratty sneakers and black jeans, and that other teenagers are here with me, instead of old men in suits and ties. It feels as if we've crossed into another dimension, an upside-down one.

Ming-lai unrolls a giant black Bauhinia flag across the

atrium. Hesitantly, I start taking pictures again, until I notice Suki destroying the red Hong Kong emblem, painting over the words PEOPLE'S REPUBLIC OF CHINA. She moves on to a copy of the Basic Law next, ripping up the pages of our constitution like it's fodder for recycling.

I snap my cap back on my camera lens and race up to her, heart pounding. She's gone too far this time. "Suki, you'll go to jail for this!"

"I'm wearing a mask," Suki retorts, not even glancing at me. "And they're trashing the CCTV footage. No one will know I was here."

Sure enough, protesters are demolishing the computers and security cameras, cheering as the expensive equipment splinters into pieces. I imagine the headlines tomorrow, and what Mom will say about us. Marching in the streets is one thing, but sacking the LegCo building? The place that has represented our government and democracy for decades?

"Shouldn't we try a different approach?" I ask, trying to keep my voice from shaking. "We could vote, or—"

Suki scoffs. "Maybe that works in America, Phoenix, but not here."

"We could try to change the system from the inside. We have a democracy—"

"Which is a *sham*." She whirls around now, her eyes blazing. "Do you know the electoral system is designed so that a majority of the popular vote will only ever elect a minority of seats? No matter who wins the vote, Beijing will *always* hold the majority. Do you know our elected legislators can't introduce a new bill without consent from our dear chief executive? Do you know the last candidates we elected to office were disqualified because they 'didn't take their oaths properly'?" Suki speaks so rapidly her words blend into one another. "Peaceful protests don't work," she spits out. "You can't play by the rules, Phoenix. Not when the system's rigged against you."

Someone puts a hand on my shoulder. I turn to find that Osprei's joined us. "This isn't a violent protest, Nix," he says. "We're not targeting anyone. We're just here to make them listen to us."

"To make them see how fucking furious we are," Suki hisses. Then she shakes her bottle of spray paint and moves on to graffitiing the seats. She's only targeting certain ones— where the pro-Beijing legislators sit.

"Look around, Nix. Take photos," Osprei says under his breath. "Check out the library." Then he pauses, his eyes darkening. "But get back here before midnight. We leave together, remember that."

I nod and scurry out of the atrium, gripping my camera so tightly it leaves red marks on my palms. Down the hall, the library is untouched and empty, and I don't understand what Osprei wants me to see here. Then I spot the barricade and the handwritten sign before the entrance, clearly scrawled in haste: *Please do not damage the books. Hong Kongers, add oil!*

Suki and Osprei are right; this isn't violence merely for the sake of violence. This is targeted. Focused. In the atrium, only certain symbols are vandalized. Even in the cafeteria, protesters taking drinks from the refrigerators leave cash behind as payment. I take photos of the wrinkled bills and coins, the handwritten signs, hoping I can paint a different narrative from the one that will inevitably be broadcast tomorrow.

And then I get the AirDrop message: Police are coming. Leave together.

I rush back to the atrium, which has descended into an argument worthy of the legislative floor.

"If we leave now, they'll call us rioters!" Ming-lai is shouting, ironically, from behind the podium. "They'll say we ransacked the place and left like triad thugs. We need to stay and stand our ground."

"They have tear gas," Suki argues. "Remember our motto? *Be water.* We need to know when to fight and when to run."

"You can run if you want," Ming-lai says. "Like your uncle." Her eyes bulge. "You—"

"Suki!" Osprei grabs her from behind, holding her back. He whispers something in her ear, and she stops struggling, though her eyes still incinerate Ming-lai.

"I have nothing left to lose," Ming-lai says. "I'll stay even if no one else does."

"No," Osprei says, his mouth set. "Jat cai zau. We leave together."

"Ging caat!" Wing-chi and her girlfriend rush back in through the side entrance. "Let's get out of here and regroup outside!"

"I will not go—"

Osprei grabs Ming-lai by the shoulders and hauls him toward the door, ignoring his protests.

"Jat cai zau!" Wing-chi's girlfriend starts chanting. Others join in. "Jat cai zau!"

Outside, the cool night air engulfs us. I feel relieved to be outside again, in the open, without the blinding fluorescent lights to incriminate us. The police have raised their flags warning of tear smoke. The surface streets have cleared out of everyone but black-clad protesters and volunteer medical teams. Up above, on the footbridges, the tunnels swarm with bystanders who lean out over the railings, watching the action below. Many of them wave signs; others hold cameras and tripods. But most journalists won't venture down below.

"Stick to the side," Osprei warns me as he straps on his gas mask. "And stay out of the way."

I nod, making sure my own gas mask is secure. In the shadows, I take out my camera once again and get to work, emboldened by the dark. There are two boys that look like brothers spray-painting the same message together across the giant LegCo columns: *It was you who taught us that peaceful protests were futile.*

Chills run down my spine. This is a very different education from what I was taught in school.

On the opposing column: *Am I next? Will you shoot me too?*

Glass shatters up ahead, followed by the sickening pelt of rubber bullets. I hear a hair-raising scream and watch as a girl picks shards out of her boyfriend's arm. He leans in and kisses her, despite the unfurling scene around them, and I stoop to capture the moment.

Behind them, someone's holding a smoking plate. I recognize what's about to happen. Flames writhe and flounder in the street. A police officer, caught unaware, screams as he falls to the ground, thrashing like a vehement snake.

I feel tears prick my eyes, though I don't know why. I force myself to keep taking photos, turning numb to the pain of those around me. The police descend on us, clubbing, spraying, tackling. Umbrellas fly through the air, along with arrows, even ceramic tiles. It's total pandemonium and I want my camera to capture this.

When a still-smoking shell rolls by my foot, I scramble up onto a concrete ledge, then pause at the top, lifting my mask and taking in this bird's-eye view. I change the aperture and shutter speed, trying to adjust for all the motion and light. It's funny; up here I can see more clearly what's happening. Down below, it's all just blurs of movement, disjointed sound and color. I increase the ISO, trying to capture the brilliant night lights, when a tear-gas canister explodes.

I hear screaming and don't understand it's me. I can't see Osprei or Suki or anyone I know. My eyes burn like the sting of a thousand bees; I press my palms into my eyelids, but it only makes the pain worse. I can't see anything. I'm crawling on the ground, overcome with nausea, panicking.

"Phoenix!" I recognize Wing-chi's voice a few feet away from me. The sounds of a crash echo beyond us, and now the terrifying cascade of bullets: open fire.

I force my eyes open against the pain and see Wing-chi lying on the ground, bleeding. Her right arm is bent in an unnatural, crooked position. Her beautiful face is ravaged with blood. "Light it!" she cries. With her left hand, she fumbles with her cigarette lighter. "Light it now!"

She's gesturing to her backpack, to the petrol bomb inside. I can't think fast enough. The police are marching toward us; the protesters' front line of defense has scattered.

I watch the ging caat raise their guns; their figures are foreign; their figures are familiar. But I must be imagining things now.

"Phoenix!" Wing-chi's voice sounds like it's coming from across an ocean. "Now!"

I don't know what to do. I grab the bomb and uncap it. Then I hold the rag to Wing-chi's lighter; it catches easily. The protesters are shouting all around me: *"Justice for Hong Kong! Five demands, not one less!"*

I run forward, throwing the bomb. It flies from my hand like a feather, slowly, like time has stilled.

The bomb lands on the ground. Then I run.

I hear a rubber bullet whiz past. I don't know if I'm in my body or out of it, but I feel every sensation tenfold. The bullet strikes the girl in front of me, who lets out a terrible, wrenching shriek. I'm reaching out for her when the force of an impossibly heavy body collides into me.

The first thing I'm cognizant of is the clatter of my camera meeting concrete. The shattering lens and the crunch of plastic and metal. I know immediately my camera will never take another picture.

And then the pain hits me. Someone's atop me, the weight of his body forcing me to the ground. The baton strikes me in the head, and I cry out, the pain like nothing I've ever felt before. The next blow lands on my shoulder. My arm gives out; my skin scrapes the ground. Blood...who knew blood could be so hot?

His legs straddle me, pinning me in place on my stomach. I can't move, I can't breathe. "Please!" I scream, but my voice is lost in the crowd. The gun on his hip presses against me, a constant reminder. Flashes of fire dance in my vision, like smudges of sunspots that linger even after you've closed your eyes.

Then I hear a shout: "Get the fuck off her!" Suddenly, I'm freed, and I roll over on my back, gasping. There's the muffled sound of a scuffle, then pressing darkness, and the next thing I know, someone is holding me in his arms, running, then lowering me against the shelter of a retaining wall. "Phoenix," he whispers.

My vision is blurred with tears. "Who..." I start to ask, until a new voice interrupts. "Oh my God, Nix!"

I rub my eyes. "Osprei?"

I hear him skid to his knees beside me. "Hold still," he says, before pouring a cool liquid over my face.

My eyes still smart, but I can see clearly now. Osprei kneels before me. No one else. Was I imagining things? Why did that stranger's voice sound so familiar?

"Aa Mui." He drags me to my feet. "We have to get outta here."

We limp toward the alley and try not to breathe in the thick scent of char in the air. My mask is gone, along with my camera and backpack. "Where's Suki? And the others?" I ask as we make slow progress down the alley, trying to escape the incoming flood of backup police.

"Wing-chi went back to grab Suki," Osprei grunts. "We need to go faster. We'll meet them away from the center."

The alley opens up into another crooked side street, and sounds of the fighting grow distant.

"Osprei!" Suki and Wing-chi approach from the other end of the passage. Suki is unharmed, while Wing-chi limps, her arm in a makeshift sling. But we're not the only ones who heard her shout.

Farther back, at the very end of the road, behind Suki and Wing-chi, two cops materialize against the gloom. "Freeze!"

Osprei tries to force me to duck behind a dumpster, but it's clear the cops have spotted us. "We need to find a place to hide," he says between his teeth, pulling me into the shadows as they advance.

"They're blocking off the street!" Suki's warning rings out. "Run!"

And then we spot the second pair of cops—this time behind us—and we know we're done for. I grab Osprei's hand and start to sprint, never mind the coursing pain in my shoulder and the chemicals stinging my eyes and the police stampeding closer by the second.

There are furious shouts in the distance and the sounds of a sudden collision. Overhead, I hear the whirring of a helicopter. Wing-chi and Suki fall into step beside us as we all sprint toward the same backstreet, the last one left between us and the ging caat hedging us in.

Suki pushes me forward as I start to stagger, gasping. "Almost there!" she pants, and then she cries out because she sees it just as I do: the fence at the end of the alley. We're trapped.

I can't stop thinking about what Mom told me: If they arrest us, it's up to ten years' jail time.

Osprei curses. Suki glances over her shoulder at the ging caat approaching. They've slowed down now that they've caught us at a dead end. She takes a few steps back, then charges forward.

"What the hell?"

She leaps onto the ridge at the center of the fence, then scurries up the rest of the way and throws herself across. "Hurry!" she shouts from the other side. The cops shout too, rushing toward us.

Osprei gets to the fence first but pushes me forward instead. "I can't do it," I whisper, gaping up at its enormous height. "Just leave me behind."

"Fuck, Nix, no!" he shouts. In a blind, dizzying second, he's boosted me up, arms shaking, and I scramble for a foothold, my hands clenching the top of the fence so tightly I feel the metal pierce my skin. Then, with teeth gritted and eyes squeezed shut, I drag my entire weight up and over, letting myself tumble across to the other side.

Suki half catches me, half falls with me. We pitch over onto the ground, then pull each other up as Osprei vaults over. Wing-chi is next, her face appearing over the lip of the fence and her hand reaching out—

And then she disappears back over the edge. There's grunting and swearing as I hear the cops pin her to the ground. Osprei curses and Suki screams bloody murder, running toward the fence as if prepared to fight again.

Osprei grabs her before she can go more than two feet. "Call Sam-ying!" Wing-chi shouts through the fence. "She'll know what to do!"

Suki and I are both crying. "Hoeng Gong," Suki screams through her tears, "jan gaa jau!" With that, she grabs my hand, nods, and pulls me into a sprint.

The cops are everywhere, even on this side of Central. Someone spots us running. "Cockroaches!" one shouts. "Grab them!"

We turn a corner but it's no use; there are more of them swarming the streets. "This way!" Suki hisses, circling back toward Admiralty.

"What are you doing?" Osprei demands.

"Just trust me!"

We turn onto the main boulevard, easy targets under the bright streetlamps, and I wonder if Suki's gone mad, if she's planning some kind of suicide mission. Ging caat accumulate at the intersection and start waving and pointing. It looks almost as if we're about to dive straight into them. I'm slowing in terror when Suki seizes me, hauling me toward the sidewalk, toward the stairs—up the stairs—

To an old church. Suki bangs on the doors and, like a miracle, I hear the sounds of a lock unlatching from inside. But it's impossibly slow, and the cops are onto us; they're close enough that I can see their clothes, torn and bloodied, their furious faces, as if they want to eat us alive—

The doors fly open, and we fall inside. I catch the ging caat's gleaming eyes in the dark just before the doors bang shut.

We collapse in a heap on the old wooden floorboards. The warm yellow lights from the altar candles flicker across the chapel, illuminating the other protesters huddled against the benches and walls, hunched against each other as if afraid the building will come down in an earthquake.

The air smells of incense and rosemary and musty books, like every other church I've been inside. *How do all churches manage to smell the same?* I wonder, because it's easier than wondering about Wing-chi waiting in jail, or Kai, who might still be out in LegCo.

Around midnight, an elderly woman approaches our group to offer water and fruit snacks. I barely feel the water going down my throat; I think I'm still in shock. I keep staring at Suki and Osprei, willing myself to believe they are alive, they are with me. We made it out together, or did we? Can you ever make it out?

There are still so many others out there. Tin-lok, who escaped to Taiwan. Ming-lai, who tried to stay at LegCo. Wing-chi, who let us run first. Will they blacklist her now?

I start to shiver uncontrollably, even though sweat coats my skin and the church is overheated from all the bodies pressed together. "It's okay, Phoenix." Suki puts her hand on my shoulder and I jump, recalling the feel of that police officer's touch. The way he shoved himself atop me, like I was a feral animal to subdue. "We're safe here. Churches are off limits to ging caat."

The idea falls over me like passing clouds in a gale, there and then gone. I tell it to myself over and over: We're safe. We're safe. We're safe. As if I can repeat the words until they hold true. But I know they're not. Because there's still tomorrow, and the day after, and the day after that.

I remember at my first protest Charlie said we were on the losing side. He was right. The Hong Kong government has their officers, firearms, ammunition. China has a hundred times our population and a hundred times our might. We're just a small island really, compared to a giant. We're just kids compared to the largest army in the world.

I think back to my stupid, naive hope when I first started documenting the protests on social media. I hoped that the world would see us, that they would acknowledge us, and that they would help us.

But it seems we're alone.

"What happens when the news coverage ends?" I rasp, thinking of Mom's cynical predictions. "This year, next year. What happens when the world grows bored and forgets about us?"

Suki turns her luminous gaze on me. She doesn't deny it, as I hoped she would. She doesn't tell me it'll all get better in the end. Instead, she takes my hand. "We're still here," she says. "And we won't forget, *ever.*"

My eyes well with tears, that hot, choky feeling building in my throat.

The doors open once more and several teenagers dressed in black rush inside, gasping for breath. One of them is clutching his forehead—a head injury. They help him to the bench carefully. His friend is weeping beside him.

I shake my head, terrified and ashamed of my terror. Again I think of being thrown to the ground, a cold gun grinding into my bare skin. My stomach swoops at the mere memory, and I know I can't do it again, I can't. "I've never felt so…so scared," I admit. I feel like such a coward.

I draw my knees to my chest, but Osprei tries to hug me anyway. "Aa Mui," he says. "You don't have to be a front-liner. There are other ways to fight."

I put my head on my knees. I think of all my Instagram followers, the things they comment on my posts. They're always amazed by the size of the crowds, the number of weapons, the sheer force of the fires. But they don't actually know what it's like, not really. A hundred people, a thousand, ten thousand: It doesn't matter the number, the crowds always feel bigger in real life. The batons feel deadlier when they're in your face. And the fires feel hotter when you're standing in front of them.

I want people to understand what it's like to live here. Not just what it's like to be a frontline protester, but also what it's like to be a little kid like Robin, maybe even what it's like to be a mainlander like Kai.

I want my parents to know that those who choose to remain silent still choose a stance. That there's no neutrality, and in the end, your silence won't protect you.

I want my friends overseas to know more than what photos I take. I want them to know what I think and feel: how overwhelming the fear is, how blinding the pain. And still, I want them to know what it's like for your sau zuk to take your hand, pull you forward, stick together, look out for each other.

My interview notes with Tin-lok are still on my computer, untouched. Suki told me to wait until he settled into his new Taipei home. Then I put the article on hold because of all the other crap going on in my life. Time flew by and I forgot. But now I know I really do want to write it. I have so many ideas for how I would frame the story, where I would begin the narrative. Maybe at the moment of his arrest? Or much earlier than that, when he first had the idea to open a shop for banned books? My fingertips tingle as if I'm already typing at a keyboard. I want to work on it as soon as I get home.

We have a long while to wait first. All night we hold vigil

in the chapel, watching for daylight to break. Around five in the morning, someone AirDrops the news that the ging caat have cleared out, that it's almost safe to leave. I wake from a restless nap to check my phone, which is miraculously unharmed, except for a few scratches on the screen. Kai's texted to ask if I'm safe, and when I reply, he seems immensely relieved. Even though I didn't see him at LegCo, it's comforting to know we were both there, together.

One voice in the benches starts to sing, and then others join in:

"Amazing Grace, how sweet the sound, that saved a wretch like me..."

I glance at Osprei, who's started singing along, though he hardly knows the lyrics, though we've never really gone to church except for Easter and Christmas. In this moment, I wish Mom and Dad could be here with us. There's a surreal certainty I feel—that if they were here, that if they could hear the echo of our voices across the city, they too would understand.

Amazing grace, how sweet the sound.
That saved a wretch like me.
I once was lost, but now am found.
Was blind but now I see.

Suki is smiling at everyone around us with tears in her eyes, singing along in her husky voice.

Was grace that taught my heart to fear.
And grace, my fears relieved.
How precious did that grace appear.
The hour I first believed.
Through many dangers, toils, and snares,

I have already come.
'Twas grace that brought me safe thus far.
And grace will lead me home.

The world is shimmering and distant through my veil of tears. The altar ripples in my vision; the candlelight distorts into stars; the people and faces and eyes turn into feelings and richness and home. Even when we stand against an impossible mission, even when we know with certainty that we will not have a happy ending to our story, we have one advantage in this world. We look out for one another. We know we are nothing alone.

But we are everything together.

20

Kai

TWENTY-FOUR HOURS LATER AND THE BATTLE still rages on outside. Classes are cancelled, offices are closed, businesses are shuttered. My dorm is silent when I return an hour before midnight. Most beds are empty.

I'm only here because of a head injury. Medics sent me home with orders for bed rest. Instead, I'm searching the news endlessly, like picking at an open sore. I can't stop.

"Police officer drags female protester and beats her with baton." There's even an accompanying video.

"Seventy-two people injured, two in serious condition."

The hatred and vitriol are overflowing online. "Carrie Lam, your hands are red with the blood of our children. Hong Kong police, you are Communist slaves. You know the law and break the law. You delight in the pain of our people!"

I shove my phone under my pillow before I can throw it.

You don't understand, I want to tell them. You don't understand what it's like. When the mob is coming down on you, when you can't think, when you're getting sucked under, dragged by the tide.

The scent of ash clings to the air, and I get up to close the window. Hong Kong's become a war zone.

My phone starts ringing. It's Phoenix—her eleventh time calling today.

I decline the call. I don't want to talk right now. Not when I feel bile in my throat, not when I can still hear the screams of protesters begging me to let them go. Not when every single one of them reminds me of her.

I can't face her. I can't face her and lie.

I set my phone down just as it starts ringing again. Phoenix.

I stare at it blankly. *What if she's injured? What if—*

I grab my phone. "Hello?"

"Where were you?" she exclaims, nearly blasting my eardrum out.

"It's been a long day," I start, wincing. I know these kinds of replies solve nothing. "Sorry I missed your calls."

In the background, I hear her running down the stairs. "Can we meet up? I want to give you your birthday gift."

"What?" I almost laugh aloud from shock. In all the chaos, I forgot my own birthday. "Today's June tenth?"

"We have exactly thirty-six minutes left to celebrate." I hear a door sliding shut on her end. "Let's hurry before the day's over. Where should we meet?"

"You shouldn't leave your neighborhood," I say quickly. Repulse Bay is far enough from Admiralty that she might not understand how bad the riots are right now. "It's not safe out."

"I'm sure it's fine," she says. "I'll ask Uncle Chow to drive me—"

I imagine her car getting stuck in the road, barricaded by protesters. I imagine the mob descending on her and the police firing tear gas—

I swallow hard. "I'll come to you. Just stay in Repulse Bay. I'll text you when I'm there."

"Are you sure? It's far for you…and late. Why don't we meet in the middle?"

"It's fine. Stay put, okay?"

Before she can argue, I end the call and grab my wallet. I can't believe I'm making the trek across the island when most of the train stations are closed, the city's under lockdown, and I've gotten less than six hours of sleep in the past forty-eight hours. All for some birthday gift when I don't even want to celebrate my birthday. But the other option—Phoenix being stubborn, Phoenix sneaking out, Phoenix getting caught in the skirmishes—is much, much worse.

My options have always been shit.

I don't make it by midnight. By the time I get to Repulse Bay, it's already June 11, and my birthday is over. Still, Phoenix meets me by the beach, excited as a little kid on New Year. Her face is bare, her long hair pulled up in a messy bun. I like seeing her without her fancy getup, because she looks less intimidating, less made of money. She looks like someone who could actually like me, who could exist in the same world as me.

"What's this?" she asks, touching my cheek. Her voice is soft, nearly lost beneath the sound of waves lapping at sand.

"It's nothing," I say, my hand going to the bruise. I didn't think she could spot it in the dark, but her eyes miss nothing.

"Are you hurt?" She frowns. "How long did you stay at LegCo the other night? I didn't see you."

If only she knew. I watch her chew on her lower lip, and without thinking, I tug on it. She releases her lip, smiling at me. I want to kiss her. "How's SAT practice going?" I ask instead, sliding my hands into my pockets before I do anything I'll regret.

"I need to have a talk with my mom about it, but I've been putting it off all week because she's in the middle of a mental breakdown. Divorce stuff." She sighs. "And I have to deal with the international college fair tomorrow."

It'll probably be cancelled due to the lockdown. But only a police officer would know that. "Lucky you," I say instead.

"I guess." She looks unconvinced. "Mom's hoping I'll kiss up to the Yale guy. Apparently Charlie's dad knows him from lacrosse or something."

I don't know what lacrosse is and don't mean to ask. Again, I'm reminded of the distance between our lives, the fleeting nature of our time together. She is leaving to go abroad, to do big things with *passhion*. She will leave. And I will stay.

"Anyway." She flashes me a wide-toothed grin as she pulls out a wrapped parcel from her backpack. The wrapping paper is shiny gold, the kind of foil that's extra thick and costs twice as much at the art store. Suddenly, I don't want to open it. I don't want to know what's inside.

She doesn't see my reluctance. Instead she holds up

her phone and takes a picture. "What was that for?" I ask, stiffening.

"I just want to remember," she says, leaning back to take another shot. *Because soon, this will all be past tense for her.* "You're so beautiful."

I know I must look like shit. The dark circles and purple bruises and disheveled hair. I'm not even in my usual monochrome attire because I didn't want to look like a protester. I'm wearing a navy-blue sweatshirt I haven't touched in years. It's too short in the sleeves.

"Open it."

The package is heavy in my hands—a sign it's probably expensive. Like ripping off a bandage, I tear the wrapping paper in one swift motion.

It's a brand-new Wacom drawing tablet, with 8,192 levels of pressure sensitivity, tilt response, and precise tracking technology. Just like what the art kids at PolyU own, but shinier, newer.

My hands are trembling. I picture all the designs I could build with this. I picture pulling out my tablet in class, using it at a coffee shop with other working artists and illustrators. I want this. A lot.

And I know I can't have it.

"I can't take this," I say, shoving it back into her hands. "It's too much."

"What? Of course not." She returns it to me. "It's nothing."

Nothing. The word cuts like a knife. "I can't afford this."

"You don't need to afford it." Her voice is soft and coaxing. "I already bought it. C'mon, just take it. It'd be too much of a hassle to return now."

"But…" I was wrong to think this could work, that we could ever understand each other. "Phoenix, I can't accept this. You have to take it back."

She's smiling at me like I'm just being polite. Like she knows I'll say yes in the end. As if I'm some pity project to her. "I saw how much you wanted this when we passed through Wan Chai last Sunday. It made me happy to buy it for you. Just let me be happy, okay?"

"But—" My eyes fall shut. "I can't pay you back."

"That's what a gift is," she says, as if I'm a child.

The exhaustion of the day, compounded by the shame, the guilt, and beneath it all, the bitter undercurrent of unappeased wanting…It's too much. I thrust the box back into her hands with more strength than I intend; she stumbles back and I almost apologize, but instead I walk away.

"Kai!" she cries out. She runs forward and grabs my arm roughly. "Watch." Then she tears open the box, ripping the cardboard. "Now I can't return it."

"What are you doing?" I try to seize it back from her, but she angles away. "Stop!"

"I just want you to have this, okay?" Her voice rises. "Stop making this so complicated!"

Her words sting. "You want this to be simple, fine," I tell her. "Just say it. It's because I'm poor."

"No!" She shakes her head wildly as if caught in a swarm of wasps. "No, I mean, it's not because of that. I just—I don't care about the money, okay? It's not a big deal to me!"

I swear under my breath, because only a rich person could say something so goddamn stupid. "You don't understand me."

"How can I?" she asks. "How can I when you never let me in?" Her eyes fill, which makes me sick with shame. "Why are you so *stubborn* all the time?"

"I'm stubborn?" I say, and all at once, every long-suppressed resentment spills out of me. "Take a look at yourself! Why won't you listen to common sense? You risk your life for Tin-lok, some man you barely know. You risk your life going to the protests, staying later and later when you *know* it's dangerous. I've asked you not to go on the front lines—"

"And when you ask me, it fucking sucks!" she cries out, so loud even the waves seem to tremble. "It's like you think this is some joke to me, like a hobby, like I can just give it up and move on with my life—"

"Because you can," I hiss. "How's your life going to change because of this? You're going to America with Charlie, you're leaving—"

"But Hong Kong is my home!"

"If it's your home," I say in a low voice, "then why don't you care a little more? Do you understand what's happening now because of the protests? There are kids in hospitals as we speak. Their parents don't know if they're going to last the night. The streets are barricaded; people won't be able to go to work tomorrow. They won't be able to open shop and make a living and feed their families! The economy is tanking. Unemployment rates are soaring. People are threatening hunger strikes and suicide—"

"What would you have us do instead? Surrender quietly?" She starts pacing. "Give China the keys to our home and maybe the hearts of our firstborn too?"

"I didn't want to say this, but China's going to take over one way or another. Nothing a thousand or even a million kids can do is going to change anything, Phoenix. If we want peace—"

"Peace," she scoffs. "Maybe you've been brainwashed, living under the Chinese dictatorship for so long. What you have in China isn't real peace."

"We don't have all this fighting—"

"You don't have any dissent at all! Because anytime anyone criticizes the government, or takes one step out of line, they disappear. And the media pretends they never existed." She stops in front of me, squaring her shoulders. "When China takes over—who knows what's going to happen here? But I for one would rather fight for a chance at freedom than settle for a pretense."

"Even if people get killed."

"Whatever sacrifices must be made!" She glares at me fiercely, her eyes rimmed red.

I feel like we're speaking from opposite ends of a tunnel, and everything we say gets distorted and warped, echoed and twisted. I don't understand her. I don't understand how she can talk like this, as if she's invincible against the consequences. As if the push and pull of life won't touch her, won't drag her down through the undertow like it does the rest of us. As if your actions don't have ripples, as if you don't know you can wake up one morning and ask your ma for winter melon soup for dinner, then go to school and come home that night and find her passed out on the sofa, not breathing. And your last words to her were "winter melon soup."

And you never told her you're sorry.

"We're both so stubborn," she whispers, her voice choking up. I can't tell if she's laughing or crying. Maybe both.

I nod. At least we can agree on this.

"I can't believe I picked a fight with you on your birthday," she mumbles. "What kind of girlfriend am I?"

Girlfriend? She considers herself my girlfriend? I try not to let my surprise show on my face. She considers what we're doing, this sneaking back and forth, this evasion . . . a relationship? I know I should be alarmed, but I'm touched instead. And then racked by guilt. Because that means what I'm doing, this lying, is much, much worse.

Because it's serious for her. And as much as I don't want to admit it, it's serious for me too. That's why I've been having a hard time looking my father in the face. That's why I've started lying on my reports to Lieutenant Chan, writing "no new events" on my briefings. That's why I walked across the city to see her, despite my concussion, despite my exhaustion.

Xingxing zhi huo. A single spark starts a blaze. And the flames are catching.

"I'm sorry," I sigh, running a hand through my hair. I clench my hands behind the back of my neck. "My head's a mess."

"It's my fault," she says. "I'm sorry about what I said, about your being brainwashed. I know it's not true. I mean, look at you. You're protesting at LegCo and even getting hurt for it." She touches the bruise on my cheek again, and this time, her hand lingers. "I hate those fucking cops more than anyone else in the world."

A cold chill runs down my spine.

"It's late," I say. "You should get back."

"Do you forgive me?" she whispers, peering up at me. Her eyes are so wide, and so open, I can't imagine lying to this face. And yet I do, time and time again.

"There's nothing to forgive," I say quietly, and the words fall as only lies do: like water, passing easily through a net.

Phoenix

WE STAND ON THE BEACH IN THE HALF DARK, so close our breaths mingle. I want an end to this separation between us, a way to join our thoughts and minds so that our pasts and our backgrounds and our contexts don't matter anymore, and the only thing that matters is this. *I'm falling for you,* I want to tell him.

But I don't. Because if I do, I'll scare him away. I feel as if I'm holding a wild bird in my hands, one quick to spread its wings and fly. *Stay a little longer,* I want to say, *stay for me.*

Instead, I speak without words, in the only way I know how. I reach up and twine my fingers through his hair.

Then I kiss him.

Maybe it's because of his exhaustion, or the fight we just had, but he answers more readily, pressing deeper, harder, more demanding than he ever has before. As if he's trying to mark me, as if he knows how much power he has over me. I feel him forcing our lips together, our tongues together, his hands in my hair, on my back. The want is overwhelming, irresistible. And why resist? I start unbuttoning my shirt. It takes him a second to understand, and then he draws back, gasping for breath.

"Lifeng," he says, and there's an unmistakable question in his voice.

I nod. I'm ready. We come together again, my mouth opening beneath his, and that's when someone honks at us from the thoroughfare and we jump apart. The car is already racing past us down the street, but we remember we're out in the open. Kai buttons my pajama shirt higher than it was before, up to my throat.

"C'mon," I say, breathless, picking up my bag from the sand. "I know a place we can go."

I take his hand and lead him down the street toward my country club, which sits on the beachfront. Mom pays full membership fees for us kids, but I never go because my brain hates exercise and my skin hates tanning. (I give the word *sunburn* a whole new definition, seriously.) I figure if official guest policy is one guest per member, we're not breaking any rules.

There's just the small issue of open hours, but time is relative, right?

"The fence is broken in the back," I explain, leading us toward the parking lot behind the club. I can't take all the credit; Osprei was the one who discovered this trick. It's where he brings all his lady conquests because the security cameras don't work.

Kai reaches through the gap in the fence to unlock it from the inside. We tiptoe along the garden path to the swimming pool, which is brightly lit despite the hour. Lights glow from beneath the water, turning the surface of the pool into what looks like hundreds of rippling, blue-green gemstones.

I glance at Kai; he's watching me. His face is cast in shadows, highlighting all its angles and sharpness. A few strands of hair fall over his forehead, hiding the fresh cut by his ear. His eyes are lidded and dark, starless. I guess I'll have to accept the mystery of him, to know there will always be more to know. Some small part of me thinks this won't last, that we're too different, that we won't be able to manage the future. The thought only makes me want to cling harder to him now. I guess I've always been a little masochistic; I've always wanted what I can't have.

Without breaking from his stare, I unbutton my shirt again, my hands shaking with nervous energy. I watch the knot at his throat pulse, the tendons along his neck thrown into sharp relief.

My bare skin prickles beneath the intensity of his gaze. Briefly, my thoughts recall Officer Ho Yi-tung—his unwanted leer, my utter humiliation—but the memory fades as if relayed through poor radio reception, lacking power. Kai is nothing like him. I felt helpless around that officer; I feel safe around Kai.

I smirk at Kai now. Then I walk a few paces back and take a running leap into the pool.

The water is ice cold. I come up gasping for breath, smoothing my hair back, off my face. Before I can wipe the water from my eyes, I see a blur in the air and then a giant splash hits me in the face. Kai pops up beside me, grinning.

I've never seen him without a shirt before. He picks me up in the water and I trail my hands over his broad shoulders and arms. "Why does an artist need these kinds of muscles?"

He gives me a crooked half grin. "Artists are vain creatures, you know," he says. Then his voice drops, as if admitting a secret. "We're drawn to beauty."

I tilt my head at him. "Then you think I'm pretty?"

"I don't just like you for your personality, if that's what you're asking."

I laugh. We frolic in the water until it gets too cold. When we get out of the pool, I'm inspired by the sight of water beading on his bare skin, his wet hair, so dark it looks like newly ground ink.

I practically attack him, though my lips are already swollen from kissing. He responds with equal force, lowering me to the lounge chair by the pool, then raising himself over me. Everything's happening so fast. My breathing goes unsteady as his thumb brushes the inside of my thigh, as he works his mouth down my neck, to my collarbones, my breasts, trailing kisses down my stomach. I've never felt this kind of thrill before. *No wonder Osprei is a fool for love,* I think. It's better than a drug.

"I have protection," I say breathlessly. "In my bag—"

Kai raises his head, his eyes dark with lust. Then something in them clears, and he surfaces as if from underwater. Abruptly, he sits back. Then he stands, scrubs his face, and walks away.

I rise too, confused. "What is it?"

He's clutching at his hair as if he wants to pull it out. "Lifeng, I can't."

It takes a second for me to understand, as if there's a lag. I pause. "Oh. Are you a...virgin?" I color as soon as the words are out of my mouth. "Not that there's anything wrong with that, if you are," I add. "I don't want to pressure—"

A laugh escapes him. It sounds almost like a sigh. "It's not that." He turns to me at last. I can still see the heady desire in his eyes, the hunger that matches my own. "I'm sorry, Lifeng. Just, I can't. It wouldn't feel right." His mouth twists, his expression lost somewhere else, far away.

There's something he's not saying, something he's hiding from me. I open my mouth to argue but he's already drying off with one of the country club towels. He hands one to me, then wordlessly pulls on his jeans. I'm standing there like a mannequin when he retrieves my pajamas from the ground and passes them to me. They smell like chlorine.

"All right," I say, because Robin would tell me to take Sun Tzu's advice and know when a battle is lost. I slide on my pajama bottoms slowly and reluctantly. He's already changed; he starts helping me with the tedious buttons on my shirt. I don't get it. He says he's bad for me, he says he's a bad person, but all evidence points to the contrary. I've never met a boy like this, who notices the small things, listens more than he speaks, crosses town just so I don't have to walk in the dark.

I was wrong about him before. Kai is like me; we're both diaspora kids. He might come from Shanghai, which couldn't be more different from North Carolina, but we both know what it's like to be separated from everyone else, to not find a mirror in your peers. We both know what it's like to exist in between, neither here nor there. I think about my feelings toward America: that dual sense of responsibility and powerlessness. Is that also how he feels about China?

"What is it?" he asks, voice low.

I'm drinking in the sight of him, because I know I'll only get to see him a few minutes more. How do people live like this, I wonder—how do people live when they're in love? "Nothing," I say, "just thinking about how much I like you."

I smile at him, but his eyes look sad, weighed with fatigue as if he just turned a hundred and not eighteen years old.

Outside my house, I force him to take the drawing tablet, and this time, I win. As we say goodbye, I hold my breath, then watch as he slips into the shadows.

That night, I fall asleep and dream of treasure chests, locked and shuttered. When I find the key, my hands tremble as I unlock the coveted chest, only to find that I am too late. The waiting gems have turned to dust, which dances away in the wind.

Phoenix

I'M AT MY SUMMER SAT COURSE WHEN THE news breaks. The other students start whispering and checking their phones, although Ms. Chiu has already threatened to break the next phone she sees. (We're beginning to suspect Ms. Chiu has some unresolved anger issues going on.)

"What's happening?" I whisper to my partner, Ruby. Ruby goes to Whitney with me, though we run in different circles.

She shoots a glance at Ms. Chiu, who's concentrated on writing algebraic proofs on the chalkboard. "Suicide at Admiralty. Someone jumped off the rooftop at Pacific Place." She hesitates. "Apparently, he did it in protest."

"Who?" It comes out much louder than I intend. My mind flashes through the possibilities so fast I feel whiplash. *What if it's someone I know? What if...*

I can't bring myself to finish that thought.

Ms. Chiu turns to glare at me. "Did you have a question, Ms. Lam?" she asks, the chalk in her hand poised like a weapon.

"No," I say. "I mean, I would like to use the restroom."

She nods. I'm in a daze as I grab my bag and run out of the classroom. When I'm safely in the hall, I pull out my phone. The first article I read doesn't identify the victim. Instead, it talks about the yellow raincoat the guy was wearing. On the back was written: *Carrie Lam is killing Hong Kong.*

I find his name at last—it's no one I know. I let myself exhale, but it feels performative; the relief doesn't take over as I thought it would. I still feel that same taut, coiled energy in my limbs, like a clock wound too tight, ticking too fast. Each second stunted, each minute limping, lopsided. Time has a fragile feeling to it, as if I could blink and wish the days away.

I just want everything to slow down.

Is this how Mom gets when she has one of her panic attacks? Like her skin is stretched too tight, like her insides are a tangled mess of knots? I hide in the bathroom and sit on the toilet, waiting for my breathing to even out.

Kai has texted me. So has Suki, Charlie, even Robin. I'm getting dozens of DMs on Instagram. I know I should be making a post about it, updating my followers and acknowledging what happened. I'm getting in over my head. I've overcommitted, tied too many knots. No string left.

"Phoenix?" There are footsteps outside my stall. "Are you in there? Ms. Chiu is getting worried."

"I'm fine," I say. "Just girl problems, you know."

"Oh, okay."

My phone lights up with a new text, from Charlie: I need to talk to you. It's important.

I open the chat window to reply, but then turn off my phone instead. I don't know what to say; I don't want to talk. Charlie's supposed to be my best friend, but we've grown apart lately. He knows it too, though it's gone unsaid. In the absence of a loud fight, our friendship has simply withered, like a riverbed drying out in the sun, cut off from its source. I can't tell if it's because of a small thing, like a busy schedule, or if the root is much deeper. Is it because I've changed? And my dreams—have those changed too?

I don't know what I want anymore. Some days I want nothing; some days I want everything. Too many thoughts crowd my head, each demanding air and water and light to grow.

I think of the police officer who chased me the night of Tin-lok's escape, Officer Ho Yi-tung. I remember his scalding eyes on my body, his gaze like a blistering poker. I remember shivering against the empty night, wanting so badly to run. I think of Kai's low voice as he tells me that I don't understand. His hungry lips, of the wanting that sometimes overpowers me until I can't think, can't breathe. I think of reading Suki's interview in the *Guardian* and feeling so proud I wanted to cheer for her from my bedroom window. I think of Mom, of her unhappiness, stifling as an airless room. I think of my broken family, how it always feels like we're waiting for something, on the brink of something. What are we waiting for? I don't know. I'm waiting too.

I get up and unlock the stall, then wash my hands to keep up the pretense. The cold water burns my skin. I glare at my reflection in the mirror. I can't make everyone happy; I've never been able to do that. It comes with being part of two worlds, never fully belonging to either. But I can start by being honest with myself.

I'm not going to America for college.

I'm not leaving Hong Kong.

I don't bother returning to class. Suki texts me as I head down the hallway. You coming to the protest tonight?

I'll be there.

When I get home, Mom is nowhere to be found. Instead, Robin pounces on me in my closet as I'm changing into my protest clothes.

"Mom was upset you missed your college counseling appointment yesterday," Robin says in her hoity-toity, told-you-so voice. "She drank from the forbidden cabinet because of you."

Tian ah. The forbidden cabinet has no magical wonders like its name might suggest, only some very old, very expensive French wine she usually cracks open around holidays or special occasions. As we've stopped hosting parties since the divorce (whoever said misery likes company has never met Mom), she's taken to staking out the entire contents of the forbidden cabinet for her own pity parties. Robin informs me Mom's been marathoning K-dramas and crying on repeat, while drinking wine to "replenish her electrolytes."

"Mom thinks you're purposefully trying to fail your SATs to punish her. Because of the divorce."

"Mom needs to get over herself." I throw on a colorful

hoodie over my black T-shirt to disguise my protest gear. "If I fail my SATs, it'll be because of me, not her."

"Oh, so you are still taking them?" Robin has the habit of picking apart my words with the intensity of a surgeon. "Because that's been kinda up in the air too."

"How'd you figure that out?" I ask, swinging toward her. She's still in her pajamas despite the fact that it's four in the afternoon. I'm also not sure when she last washed her hair.

"Well, you haven't mentioned Yale in, like, forever," Robin says, hugging my Tata plushie to her chest like a shield. "And I saw you looking up HKU Law's acceptance rate. You want to stay in Hong Kong, don't you?"

"Robin! You checked my computer search history *again*?"

Robin widens her eyes and bats her lashes in false innocence. She learned how to play cute from watching Osprei's annoying ex-girlfriend and I still haven't forgiven him for that. (Next time he brings home any girl whose legal name starts with Sweet and ends with Baby, I know to raise some warning flags.)

I stuff my protest gear into my backpack and head downstairs, Robin at my heels. In the kitchen, there's red bean soup warming on the stovetop. I breathe in the sweet fragrance, hit by a wave of nostalgia. We only used to eat red bean soup when Dad was home, because it's his favorite dessert.

But I guess Mom isn't waiting for him anymore.

"I'm just saying," Robin says, spooning out a bowl of soup, "Mom won't be happy if she finds out."

"Finds out what?"

We both jump.

Mom stands in the living room doorway dressed in a formal gray pantsuit. She looks like she's going to the courthouse—that, or a funeral parlor.

"When'd you get home?" I ask, stunned that Mom crept up on us so soundlessly. Now that I'm seeing her in the flesh, all my hard-won courage deserts me. I'll tell her the truth another day, I decide. (My powers of procrastination are unparalleled.) Besides, I'm running late.

I hook my backpack onto one shoulder and turn toward the back door, keeping my head down.

"Where do you think you're going?" Mom asks. In her pantsuit, she looks like she's a judge about to deliver me my sentence.

Robin looks at me with big eyes. Her spoon frozen in midair, she mouths, *Sorry.*

I sigh, making a gut decision. I can't put this conversation off any longer. I set my backpack down—it's heavy with all my protest gear—and take a seat at the kitchen counter.

"Mom—" I start. This is so much harder than I thought it would be. "What would you and Dad think if I decided . . . not to take my SATs?"

Mom stares at me, bewildered, uncomprehending. "Would you take the ACTs instead?"

My tongue isn't working properly. It feels like I have cotton balls stuffed in my mouth. "I want to go to university here. In Hong Kong."

There's a stunned silence.

"Phoenix, you can't be serious." Mom looks as if she

thinks it's April Fools' Day, as if she's waiting for me to shout "Just kidding!" "You've always wanted to go to Yale. It's been your dream for years."

"It's been *Dad's* dream for years." I swipe my clammy palms on my pants. Slowly, understanding dawns on Mom's face. "Hong Kong is mine."

"She wants to apply to HKU Law," Robin pipes up. "Apparently, it's ranked eighteenth in the world. And first in Hong Kong, but you know that."

I squeeze Robin's hand under the counter. Mom lets out a deep breath as if preparing to meditate. "This is about the protests, isn't it? If you think your father and I are just going to accept this and let you throw away your dreams, just for some...some passing trend—"

"The protest movement isn't a trend!" I stand too quickly and my stool tips back, crashing to the floor. "Hong Kong is my home and where I belong. I want to study here—study its law and politics and history and learn at one of the best institutions in the world."

"But Yale is a top university—"

"So is HKU," I say. "You and Dad would recognize that if you cared more about my actual education and less about our family image and social status."

For a moment, the only sound in the house is the fallen stool clattering against the kitchen tiles. Then Mom shakes her head. "If you're staying for the protest movement, you're more foolish than I thought. This so-called movement will end in mere months. By next year, China will have taken control of the island. And you'll be thanking your parents that we paid in blood, sweat, and tears to get you an American degree, Miss Phoenix Lam." Her voice turns harsh, remorseless. "This isn't your fight. This is beyond the scope of our lives, beyond what any of us can control. The only thing we can do is protect our own."

I look from Mom to Robin. I've heard variations of this sentiment from Charlie, Tin-lok, my grandparents. But what they don't get is that we're not defining "our own" in the same way. My own is not just Robin and Osprei and Mom. It's not even just the friends I can name off the top of my head. It's everyone in Hong Kong, everyone who's fighting for a chance at a better future.

I grab my backpack off the floor. Despite the hardness on Mom's face, I can tell she's anxious on the inside. I know she's in a difficult position. She wants what's best for me; she doesn't want to lose face in front of Dad; and she knows any bad behavior on my part reflects poorly on her. Things are tense enough as they are. I've just made our next family get-together ten times more awkward.

But they could understand if they tried. Mom and Dad are both Hong Kongers, both born and raised here. They both have grim stories of growing up under British occupation, chafing under colonial rule. Now that they've overcome those hardships, they think they're untouchable in their Repulse Bay neighborhood. And maybe they are. But every generation has its own story, and this is mine.

"Phoenix, I'm *tired*," Mom says, a sulfurous note in her voice. "Can't you see that?"

Something snaps inside me. "We're all fucking tired,

Mom." I hear Robin gasp. "None of us want to go out protesting every night. We're doing this because we have to. Because the alternative is worse."

I head toward the door. "I'm not asking you to agree with me. I'm asking you to let me make my own choices."

Kai

"ZOUSAN." SERGEANT LEUNG WAVES IN GREET-ing as we pass another squad on our way back from patrol training. "How'd it go?"

"We lost them again," the squad captain answers, face weary. "They knew we were coming."

Marco jabs me in the side. "See what I mean?" he mutters under his breath as we head to the showers to wash up. "How do the protesters always know where the police are? It's like they have a tracking device on us."

I yawn. Between late-night swimming with Phoenix and early morning patrol training, I've gotten close to zero sleep. "Actually"—I yawn again—"maybe they do."

Marco grabs his toiletries from under his bed and slings his towel over his shoulder. "What do you mean?"

I rub my eyes. I can't believe we still have afternoon

classes after this. It'll be a feat if I don't fall asleep at my desk. "Do you remember the sting op from a few weeks back? One of the HKU students I met there is a computer science major. Ming-lai. He designed this program that consolidates every single livestream out there into one solid fucking map—it has a street view of all of Hong Kong Island, even New Territories. He shared the link with us on Telegram."

Marco's eyes go round. "And it tells you exactly where the ging caat are?"

I nod. "I think it even shows recommended escape routes. He's crowdsourced from, like, hundreds of volunteers. It's all self-reported. By the way, can I borrow your shampoo? I'm out."

"Wai!" Marco whacks me hard enough to bruise. "This is *huge*. We need to get that site taken down. If even Raptor squad can't catch the protesters, how can anyone else?"

Like waking from a dream, I slowly come to. My face heats. "I don't know...."

"You just said you knew the mastermind behind this. Ming-lai, was it?"

I brush past him toward the corridor. I'm too tired to think about this right now. "C'mon, we'll be late for class—"

He grabs me. "Kai, listen. You wanna get in your dad's good graces? Tell him this."

I wrench out of his grip. "What the fuck?"

Marco's face is uncharacteristically serious. "It's not my business. I get it. But I'm not that oblivious, okay?"

I choke. "Don't presume you—"

"Even if you don't snitch on the kid, someone else will. A secret that big—it'll leak one way or another. Why not take the credit for it?" He shoulders past me toward the restroom, and I think he's dropped the subject until he adds, "If you don't, I will."

And now I'm wide awake. He's right. Hundreds of people are in on the secret, though they may not know Ming-lai's real name. And ever since I blundered the Tin-lok sting, Father hasn't spoken to me in weeks. Not that I've even *seen* him since. I wonder how he's doing. If he's eating, sleeping. He didn't come back to the apartment at all last weekend.

"I'll do it," I say, though Marco can't hear me over the shower. *My actions won't cause a ripple,* I don't say. Ming-lai is bound to get arrested one way or another. So what if I'm the one who pulls the trigger?

Ming-lai means nothing to me. But someone else does. And if she finds out...

"She won't find out," I say aloud, so confidently I even believe it myself.

I'm a practiced liar.

A few hours later, Father interrupts our lunch break. He has a paper in his hand. I recognize the yellow seal; it's a warrant. He scans the cafeteria. At first I think he's looking for me, until his eyes halt on Lieutenant Chan. "I'm bringing Twenty-Four."

I jump to my feet. The other trainees start whispering immediately. Marco pulls my plate toward him, knowing I'm not going to finish it now. He spoons Mapo tofu calmly from my dish to his own.

I'm everything but calm. I approach like a wild animal, cautious but hungry. "Are you sure that's wise?" I hear Lieutenant Chan ask. "He's still a trainee."

"I can look after my own son."

My eyes widen but I force my face to remain impassive. A tingling fizz spreads through my chest, like the warmth of alcohol.

"Let's go," Father says.

For the first time, I think. He called me his son for the first time.

There's half a dozen of us, including me. We squeeze into the elevator of Ming-lai's apartment, then pile out into the narrow corridor, which is just as stale and airless as I remember it.

"Open up." Father bangs on the door. "Police. We have a warrant."

Through the thin walls, I catch a muffled gasp followed by heated whispers. The old wooden floorboards creak and groan. They're trying to escape.

Father grimaces and signals for the hydraulic door breaker. He locks his elbows in place, fitting the heavy machinery to the door. Inside, I can still hear footsteps scurrying across the floor, and I recognize the futility of it; they don't stand a chance.

With one practiced motion, Father breaks open the door. I catch a flurry of movement before he rushes in, followed by the other officers. I'm last inside.

The kitchen and sitting room are empty, but the windows

are open, and they threw something that smells like gasoline into the building air shaft. We're not getting that out anytime soon.

Father scowls at the empty state of the apartment and draws his gun.

A ringing sound fills my ears. "Sir!"

He ignores me, moving down the hall with his gun raised. *What if Phoenix is here?* I think, panicking. Then I wonder, how could the thought not have occurred to me earlier?

Easily. Because I don't think. It's simpler not to.

I stumble after my father, so sick to my stomach I'm afraid I might throw up.

From the bedroom, I catch an undeniable flash of light. Father shoves the door fully open with his foot. "Hands up!"

There's only one person inside. A pale, dark-haired boy standing over a computer. Slowly, he turns and lifts his hands in the air. My breath whooshes out of me. It's not Ming-lai. It's Osprei.

He looks at us with cool appraisal, his brow cocked. He can't possibly recognize me beneath my helmet, but still I tense.

"Hello there," he says, somehow appearing casual even with his hands raised. "I don't recall inviting you in."

"Face the wall," Father says, taking out his zip ties. He pulls Osprei's arms behind his back. "You're under arrest."

Then Father turns to me. "Twenty-Four, guard him while we search the premises."

I look at him in outrage, but he's already moving on. I don't want to be left alone with Osprei; it's the worst job I could possibly get.

Osprei is humming a childhood lullaby, unperturbed. I avoid making eye contact with him. For something to do, I move toward the desk and try turning on the computer. It's clearly overheating because its fan is making loud whirring noises.

"Don't bother," Osprei says, from the wall. "It's wiped."

The keyboard is missing several keys, and the desk lamp is broken. Ming-lai doesn't even have a bed frame, only a sagging mattress. He's clearly poor, poor like me. He doesn't belong in the same sphere as Osprei, or even Suki, who is at least middle class. What is he doing wasting his time with this damned protest movement? Who does he think he is, that he can change the government and the law and the ways things are done around here with a few posters and a dying laptop? Why do any of these kids believe it? How *dare* they believe it?

I resent them, I realize. I resent them because I made my choice when I enrolled in the police academy, and they made theirs when they took to the streets. It's people like Ming-lai and Suki, and even Phoenix, who dare to follow their "passions," who dare to dream bigger than themselves.

If I don't have that right, why the fuck do they?

I step back from the desk. That's when I notice a comb sitting next to the wireless mouse. There are long strands of purple hair tangled up in the wooden teeth. I touch the hair; it's still wet. *Suki.* She's here.

"All clear," I hear Father say from the living room. "Let's move out."

You missed a cockroach, I could say. She's hiding here, somewhere. So is Ming-lai. I think Osprei is protecting him.

Because Osprei knows, with his connections and his family lawyer and his wealth, he will not lose his trial. But Ming-lai would.

But what if Phoenix is here too? She wasn't supposed to be here last time either. And still, she followed me—into that locked stairwell. Then we spent the night together.

I remember waking up in the morning and looking into her sleeping face. I remember wanting to kiss her. I remember thinking she was too good for me.

But we *all* want more than we're given in life—isn't that just human nature? I was the one who made the wrong choice; I see that now. I was the one who settled. Ming-lai made his own options. Despite the risks, despite the lack of a safety net. He's staked his entire life on this movement. When I enrolled at the academy, I went with the flow, like water. It wasn't what I wanted to do, but I didn't think I had a choice. I didn't think people like me ever did.

"Clear?" Officer Wang asks me, leaning in through the doorway.

I nod. "All clear."

At the station, Father files the paperwork on my behalf. I'm heading toward the exit when I hear a familiar voice at the front desk. My stomach lurches.

"Let me see him, *please*," Phoenix says. Suki is with her.

The desk receptionist checks his file. "His bail hasn't been posted yet, miss."

"He's my brother."

"Come back in a few hours."

"It's okay, Phoenix," Suki says, taking her arm. "He'll be fine. There's no evidence against him."

Phoenix turns around; I throw myself back against the wall before she sees me.

If Phoenix finds out I arrested her brother…she'll never forgive me.

Father finds me in the hallway. He's already shrugging on his jacket, preparing for another patrol. "Gaa jau," he says, clapping me on the shoulder as he walks by. "You just caught a terrorist in the making."

I nod leadenly, then head out back to the smoking area. I crouch on the ground, trying to steady my erratic heartbeat. I got his attention, his approval. That *was* what I wanted, wasn't it? For him to recognize me as his son, for him to see me, to know me. But he doesn't see me, not really. Because the image I've shown him—it's a lie.

I'm not like him. And no matter how hard I try, I never will be.

Phoenix

SUKI AND I ARE BOTH WAITING OUTSIDE WHEN Osprei gets out on bail. He kisses Suki, then hugs me. I want to box him for looking so carefree.

Taking one look at my face, he bursts into laughter. "Don't worry so much, Nix!" he says. "They couldn't charge me for more than unlawful assembly. All the evidence points back to Ming-lai."

"Not here," Suki says lowly, shuffling us toward the MTR station. We merge into the throngs of people, but she keeps glancing over her shoulder, as if afraid of being tailed. "He's hiding in a fumou's basement right now," she says quietly. "But we need to smuggle him off the island. He'll go to prison if he stays."

Fumou means parent, but it's also the name for older folks who support the frontline protesters behind the scenes. They give us rides at night, drop off supplies, even offer hiding places for protesters wanted by the police. Most of these people are complete strangers, willing to sacrifice their time and money and future to help us.

It's astonishing to see this change that's come over Hong Kong—where before, in a city of seven million, neighbors couldn't be bothered to learn one another's names, now real solidarity has risen among us. I see strangers leaving coins at the MTR stations all the time because they know we can't use our Octopus cards to swipe through the turnstiles; the police track our identities that way. Other folks bring bags of colored clothing to the MTR so we can change out of our black clothes before we leave the scene of the protest. Still others leave their grocery stores open at night, with signs saying PROTESTERS, TAKE WHAT YOU NEED. HONG KONG, ADD OIL!

"How long can he hide there?" I ask as we weave through the teeming Mong Kok night market.

Suki frowns. "The fumou said however long he needs, but she's too generous. We don't want to take advantage of her. She can help pay for the cost of the boat ride, but she can't get him there herself. We'll need to do that on our own." Then Suki cracks a grin. "Besides, Ming-lai is begging us to get him out as soon as possible. Apparently, he's playing babysitter to her two toddlers. Twins. And you know how he is with kids."

Osprei snorts. But I'm stunned. "She's letting *her own kids* play with him?" This boy who's wanted by the police?

Suki shrugs. "She trusts him. We trust her."

"Do you even know her name?"

Suki shakes her head, the overhead street sign casting her face in a dark red glow. "I don't need to. It's like this—no one trusts the authorities anymore. So we trust each other instead."

I glance back at the police station in the distance, with its graffitied exterior that they still haven't managed to scrub clean. It's true that no one trusts the cops anymore, or the government. That happens all the time, in history and around the world. But instead of devolving into cynicism or anarchy, we've turned to one another. We've built a real community.

I smile for the first time all day. Osprei grins back at me.

"I'm still mad at you," I say, my scowl returning. "Why didn't you hide too?"

"They wouldn't have believed an empty apartment," Osprei explains. "Besides, my guess was right—I thought they wouldn't ask for my ID before they arrested me. They assumed I was Ming-lai. By the time they brought me into the station, it was too late. Ming-lai was long gone."

I sigh. Osprei is so cocky, sometimes I worry he'll jump off a cliff if it means getting to play hero. "But did you really have to take the fall?"

"Ming-lai couldn't," Osprei says, before pausing in front of a rice-cake stand. "He's already been arrested once for inciting secession and resisting arrest."

"Someone sold him out—I'm sure of it," Suki says darkly, looking like she wants to murder that person. "They knew too much for it to be a coincidence. I just can't figure out who. Only the HKU kids knew his real name."

Suki's lost in thought—until Osprei takes her hand. "Enough scheming," he says, a twinkle in his eye. "Aren't you going to celebrate my homecoming?"

"You were in jail for less than six hours!" She giggles

and kisses him anyway. "Thank you for protecting me," she whispers.

I wrinkle my nose and formulate my escape route. Something tells me they'll be occupied for a while. My phone rings then, and I bless whichever telemarketer is calling me. But when I check the screen, it's Charlie.

I frown. I don't know why I've been avoiding him, except that my gut tells me I won't be happy with whatever this "important thing" that he wants to talk about is. Still, I can't ignore him forever. He's my oldest friend, and I owe him more than total silence. "Hey," I answer at last. "What's up?"

I hear bass vibrating on his end, blaring music and laughter and shouting.

"You picked up." His voice sounds slurred, unfocused. "Nix."

"Where are you?"

"Some club in Mong Kok. My cousin's visiting from Cambridge, remember?"

"Oh." Phil is Charlie's cousin twice removed; I wish he were *more* removed from Charlie's life. Last time he visited, he asked if I had any Asian friends looking to bang a white man. I told him he could go fuck himself.

"I didn't expect you to answer," he says, apparently moving somewhere quieter. The booming music recedes. "Have you read any of my messages?"

"I've been busy," I say, before adding, "You said you're in Mong Kok?"

"Tung Choi Street," he says. "Why, you close by?"

I raise my head to get my bearings. Osprei is currently

feeding Suki rice cakes. There's a lot of tongue action going on. I turn away hastily. "I'm a couple of blocks away, actually. On Nathan Road."

"Who are you with?" he demands. "The Chinese boy?"

It's not a derogatory word, but the way he says it makes my shoulders tense. "No," I say, "Kai's at work. I'm with my brother."

He sounds relieved. "Wanna come meet me, then?" he asks. "I've been meaning to talk to you."

"About what?"

"Eh..." He's not fully coherent right now. "Let's talk face-to-face."

I try thinking of an excuse to avoid Phil. "I don't want to interrupt your cousin-bonding time."

"Phil's off with some girl right now. That's all he wants to do in Hong Kong."

Gross. At least I don't have to see him, then. "I'll be there in five," I say, waving goodbye to Osprei and Suki. Only Suki's polite enough to wave back. "Text me your location."

By the time I arrive, Charlie and Phil have apparently moved from an EDM club to a dive bar on Sai Yeung Choi, only a couple of blocks from the Mong Kok police station.

Despite the proximity of the station, the streets are alive and thrumming with noise, partygoers spilling out of the bars lining the alleyway. Paper lanterns and Christmas lights are strung across the rooftops, sending warm orange light skittering across the cobblestoned streets. Friends stroll along the sidewalk while couples sit on the curb, drinking beer and leaving crumpled cans in the gutter. It's almost eleven in the evening, but Mong Kok never sleeps.

Charlie's at a seedy pub I've never heard of near the end of the alley. I double-check the address before venturing inside. Although it's dark, I spot him immediately. He's collapsed on a bench against the far wall, his complexion beet red, his hair mussed as if he just fell on his face. He probably did, once or twice. Phil, to my relief, is nowhere to be seen.

Charlie may have over a foot on me, but my alcohol tolerance is higher than his. I won't let him live this down, especially since it looks like I'll have to play babysitter tonight. "C," I say, taking him by the arm, "you're absolutely shit-faced. Let's get you home." I'm a little annoyed. I thought we'd have a drink and chitchat for a bit. I'll probably be spending tonight cleaning up vomit instead.

When we get out of the bar, the cool night air seems to wake him. "Hold up," he says, raising a hand before he belches. I take an automatic step back. "I already threw up," he says.

I scrunch my nose. (At least we got that out of the way.) "Phil should know by now you can't handle your drink," I say. "He does this to you every time."

"I think he finds it funny," Charlie says miserably.

"What an asshole."

"He's my cousin."

I keep quiet at that. I know how it is with family. You're stuck with them.

Before we can go any farther, Charlie plunks down on a newly vacated bench. "Can we sit for a bit?" he asks.

I look down at the bench dubiously. It's sticky with something that I hope is just spilled beer and not piss. I perch on the far edge.

He leans forward. His pupils are huge. "I need to tell you something."

"I'm listening," I say, drumming my fingers against my thigh. I know what he's going to say; he's going to bring up the protests. He thinks I'm getting involved with the wrong crowd, as if Suki and Ming-lai aren't straight-A uni students but members of a triad gang.

"It's about Kai."

Well, that's a plot twist.

"There's something off about him—"

"C, we're just friends, okay?" I say, lying through my teeth. "I'm perfectly experienced enough to decide—"

"No, you're not. You're naive and altogether too trusting, and on top of that, too reckless to listen to anyone's opinion but your own! He's done something to you, Nix. I don't know what it is, but I don't like it. He's changed you."

I start to stand but he stops me. "I didn't want to tell you this," he says, "but I did some digging. I went to HKU last week. I knew Kai was hiding something. He said he was a design major, right? Well, I waited outside the arts building for ages and never saw him once. When I asked some art students about him, they said they'd never heard his name before!" He takes a breath; he's worked himself into a fit. "He's not who he says he is, Nix."

"Bullshit," I say. Charlie's really gone too far this time. "There's probably hundreds of people in each class. How do you even know you went to the right spot? Let me make my own choices, C. And stop camping outside random buildings. If Kai finds out you're stalking him..."

"Then what?" Charlie asks snidely.

"I don't know, but he'll think I put you up to it."

Charlie throws his hands up in the air, because clearly, he *is* doing this for my sake. And I appreciate that he cares for me. But this argument is null and void. "Now it's your turn to listen, C. You're right that Kai isn't what he seems." I pause, choosing my words carefully. It's hard to describe. On the outside, Kai can appear cold, abrasive even. But once you get to know him…he's kind. Softhearted. A nyunnaam. Not that I can tell Charlie this. "But what he's hiding isn't bad. It's just private. And it has nothing to do with you or me."

Charlie opens his mouth like he's about to ask. I shake my head. No way am I telling anyone about Kai's mom—and his guilt over her death. I change the subject. "Why don't you come with me to the rally tomorrow? Some of our classmates will be there—it can't get more mainstream than that. Did you see how many people are going on the Facebook event?"

Charlie scoffs. "The whole thing's a show. What are you going to do there? Take a walk? Hold up some signs?"

I draw back sharply. "I'm going to photograph and write about it. In English. The world needs to see what the ging caat are like. They need to be held accountable for their actions."

He gives me a look, one that reminds me of how Dad used to look at Mom—with complete derision. "There are professional journalists who can take those. Besides, there's thousands of photos on the internet already."

"Not like the ones I need," I say, jerking to my feet. "You know most journalists don't risk getting up close."

"Because they don't have a death wish!" He rises and grabs me by the shoulders, not gently either. "What's gotten into you, Nix?" he demands. "Tell me. Why are you doing this? Who are you trying to prove yourself to? Is it Kai?"

I try to shake him off, but he doesn't budge. Charlie's only handsy like this when he's drunk. "You just don't get it." Charlie doesn't understand. Neither do my grandparents, who came over last weekend to beg me to stop stressing Mom out; they know Osprei and I have been showing up at the protests. "Protesting doesn't work," Po Po told me. "The powerful will win and the world will move on. Your life won't be affected."

"Nix, the protests are dangerous," Charlie says, as if I don't already know that. As if I don't have glaring bruises on my shoulder and sternum to remind me of the ging caat every time I take a shower. He grasps my hands now. "You know how much I care about you. If you were hurt..." He has that look on his face like he's about to take an exam and he knows all the answers. The steely glint in his eye scares me.

His arm tightens around my waist so that I'm trapped against him, and suddenly I'm reminded of the feel of that officer's hands against my skin, his taking eyes, his total confidence as he looked me over, as if he owned me completely—

"Get off!" I shove him hard. He staggers back, caught off guard. People are staring. "Sorry," I say quietly, seeing his humiliation.

He blinks back what look like tears of rage. "You've changed, Phoenix," he says between his teeth. "You're not the person I thought you were."

All my pity dissipates, like water in summer heat. "What's that supposed to mean?" I ask. "We all change, C. We're sixteen; we're supposed to be changing."

"Not like this. You used to care about bigger things—like getting into college and getting out of here. You used to have big goals!" he shouts, his voice carrying.

"No, I used to have *your* goals. Everyone keeps telling me what they want from me and I'm so sick of it! It's not bigger or better to get into an American university, no matter how prestigious it is. If I want to stay in Hong Kong, why does that make me a traitor? Why can't I protest on the streets and fight for what I believe is right?"

"Because you're not like the rest of them! You're better than them, you're..." He trails off abruptly, as if censoring his next words. More people are watching now. But I don't care anymore.

"I'm what? Richer? More privileged?" I snap. "Just spit it out, Charlie. You think we have a future and they don't."

He flushes but holds his ground, his eyes sparking. "Of course they have to fight for this. They were always going to stay in Hong Kong."

"But we can leave." I finish his sentence with barely repressed contempt. "*You* can leave, Charlie. But I'm not going to."

I whirl away. That's when he grabs me.

Kai

"LET GO!"

I hear her before I see her. At the high-pitched shriek in her voice, I shove my way through the crowd. There they are, at the end of the alley. The white boy's grabbed Phoenix's wrist, yanking her toward him.

One moment I'm standing there, thoughts blank. The next I'm in his face, wrenching him back. Phoenix stumbles in surprise, losing her balance and falling. I glare at Charlie, then turn to Phoenix, positioning myself between them.

"Are you okay?" I ask, my voice low and barely controlled. With every breath, I will my anger not to implode.

She nods, looking badly shaken. I'm about to offer her a hand when Charlie lunges from behind. I twist and shove him back.

"Get your hands off me!" he snarls. He swings a clumsy punch at me, but I sidestep him easily. He's drunk off his ass.

"She told you to let go," I say, advancing.

There's terror in his eyes. The thought passes through me but doesn't leave a mark. The only thing that registers is anger.

He charges, running at me headfirst. I duck and flip him over me; he lands on the ground with a loud *thunk.* The crowd exclaims, muttering among themselves. Hong Kongers are busybodies. I'm not following police protocol here, but I'm not in uniform either.

"What the hell do you think you're doing?" Another white boy, equally blond, equally tall, emerges from the crowd. He has an arm slung around a Chinese girl, who stares in alarm at Charlie sprawled on the ground. She untangles herself and backs away.

"Phil," Phoenix says, scrambling to her feet. "It's not—"

He eyes me. "You punk—"

Phil launches himself at me. This guy is sober, and stronger too. I try to back up but there's no room with all the people around us. He attempts to grab me; I dodge. He feints, then lands a solid blow to my jaw. My ears are ringing. There was something sharp on his hand—a ring.

"Kai!" Phoenix's voice sounds far away.

I see a hazy blur before he jumps me, and then we're both rolling on the ground. He aims at my head, but I twist and his fist smashes against stone instead. He swears; I hook my legs around his and flip us, so that now I'm on top, pinning him. "Calm down," I say, panting. I don't want to deal with another arrest.

"You little chink," Phil spits out. "You think you can get away with this?"

I jam my elbow into his throat so that he gags. "Shut up."

I know what I'm doing is illegal. I know there's a crowd of people forming around me. I know Phoenix is watching and I know Ma hated when I fought. But all these thoughts are distant in my mind, and my hands move as if of their own accord, following a different master, one born of anger.

"Phil!" Charlie cries out.

All my suppressed fury and resentment over Hong Kong, over my father, my mother, my damned life; it's seeping out of my hands, and my control, so hard won, slips—

I press down, slowly. He chokes.

"Kai." Her voice is familiar. "Stop."

And then reality floods back. I let go. Phil's face is red. He hacks out a cough as he sits up.

Phoenix tugs at my sleeve as I stand. "How did you find me?" she asks.

"This is my route to the MTR." I try to point down the street, swaying. Why do I feel so light-headed? "I was heading back to the dorms when I heard shouting...."

"What dorms?" Phoenix asks, before her eyes widen. "You're hurt."

I touch my head. Blood trickles down my temple, but I can't register the pain. My whole body feels numb. "It's not serious."

She takes a closer look and her lips part in horror. "Kai, you're bleeding. A lot."

"Fuck!" Phil's gotten his breath back. "How dare you—"

"Phil." Charlie's standing now, looking miserable. "Let's just go."

"I'll sue you—I'll—"

Someone from the crowd shouts at him. Others join in.

"We need to go to a hospital," Phoenix says urgently,

trying to cup her palm around my temple. "You could have a concussion—"

I shake my head, then grimace. That hurts. "No need," I say. "I'll just go home and sleep it off."

"What? No!"

"Lifeng." The thought of explaining it to her all over again leaves me exhausted. "I've had enough of hospital bills."

Her eyes soften with understanding. "Do you have a first-aid kit at home?" she asks. "I can help you."

The adrenaline is fading. I remember how little I've slept and am hit by a wave of dizziness. Phoenix grabs me, trying to steady us both.

"What did you say?" I ask, looking down at her.

She grabs my bag off the ground and slings it over her shoulder, then starts leading me down the street. I let her, until she says, "Which way to your apartment?"

"You can't go there!" I wince and lower my voice hastily. "Sorry. You just—you can't come to my apartment."

Her face shows her hurt. "I can't let you walk back alone."

"I'll be fine."

"Kai, if you saw what you looked like right now..."

It's true that passersby are shooting me odd looks. I rub the back of my neck. "My apartment's quite small...."

It's a weak excuse, but she doesn't press me on it. "Why don't you come back to my place instead? I can call Uncle Chow right now. You shouldn't walk anyway."

"Your place...?"

She lets go of me and takes out her phone. Without her support, I have to lean against a wall for balance; I must be worse off than I thought.

"The intersection of Tung Choi and Boundary Street, yep. Come quick."

"Wait, Phoenix—"

She hangs up. "It's settled."

"But your family. And Osprei—"

"No one will see us," she says. "Trust me. It's a big house."

I can't comprehend a house where the people living inside don't cross paths. I'm too tired to argue further, though I know I should. Sergeant Leung will have my head when I return to the academy late. I slump to the ground, deciding to just sleep here.

In what feels like mere minutes, Phoenix is nudging me awake and pointing at a black car in front of us. There's an older man taking hold of my shoulder and pulling me up. He looks vaguely like my father, the same coloring and strong jawline, but by the way he's speaking to me, as if I'm a child, the way he's holding me, as if I'm fragile—I know it can't be my father. My father, who despises weakness.

"Thanks, Uncle," Phoenix says from far away. "I'll grab his bag."

My eyes fall shut. The darkness is pressing, heavy and warm. As the man helps me to the car, then settles a blanket over my shoulders, I imagine he is my father, and that I'm a child, five again. I hear the engine start, and feel the car pull away from the curb. Memories return to me as vague half-truths, distorted as if through warped glass. In the dark, I try to recall what it was like to be a child, to trust your parents loved each other, to trust they would protect you, to trust that, no matter what, they would keep their word.

Phoenix

WHEN UNCLE CHOW PULLS INTO OUR DRIVE-
way, I tell him to turn off his headlights so as not to alert
Mom. I consider sneaking in by way of the sycamore tree,
then remember no one's home anyway. Robin's at sleepaway
camp, and Mom stayed over at Po Po's, since Robin's not
coming back until the day after tomorrow. As for Osprei…
he'll be wherever Suki is.

"This is your house?" Kai asks, stepping out of the car
blearily. He looks at the front entrance, then at me, as if trying to find the resemblance between my face and a door.

I let us in quickly. With no one else home, the house
feels more cavernous than usual. I try to hurry us through
the foyer, but Kai's attentive gaze doesn't miss a thing—not
the crystal chandelier glittering from the ceiling, nor the
antique Qing Dynasty hanging scrolls above the stairway.

His face shutters, growing more and more distant by the minute.

I point him in the direction of my bedroom while I run to the kitchen to grab the first-aid kit. When I get back to my room, I find him sitting on the floor in total darkness. I switch on the light, then crack open a window for fresh air. It's disconcerting to see him in my childhood room. Like two worlds merging together.

I kneel beside him, wringing out a damp cloth. His eyes are lidded and heavy with sleep; he barely speaks as I clean his wound with a wet towel, wiping the crusted blood off his skin.

He asks in a low voice if I'm okay, and I tell him to hush. Of course I'm okay. I'm with him.

I tap the gash lightly, running my finger over its length. "You might need stitches."

He gives an infinitesimal shake of his head. "It's more shallow than it looks. Head wounds always bleed like hell."

I frown. He sounds like he knows this from experience. "I have surgical tape," I say, digging through the first-aid kit.

He gives me a sidelong grin. "I'm counting on you to keep me pretty."

I try to smile back, but it's hard to feel unworried when I just saw him get into a brawl on the streets. Charlie was drunk, but that's still no excuse for his behavior tonight. I never knew he had it in him. I guess we're both changing; we're all revealing new sides of ourselves.

Kai exhales sharply when I press the alcohol swab to his open wound, but other than that, he makes no sound. His expression doesn't change, not once. That's why I never know what he's thinking. He doesn't even react to pain.

But I saw his face as he pinned Phil beneath him. I saw his face and flinched. I didn't recognize him then. His expression was cold, ruthless. He looked, in that moment, like he could kill. I was afraid—for him or of him, I wasn't sure. I had no idea what he was capable of.

There are sides of him I don't know about either.

I pat the bandage to make sure it's secure, then shut the first-aid box. "Done," I tell him.

I'm about to rise when he leans forward and cups the back of my neck, drawing me to him. He kisses me on the forehead, then smiles. "Xiexie."

I smile back this time. "Will you sleep over? It's so late." I glance at the mounted clock. It's almost midnight.

He gets to his feet awkwardly. There's an uneasy note in his voice. "Your family..."

"They're not home right now. You can sneak out through my brother's room in the morning. It's foolproof." I jump to my feet. "I'll show you."

I lead him along the upstairs hallway to Osprei's room, which I haven't ventured into for ages. It smells of booze and cologne. I crack open the east-facing window, the view obscured by leafy branches. "See this sycamore tree? You can climb down from here and go around the back, past the hedges. It's how Suki comes in and out all the time."

Kai's eyes are big as he takes in the size of Osprei's room: the drum set that Osprei's touched fewer than ten times (and that's a generous estimate), the latest-edition PlayStation that he uses about once a year (he's too girl crazy to get into video games), and the king-size platform bed neatly made (by our housekeeper, Auntie Mok).

"This room feels bigger than my whole apartment," Kai says in a matter-of-fact voice.

I fiddle with one of my pearl earrings. "It's supposed to be the master bedroom actually, but no one wanted it. Mom thought the feng shui was off, and Robin and I both wanted a different view." I blush, self-conscious. "The other bedrooms all overlook the ocean."

"Osprei didn't mind?"

"He's never home anyway," I say. "He said he would take one for the team."

"What a sacrifice," Kai says, faint laugh lines creasing by his eyes. He doesn't look bitter, only amused. "It must be nice to have siblings."

There's no resentment in his tone, and yet, I can't help but wonder how lonely it must've been for him to have only one parent growing up, and no brother or sister. No one to joke around with, tell stories with. No one to share the weight of family when the going gets tough, no xiangyi weiming to rely on.

No wonder he feels the burden of looking after his father. He's the only one who can. The only one who can carry on the legacy of the family name.

Kai studies the escape route one more time before we leave Osprei's room. I remember how strongly he reacted when I suggested going back to his apartment, how much he resisted the idea. He said his place was small. How small? And what didn't he want me to see?

Back in my room, Kai wanders over to the baby pictures hanging over my dresser. A smile flits to his lips and I'm suddenly mortified by the possibility of him discovering all the embarrassing content in my house. Quickly, I try to hide the photo of baby me picking my nose, but he catches me before I can slide the frame into my bedside drawer.

"You were the chubbiest baby," he says, wrestling the photo away from me. I try to grab it from his hands, but he holds it way over my head, higher than I can reach.

I try jumping for it. He only laughs at me. "Not fair," I say, out of breath. "You better show me your own baby photos in return. And they have to be equally embarrassing."

He hands me back the photo frame. "I don't have any," he replies. "We lost the apartment in Shanghai to debt collectors. They took most of our stuff with it."

"But...your dad must've kept some...?"

Kai looks wry at this. "He's not really the sentimental type."

I didn't know debt collectors could take more than your money. That they could take your home too. No wonder Kai hates hospitals so much. His mother's medical bills must have been astronomical. The way Kai is with money, it's like he's *scared* of it. Like it controls him, his every move. I don't understand it; I've never felt that sort of compulsion. Then again, money's never been scarce in my family. I've never thought of it beyond what it could do for me, what doors it could open. It doesn't have a life of its own, like it seems to with Kai.

He doesn't trust doctors, cops, any type of authority figure. Instead, he just resorts to dealing with his problems on his own.

"That wasn't your first fight, was it?" I ask. He was too calm; he knew exactly when to dodge, when to strike. "You have experience."

He senses my shift in mood and turns. "You don't think they'll press charges, do you?"

"Phil and Charlie?" I perch on my bed. "No way. It was hardly fair, was it? It was two against one."

"But I shouldn't have done it," he says. He cracks his knuckles one by one. "I was in the wrong."

There it is again, that weighted silence, like a missed note in a melody. I'm attuned to him now, his frequencies, and I can tell when he holds back, when there's something on the tip of his tongue.

I recall what Charlie said about how he staked out the HKU arts building and interrogated random students to see if they knew Kai. I didn't take Charlie seriously at the time, but his words seeded in my mind.

We lost the apartment in Shanghai to debt collectors. They took most of our stuff with it.

It doesn't seem like he came to Hong Kong for education. It seems like he came to Hong Kong out of necessity.

He's by the window now, glancing out at the starless sky wreathed in fog. "When does the first train arrive down here?"

"It's six AM for the bus," I answer. "Do you have work?"

He nods. "I should leave by five fifty," he says, checking his phone, probably searching the route. I watch him carefully. He never mentions his other HKU friends. Suki never sees him around campus. And he works *constantly*.

"Kai..." I say quietly. "You're not a student, are you?"

His face goes still. I notice his hand tighten around his phone.

I can't put my finger on it—I can't say for sure how I

know. There's an indefinable shame around his job, like he wants to pretend it doesn't exist. There are other clues too. The soot under his nails, the bags under his eyes. He doesn't sleep much, and he works on his paintings only in the dead hours of night. He talks about art like it's a religion, but he hardly has time for it in his schedule. It's why he's unhappy all the time. Whatever he's spending most of his day doing, it's not art. Is he a janitor, a convenience-store clerk? A parking lot valet? All three?

"I don't care," I say fiercely. "It doesn't change how I see you."

He won't look at me. "You don't understand," he says, like the words cost him.

"I want to try." I hesitate. And yet, unlike him, when something's on the tip of my tongue, I say it. "But you won't let me."

He's turned his back to me. His whole body is taut like a tuned string; he doesn't move, doesn't even twitch. It's times like these when it feels like he's not a real person. When it feels like I'm just talking to a wall, talking to myself.

"Berlin."

I raise my head. "Huh?"

"You once asked me where I would go, if I could go any-where in the world." He clears his throat. "It would be Berlin."

"Why?"

Slowly, he sits on the floor again and leans back against the wall. "Because of its art school," he admits. I watch his swallow catch in his throat. "It's the best in the world."

And I know he's telling the truth.

His unhappiness hurts me, like it's my own. I think of

him stuck in some dead-end job here in Hong Kong, working long hours in order to care for his father, in order to relieve his unending sense of guilt. He's living for a ghost of the past, a dead person. But I know I can't say this aloud. "Your art makes you happy," I say tentatively, like it's a statement but also a question.

He plants his palm into the carpet, watching his hand disappear into the thick threads. "Your carpet is softer than my bed," he says.

I won't let him change the subject. "Why don't you apply? They probably have scholarships."

He shakes his head. "I thought about it once," he says. "But not anymore. It's not for me."

"But are you happy here?" He doesn't speak; I wait. The air feels fragile, delicate as a butterfly's wing. "Are you happy with...everything?"

"I have to be," he says, an obscure emotion clouding his voice. He looks out the window, his expression vague and distant. Not for the first time, I wish I could follow him to wherever his thoughts lead. "I don't have another future."

"Kai—"

He lets out a breath. "Sure, I used to dream of more—of traveling abroad, art school maybe, but...I know my place now. Those dreams have passed. I've changed, Lifeng. Surely you understand that?"

Your mother died, I think. *That changed you.*

He looks at me with imploring eyes. I know what he's asking of me. He wants me to drop it. It's cruel of me to keep pushing like this, but with Kai, I'm never satisfied. I always want more than he can give.

I pat the bed. "I get it," I say, forcing brightness into my voice. He gets up and sits beside me. "You know, I've also had some change in plans. I'm not retaking my SATs. I want to stay here for university." I pause. "Maybe even go to…HKU. Like Suki."

His eyes widen, but he still looks *so fucking sad*. "I'm happy for you, Lifeng," he says. "You'll get in, I know you will."

I fall backward, making the bed bounce. "Is it even worth it to sleep? How many hours do we have left before you leave?"

"Five," he says with a sigh. Then his voice lightens. "I made something for you."

"Really?" I sit up again, watching as he opens his bag and riffles through it. He takes out his drawing tablet and sets it in my lap. I turn on the screen. Then I gasp.

It's a painting of a dark street lit by rippling lampposts. There are police officers in the foreground, but they're not the focus of the piece. Their faces are turned away, their bodies blurred. What's clear are the protesters, dressed in dark clothes, their faces bright and shining beneath the lamplight. They're mid-motion, mid-flight, fleeing in different directions from the ging caat. But though they're running, they're not afraid. Their expressions are powerful, undaunted.

It's the night of Tin-lok's escape, I realize, recognizing the Sing Yuet Street neighborhood. There are other clues in the piece. One girl has streaks of purple in her hair. Another boy wears glasses. And the girl at the center, her eyes fixed on a point offscreen, she wears pearl earrings.

His finger traces the outer rim of my ear and stops at the pearl stud. "That's you," he murmurs.

"Kai," I say, or try to say, because my mouth isn't working properly right now. "You—you're amazing."

And this doesn't feel like enough; this feels like a gross understatement. When I tried to recall the drawings on his phone, I questioned whether I'd exaggerated his talent because I'd already caught feelings for him back then. But now I know that's not the case.

"I know we don't see eye to eye on a lot of things," he says haltingly. "I don't understand most of the time why you do what you do, why you risk your life for...well, never mind. Anyway, I just wanted to show you that...I'm trying to understand. I'm trying to see what you see. And I can't talk well, so I guess this is just my way of showing that."

This painting...there's so much empathy in it, so much beauty. It's as if the person who drew this understands me completely, as if he's peering through a portal into my mind. The emotion in it is unambiguous; this couldn't have been made by a passive bystander.

He painted it as someone who understands.

"My God, Kai. How have you been holding back on me all this time? You're like the next Picasso or—"

He laughs, so brightly it makes his eyes crinkle. I've never seen him so gratified, not when I admired his style, or even his looks. I see now that his art is what means the most to him.

"Picasso did surrealism mainly," he points out. "This is naturalism." He draws a circle on my bare knee, as if doodling. "I think I'll call it...*Rageland*."

"Tian ah," I say, barely registering his words as I turn my attention back to the piece. "You have so much talent, Kai. I swear if you apply…you could even get a full-ride scholarship!" I set the tablet down. "You know what? I have an aunt in Germany! Maybe she could put in a good word—"

He laughs but stops me. "You dream big, Lifeng." He smiles with fondness, brushing his thumb across my cheek. "That's what makes you so lovely."

He leans forward and kisses me on the lips. Softly now, like we have all the time in the world. We fall back onto the pillows as he pulls me into his chest, encircling his hands around my waist.

I mean to stay awake, to stay with him, but my eyelids grow heavy. *I'll only rest for a few minutes*, I think. Then I'll walk Kai to the bus stop.

But when I wake, hours later, Kai is gone. The pillow beside me is undisturbed, and the sheets smoothed, as if he were never here at all.

Kai

MY PHONE BLOWS UP THE NEXT DAY. I CHECK my notifications after patrol training—Phoenix has posted *Rageland* on her Instagram account, crediting me.

I break out in a sweat. Hastily, I untag myself, but the damage is done. Over five thousand people have liked the photo already, and twenty of them have requested to follow me, though my account is set to private.

Of course Phoenix wouldn't think to ask me first.

I scroll through the comments on the post. Most of them are complimentary, and a few even go so far as to ask how to purchase it. Someone says they'll vote for it as the new mural at West Kowloon Park. For a second, I forget myself and grin. Then I remember that anyone from the police academy could see this. My father could see this.

Delete my username from your caption, I text her. On your IG post.

She responds in minutes. Why? You don't want me to credit you?

No.

Are you mad?

I pause before answering. No.

She calls me. I decline. I'm still at work, I write instead. I'll see you tonight.

I pocket my phone before I catch her response. Am I mad? Maybe. Should I ask her to take it down? Yes. But do I want to?

No. Not really. I want people to see it; I want Ma to see it. I want people to see me and know me. These days, I feel like an impostor most of the time, going through the motions, living life like a ghost. The only moments I feel alive are when I'm with Phoenix, and those are few and far between.

"Any plans for the weekend?" Marco comes up from behind me, slinging an arm around my shoulder. "Unless..." He grimaces. "Are you on call?"

"Thankfully, no," I say. "You?"

He high-fives me. "I claimed an ankle injury from our last round of riot control. Those gaat zaat are plucky, aren't they?"

"Don't call them that," I say without thinking.

Marco cocks a brow. "You know they call us worse," he says, but without bite.

My neck grows hot. "I know." I know better than he does, than any of the other trainees here. I'm the only one who sees them face-to-face, without the helmet, the head gear, without the fog of tear gas that turns us all into animals. I'm the only one who knows what I know and still does what I do.

Marco notes my expression and makes a face. "Loosen up, bud," he says as we head down the corridor toward the academy gates. "Why don't you come out drinking with me tonight?"

In the atrium, I hear several trainees in our class chatting. One of them mentions Whitney American School. Isn't that Phoenix's school?

"Did you hear what I just said?" Marco waves in my face. "We're going to Fairyland tonight."

"Didn't you go there last week?" I ask, distracted. I glance back at the other group of trainees, but they're leaving the atrium.

"Tried to," Marco says, without an ounce of embarrassment. "They only let you in if you come with a girl. Preferably several."

"Then why are you inviting *me*?"

He snorts. "I'm going with a group of friends from secondary school."

The glass doors slide open, enveloping us in a cloud of muggy summer heat. "I'm not going to crash your high school reunion."

"You'll fit right in. In fact, something tells me you'll be very popular."

I smirk. "Then are you really going to invite the competition?" Before he can respond, the pedestrian signal turns green; I wave goodbye.

"Where are you off to?" he calls.

I merge into the crowd, which feels like a walking sauna. "I have plans already! See you Monday."

Marco whines but waves in parting. He often complains that I disappear on weekends and sometimes even threatens to tail me. I know he won't actually; he's far too self-absorbed for that. But he is curious who I meet all the time; by the way I do my hair on Friday nights, he knows it's not my father.

My phone rings as I'm climbing the stairs to the MTR. "Hey!" Phoenix sounds breathless, exuberant.

My mouth twitches into an involuntary smile. "Hey, you."

"Something bananas just happened." She talks in a rush. "Meet me in Wan Chai? I'll text you my location."

"What is it?"

"It's a surprise!"

I'm immediately apprehensive. You never know what to expect when it comes to Phoenix.

"I gotta go. Logistics," she explains vaguely. "See you there."

She hangs up before I can ask another question. I sigh, then slick my hair back one more time for good measure, checking my reflection in the window of a parked car. My jaw is smooth of stubble, my face tanned from sun. I lift my shirt and fan the thin fabric, my skin prickling with heat. Whatever surprise Phoenix has in mind, I hope it involves air con.

In Wan Chai, the street signs are alive and flashing, sending blue, red, purple shadows across the faces of enthralled strangers. Skateboarders fly across the narrow alleyways, twisting in midair before crashing hard to the concrete, their faces damp with perspiration. Humidity hangs in the air like a curtain of warm mist, occasionally relieved by an opportune ocean breeze.

I glance at the faces of the strangers I pass, noting their delight, their boredom, their melancholy. Everyone looks beautiful tonight, but maybe that's only because I'm about to see Phoenix.

On Fridays, the world feels just a bit lighter on my shoulders. I shut off the nagging parts of my brain, the parts that blame, that condemn. I don't have to see the truth tonight. I'm just here to have fun.

Outside the address Phoenix sent me, there's only a nondescript steel door sandwiched between an herbal medicine shop and an upscale lingerie boutique. I notice other young people forming a line behind me, as if they think I'm waiting out here on purpose. I move to step out of their way. Right then, the door slides open. There's a bouncer, and behind him a tiny girl in massive heels.

She grins up at me. Phoenix.

Her dress is nearly translucent in the lamplight and shows off every inch of her bare legs. I stare, forgetting to say hello.

She laughs at my wonder. "You've seen me in a dress before!"

I close the distance between us, sliding one hand around her waist, the other curving around her hip. "Not this one."

"Do you like it?"

"Very much." I look down at her. "Is this the surprise?"

Her smile broadens. "Not even close," she says. "C'mon. You're blocking the entrance."

I turn and remember the people around us, which is how I know I'm really in deep. I'm acting like I'm drunk, and I haven't had a sip of alcohol.

"I thought you didn't do PDA," Phoenix says as she leads me down the open-air gallery toward the elevator. The doors open and she presses the ninth floor.

"I thought you didn't do heels."

She shoots me a sidelong look. "I made an exception for you."

I'm about to kiss her when the doors open on the second floor. Someone steps inside and we fall quiet, though Phoenix has to muffle her giggles. She's practically vibrating with suppressed excitement. I squeeze her hand silently.

The elevator dings. Phoenix steps out first, tugging me forward. We're in some kind of rooftop bar, which is partially enclosed and partially open. The noise is deafening up here. Old Canto-pop from the 1980s is blasting from the surround-sound speakers, at odds with the modern appliances and technology. There's an eclectic mix of people here: tall Scandinavian tourists, college students dressed in jeans, even bankers in collared shirts with rolled-up sleeves. Everyone is mingling and dancing. The air con is on full blast, which can't be cheap, but when I take a look at the menu prices, I see how they can afford it.

"Let's go to the bar!" Phoenix shouts over the din.

"Do they card here?" I ask. I'm legal, but Phoenix isn't.

She glances back over her shoulder at me and smirks. "Not if you're in with the boss." She leans over the bar to speak with the waiter. He nods and sets down his glass, then disappears into the back.

The decor is unusual—the walls covered in paintings and art prints, the bar covered in flowers, and the ceiling covered in thousands of hanging butterflies, made of some glimmering silver material. There are even birdcages in the corner, though thankfully, the only birds inside are plastic models.

"What do you think of the art?" Phoenix asks, studying my reaction. "Felix tries to showcase local artists mainly."

I turn toward the wall with its myriad ink paintings and charcoal sketches and cartoonish portraits. At first I think the assortment is random, but then I see that every painting reflects some aspect of the city. A few of these artists are incredibly talented; I take out my phone to snap a few pictures. I'll search them online later. "He has good taste."

"That's what I like to hear."

A middle-aged man appears, his hands on his hips. He smiles at me, but I recognize the appraisal in his eyes.

"Felix!" Phoenix says. "This is Kai. He's the one I told you about."

"The very artist himself!" Felix claps his hands together. "In the flesh."

The artist? I could've sworn he called me an artist.

"Listen," he says, leaning in to be heard over the music. "Fairyland is a bar, but I also fancy it an art gallery. I really believe there shouldn't be a separation between the two, you know? People come to drink and look at art. What better pairing could there be than that?"

Fairyland? This place is called Fairyland?

"I saw your piece online and reached out to this young lady to inquire about the buying process. She said I had to get your permission first, but that she couldn't tell me your name. You like the mystery, huh?"

I can barely hear him above the pounding bass, vibrating the floors. If this place caves, nine floors are a long way to fall.

"I've been searching for a piece like yours for a while now. Something that captures the spirit of the extradition bill protests. *Rageland*, is it? It's extraordinary."

I don't understand why he's flattering me. Why he's bothering with me at all. "Why are you telling me this?" I have to shout to be heard, and it makes me sound angry. That's when I realize I am.

"He wants to buy it!" Phoenix interjects. "He's going to put it up here at Fairyland." She looks at me as if expecting me to bow down in gratitude.

I just shrug. "Take it, then," I say. "It's online already." I think Phoenix catches the bitter note in my voice. Her expression changes.

Felix clears his throat. "Of course, I would compensate you fairly—"

"Suan le," I say. "I'm not going to profit off the protesters."

I walk away before he can argue. A tangle of emotions climbs up my throat. Why am I angry, exactly? I should feel thrilled; someone wants to *buy* my work. Someone wants to display it in his art gallery, never mind that it's actually a bar. He even called me an artist. Rageland, *is it? It's extraordinary.* Shouldn't that make me happy?

"Kai!" Phoenix catches up to me, panting. "I don't understand why you're mad."

"It doesn't matter."

She grabs my hand. "Stop running away!" she says, and I can tell she's mad too. "Look how many people are here. When Felix puts up your piece, everyone will see it. Everyone will see *your* art."

I hate the way she's speaking to me, as if I'm a foreigner, slow to understand the language.

"Have you ever considered," I ask, "that I didn't want everyone to know about it?"

Her brows fold. "Why?" she demands. "Isn't that the point of making art?"

Her presumption stings. "What's the point of art, Phoenix? You tell me," I say, my voice dry.

"I don't know," she snaps. "To make people feel something!"

"You should know by now." My mouth twists. "I don't do things for *people*. I'm not like you in that way."

Her copper eyes drag up to mine. "I don't know what you're saying."

"It was for you," I say quietly. And all of a sudden, the fight rushes out of me. "I made it for you."

Her lips form a silent O. I let out my breath, about to apologize, when I hear my name across the room.

"Zhang Kai En?"

Cao! Dread squeezes my throat as I recognize that voice. I consider grabbing Phoenix's hand and bolting for cover. But it's too late. Marco throws an arm around me, smothering me in his embrace. I can smell the tequila on his breath.

"You came!" he exclaims. "And you brought...a friend!" His smile practically takes over his face as he catches sight of Phoenix. "I've heard so much about you," he tells her, which is false; he hasn't. I've told him nothing.

But Phoenix looks flattered. "I wish I could say the same," she replies cheerily.

He steers her away, and I'm forced to follow. "Kai, you didn't tell her *anything* about me? I'm appalled. I'm his *one and only* friend at the—"

"Marco!" I interrupt desperately.

"Huh?" He pauses, startled by my tone.

I fumble for an excuse. "Shots?"

"Of course," Marco agrees readily. "Drinks on me!"

He propels us into his circle of friends, who are chatting against the rooftop railing. I look out over the edge and see the Tsim Sha Tsui skyline, and the dark bay below. Next to the striking city lights, the waters appear black and motionless. If I jumped in, I wonder if the waves would swallow me whole.

"Introduce us to your friend," a curly-haired girl says to Marco, eyeing me. She's standing at the opposite end of the circle, leaning against the railing as if waiting for paparazzi to take her photo.

Marco is flagging down a waiter and doesn't hear her. Instead of asking twice, she cuts across the circle and comes to stand next to me. "I'm Editha," she says, holding out her hand. I can smell her sugary perfume; that's how close she's standing. I try to take a step back, but there's no room.

"Kai." I shake her hand.

She looks up at me through her lashes. "Do you dance, Kai?"

"Terribly." Phoenix squeezes between us, handing me a shot glass. "I still have a giant bruise on my foot from the last time he stepped on me." She offers Editha the other glass, which she doesn't accept. "Trust me, don't bother with him," Phoenix says with a completely straight face.

I burst out laughing. Phoenix is jealous.

Editha arches a brow at her. "And you are?"

"His girlfriend," Phoenix supplies, before clinking glasses with me.

The vodka burns, in a good way. I collect our empty glasses and return them to the waiter. I notice Phoenix's phone lying on the bar counter, forgotten. I tap the screen to make sure it's hers, then slide it into my pocket. Thankfully, Marco has forgotten about us; I spot him in the corner, deeply occupied with someone else. I guess Yee-ching has finally forgiven him.

Back by the railing, I touch Phoenix's arm, and she smiles up at me, our fight evidently forgotten. "You left your phone at the bar." I hand it back to her. "Hoping to swap with another stranger?"

"Only if he was hotter than you." She giggles. Then her expression sobers. "Are we okay?"

"I might've overreacted," I say, voice rueful. "I don't think I'm a big fan of surprises."

She pretends to pout. "But life would be so boring without them."

The ocean breeze toys with her loose hair. I pull a long strand out of her mouth. "I don't think anyone could be bored around you."

She considers this, before an idea lights her face. "I know how to change your mind," she tells me, the corner of her mouth twitching into a devilish grin. "I have one last surprise."

"Lifeng."

"You'll like this one," she promises. "Come with me."

Instead of leading me toward the exit as I expect, she takes me down a shadowy corridor, toward the restroom. It's an all-gender toilet room, but I still don't think it's a good idea for us to go in there together. "I'll wait outside," I tell her.

"That would defeat the purpose," she says. "C'mon. No one's looking."

She pulls me in, then locks the door behind us. The

lights are tinted blue-green inside, like we're underwater. The overhead speakers play tinkling meditation music.

"Finally," she says. "I couldn't hear you out there."

I raise a brow. "You brought us here," I say, "to talk?"

"Well," she says, "if you really don't want to talk..." And then she starts to lift her dress over her shoulders.

"Lifeng—"

"God, this is tight," she says, voice muffled through the fabric of her dress. "I think I should've unzipped this first."

I laugh and spin her around, locating the zipper along her spine. She wriggles out of the dress and kicks it to the floor.

"That was much sexier in my head," she says, but I'm not really listening because I see her "surprise" now. She's wearing tiny white lingerie.

"Your turn," she says, tugging at my shirt. I let her pull it off before I pin her to the door, sliding my hand up her lifted thigh.

"Is this okay?" I murmur, and she nods, tangling her fingers in my hair. I pick her up; she's trembling against me. I can feel her quick, breathless inhalations against my skin, her mouth hovering over mine.

"Do you like surprises now?" she asks, cheeks flushed.

A laugh chokes out of me. "You win, Lifeng."

I can feel the smile on her lips. "I always do."

Kai

I MAKE IT BACK TO THE ACADEMY ON SUNDAY night, minutes before curfew, and find Marco waiting up for me.

"You sneaky bastard!" he says in a stage whisper because our roommates are asleep. "How long have you two been dating?"

"What about you and Yee-ching?" I counter. "Looks like you made up there."

An abashed grin spreads across his face. "I may or may not have shown up outside her apartment with flowers, declaring my love in the rain."

"It didn't rain this weekend."

"Metaphorical rain. Rain of tears."

I snort, rummaging in the dark for my phone charger. "You should've gone into theater."

"I considered it," he replies gravely. "But alas, I'm too

short for the stage." He slouches back onto his bed. "So, Phoenix Lam, huh? How'd you two meet?"

"Why?" I ask, more sharply than I intended.

"I mean, you do know about her...involvement, right? Eddie and Yulei were even assigned to tail her last week. Her name's on the blacklist."

I stare at him. For a second, I do nothing. Then I grab him, towing him outside. "How long?" I demand when we're in the hallway. "How long has she been blacklisted?"

Marco massages his neck, looking miffed. "I won't tell anyone about you two, if that's what you're worried about. Your career's safe."

It's an effort not to raise my voice. "I don't give a fuck about my career. How do you know she's on the blacklist?"

"Well, Eddie put up a photo of her in the locker room—"

"*What the fuck?*"

"Calm down, Kai! She's not the only one. All the blacklisted protesters—"

"All of them?" I say, seething.

"Well." He averts his eyes. "Only the girls."

My hands clench into fists. I want to kill Eddie. But I want those photos taken down even more. "Which locker room?"

"Sergeant Leung found out and took it down already. He even put Eddie on probation for it," Marco says. "Christ, Kai, it's like you live under a rock. Do you not listen to *any* gossip?"

My vision is tunneling; it might have something to do with the fact that I'm having trouble breathing. "That's how you recognized her, isn't it?" I ask in a low voice.

Marco winces. "She also gave me her name." He hesitates. "She doesn't know, does she? About you."

I swallow thickly.

"I thought so," he says, which makes me feel like shit. He took one look at me and knew. He knew I'd lie.

"Why are they following *her*?" I ask. "She's just a high school student."

"I don't know, bud. But seems like she's getting into all sorts of trouble when you're not around. They're on the hunt for that computer genius—the one *you* let slip through your fingers. You're still in the doghouse for that one," he adds, crossing his arms. "What exactly did you tell Lieutenant Chan?"

"I said I'd never met Ming-lai in person before," I say impatiently. "What does this have to do with Phoenix?"

"They know her brother's a good friend of his," Marcus says. "And they think she's involved too. My guess is they expect one of the siblings to lead them straight to their target."

I scrub my hands over my face, trying to focus. I didn't ask for details, but I saw Phoenix's unopened texts on her lock screen when she misplaced her phone at Fairyland and I found it lying on the bar. Phoenix is planning to smuggle Ming-lai out of Hong Kong. And if she's caught assisting in his escape—that's grounds for arrest. Imprisonment, even.

This is my fault. Because I led the cops to her brother. *I* arrested her brother. And now her family's on the fucking blacklist.

I lean against the wall, then slide to the ground. "Fuck." I don't know what else to say.

"Let her go, man," Marco says softly, crouching beside me. "She's not worth your job."

Marco is smarter than I gave him credit for; he picks up on implicit cues, sees all the connections between disparate parts. And yet, because I've kept him in the dark all this time, he doesn't understand this crucial fact about me.

"You don't understand," I bite out. "She's worth more than my entire fucking job."

There's a heavy, ringing silence.

"Are you going to tell her?" Marco says at last. "Because you know, if you interfere, your dad—"

"I don't care," I say, which isn't true, but I've made up my mind. It's not that I don't care about my father, about how he sees me. It's just that I care about other things more.

Things that make my life worth living.

I'm not noble like Phoenix; I would never sacrifice my future for some strangers I don't know, for a political cause or even an ethical one. And yet, I would have exchanged my life for Ma's, in a heartbeat, if I could. I would give up years of my life to have just one more minute with her, to tell her I'm sorry.

I get to my feet as if sleepwalking. I know the consequences will be astronomical, and not remotely in my favor. But the alternative is worse. I can't keep lying like this. I can't keep living this half life, hating my father, hating myself, hating even Phoenix for something that isn't her fault.

You're like water, Ma always said, *you go with the flow.* But even water reaches a breaking point, doesn't it? Even water will freeze or boil or let go of itself, of what's kept it alive for so long. Sometimes, you just let go.

Phoenix

ON JUNE 16, TWO MILLION PEOPLE COME OUT to protest. *Two million* people, on an island of only seven million.

It feels like living history.

I'm taking a photo when I catch the opening notes of a song unfurling above me: "Do You Hear the People Sing?" The crowd picks it up as I do, like a gentle mist falling over our heads, softly, smoothly.

I catch Osprei's eye. He grins at me and belts the lyrics at the top of his lungs.

Everyone is singing, a hundred voices, a million. Even the man next to me, older, gray-haired, dressed in a suit, sings along without shame. I laugh, amazed that someone my dad's age could be here too, could support us, could understand.

Shivers are running through me like mad. I don't even realize I'm crying until Suki looks at my face and laughs.

I wish Mom could see this, I think. *I wish she could feel this too.*

It's not the same as reading the news, I want to tell her. I wish I could explain the thrill of being one with the crowd, of knowing that the people around you are your sau zuk, your family, that they have your back, and that no matter what happens tonight, they'll show up again tomorrow, and the day after that. It's knowing that this is the last chance we have and knowing we won't go down without a fight. It's being tired of speaking in soft voices, of taking it, saying yessir, hanging your head as you're beaten, trod on, violated, humiliated. It's finally being able to make a sound, after years of silence, and scream.

Suki offers me a tissue. I try to wipe my eyes, but then I give up and let the tears run. I'm so happy just to cry, openly, in front of all these people who I love. *You are all with me.* I was stupid to have once thought I didn't belong here, that Hong Kong would never accept me. It's true that I'm a part of the diaspora, that I will always be in between, and yet, I can choose where I call home. There's nowhere I'd rather be than here.

The song is powerful, exuberant. The crowd is wrapped up in it, even the ones who can't speak English. They hum along, throw in Cantonese words here and there. We move down the road, marching toward the harbor in a sea of black.

"We won't let you send us to our deaths!" someone shouts as the song ends. "*Faan sung Zung!*"

It's a clever pun, and the crowd picks up the chant in unison. Directly translated, *Faan sung Zung* means "oppose delivering to China," but *sung Zung* is also a homophone for the phrase "seeing off a dying relative." The underlying message is clear: Extradition means death.

"Faan sung Zung! Faan sung Zung!"

This turns into another chant, and another. It's relentless, the energy of the crowd, one voice starting even before the last one ends, so that the noise is continuous, a running stream. *We couldn't do this alone*, I suddenly want to tell Kai. *We could only do this together.*

As if I summoned him with my thoughts, my phone rings. I pick up, confused. He's usually working at this time. "Kai?"

"Lifeng." He sounds out of breath. "Where are you right now?"

"I'm at the protest in Admiralty, but I'm leaving soon because Ming-lai—"

"Don't!" he interrupts, and I jump. Something in his voice halts me. "Don't say it," he says. "Listen. Can you do something for me?"

"Of course, but—"

"Get to the nearest MTR. Take the train to Causeway Bay, but don't get off until the last possible second. Got it?"

"What do you mean? Why?"

"If you have a jacket or a change of clothes, put that on as soon as you get off."

"Kai, you're scaring me." A new thought occurs to me; I remember Suki's paranoia, the way she kept glancing over her shoulder. "Do you think I'm being *tailed*?"

"I'll meet you at Exit A by Times Square." He exhales hard. "Just—trust me, all right?"

"I do," I say, though my pulse is skittering. "I do."

I hang up, then try to grab Osprei's attention. He's in the midst of an off-key rendition of "Glory to Hong Kong," and I have to latch on to his arm to make him see me. "I have to go. Kai needs me."

"Now?" Osprei frowns. "Ming-lai's boat docks at eight. Will you be back in time?"

"Aa Go, that's in six hours."

"Don't be late," he says. "You know what's at stake."

"I know." I know we can't afford to mess this up.

If we're caught, no one knows our sentence.

I keep glancing over my shoulder, but I don't see anyone tailing me. Maybe Kai is being paranoid. Still, I heed his warning. On the train, I pretend to scroll mindlessly on my phone before slipping through the train doors and onto the platform seconds before they shut. That's when I see him—the guy who startles, jumping from his seat a beat too late. Before he can take a single step, the doors lock, and the train shoots off into the tunnel. Was that a coincidence?

Or was he actually following me?

The back of my neck prickles. Osprei is too cocky; I never should've trusted him when he claimed he'd been let off the hook. As if the consequences wouldn't touch him, as if he could get arrested, then walk free the very next day. Just because the police let him go doesn't mean they forgot about him. Maybe they let him walk because they knew he'd lead them to bigger fish. Maybe they know about our plans tonight.

We never did find out how they learned of Tin-lok's escape.

Unnerved, I rush down the escalators toward Exit A. I don't see anyone there, so I keep going through Times Square. Then a shadow peels off the wall and joins me, matching my strides with ease.

"Here," he says, in his familiar low timbre, placing his jacket over my shoulders. I realize I'm hunching, my arms folded tightly across my chest. Though I'm shivering, it's not entirely from the cold.

"Follow me," he says, his voice low and rasping. We follow the flow of traffic into the mall, then to an underground food hall. Kai's strides are so long I have to jog to keep up. He looks around, then pulls me into a tall, enclosed booth with him.

As soon as we sit down inside, I fire off a million questions. "Kai, what's going on? Don't you have work right now? Why are you—"

He cuts me off. "You're being followed."

I feel no relief about being right. "How do you know?" I demand.

He shakes his head. "You can't go tonight," he says. "You or your brother."

"But—but we don't know when the next boat willing to take fugitives—"

"Send someone else, then," he says. "But if you go tonight, Ming-lai will be arrested. So will Osprei." His voice breaks. "So will you."

My mouth opens, then closes. "I—I don't understand," I stammer at last. "You didn't answer my question. How do you know all of this?"

He's angry all of a sudden, furious actually. The change is so swift it's like the flip of a switch. "I just do."

"Did you see someone following me? Or did you hear something? Or—"

"Phoenix," he bites out. "Don't make me lie."

"I have no idea what you're talking about!"

He looks like he hasn't slept in days. His eyes fall shut briefly. I notice the hollowness of them, the violet shadows set deep into his eye sockets. "Ask me what my job is," he says lowly.

I'm panicked and I don't know why. "Kai," I say, "we don't need to—"

"Ask me!" he snarls, and I flinch, frightened.

"What's"—I'm stuttering, my tongue not working properly—"what's your job?"

His jaw clenches as he swallows. I don't know what he'll say, but I'm suddenly terrified. I don't want to hear his response. I don't want answers anymore; I don't know why I ever did.

For the thin edge of a second, he just looks at me. Then he says: "Ging caat."

I feel the blood drain from my face.

No, I think, *that can't be. That's impossible.* "But—but I saw your ID. You're only eighteen—"

"I'm at the academy," he says, and his voice is so thick with loathing it gives me pause. "I'm the one who—" His breathing hitches. "I'm the one who arrested your brother."

I rise to my feet without thinking. I feel like I'm falling, no, *fallen*. As if I've landed flat on my back, the air knocked out of me.

"Lifeng—"

"No!" I say, because he doesn't have the right to say my name, not like that.

Memories sluice through my mind. Kai sitting next to me at the claypot rice restaurant, his dark eyes and sharp cheekbones catching the light. Kai finding me in the movie theater, sliding into the seat beside me. Kai covering my mouth with one hand when I laughed too loudly and the other moviegoers shushed us. Kai meeting me on the beach, his cuts and bruises still fresh on his face. Kai holding me in his arms, as if he cared for me, as if it weren't all a lie to him.

All this time, he's been lying to my face.

He tries to step toward me, but I back up; my heel hits the wall. "Get away from me," I warn him, my voice turning shrill. "You're a . . ." A *police officer.* "You're a liar," I say, wanting to scream the accusation at the top of my lungs. Instead, it comes out broken and tearful.

"I didn't mean to—"

"Get away from me!" I shriek. I barely see him through my veil of tears. I think of how pathetic I must have seemed to him, throwing myself on him, opening up to him—an easy target if ever there was one. He must've laughed at me with his cop buddies every time I kissed him, every time I showed him how much I cared. To think I was actually falling for him . . . "You *are* a murderer," I spit out.

He steps back as if struck. Despite the truth of who he is, his face is still beautiful to me, so familiar it feels like my own. I can't bear to know that he's a cop, just like the ones who assaulted me, who beat Osprei, who pushed that protester to jump. He looks so pained I want to comfort him. I force myself to recall the truth, the truth of who he is. I have to fight instinct, to stay back, to hate him.

It's because of the way you talk, he told me, back when we first met.

I talk too much, huh?

No, it's not that. You talk like . . . like you expect everyone to listen to you.

It hits me then: *He's a spy.* I recall his ambiguous answers, the way he never could quite say what he was doing that day. I remember how the cops showed up the night of Tin-lok's escape, like they knew the date and the time and the plan. They knew about Ming-lai too, his involvement with the livestream. They knew his real name, his apartment address.

Because Kai was spying on me all along. Not just me, but my friends too. He's been using me for information, to report our plans to the dogs.

I'm just a fucking gaat zaat to him.

I double over, my stomach churning. I feel like I might pass out.

"Phoenix?" His voice is gentle, laced with concern. "Are you okay?"

He sounds like he cares.

He lies.

"I never, ever want to see you again," I choke out. Then I run.

Kai

THE WORST COMES, AND STILL, YOU LIVE. YOU call in sick. You go home. You can't sleep so you find all your sketches of her and rip them into pieces. It's not enough. You take out your favorite drawings of Hong Kong, Tai Mo Mountain, even Shanghai. These are burned instead, which leaves an acrid scent of soot in the apartment. You open the windows, but outside is burning too. In some ways, it's satisfying.

All of Hong Kong burns together.

I unearth the Wacom drawing tablet from my backpack, lift it in the air as if I'm about to smash it, then change my mind. I'm too poor for theatrics. Besides, I can sell it online and make enough to cover groceries for a while.

I fall asleep for less than an hour, dreaming of Phoenix. I don't remember what happens, only that it ends badly. It always ends badly. This is my life, remember?

Still, I can't stop myself. After all, I'm just a puk gaai dreamer boy. So I try again, and again, and again. In the days following, I text her after work, call her, even show up outside her house on Saturday and study the face of every long-haired girl who walks down the street. I know I look like a stalker, but I can't live with the regret of not trying to talk to her.

I don't even know what I would say if I saw her. There's nothing to explain. She drew all the right conclusions: I *was* lying to her, I *was* using her. But there's more too. It wasn't all a lie, all right? There was something there, something real.

She's already lost, the voice in my head whispers. *The two of you could never work out. You're incompatible, worlds apart. Better it ended when it did, before things got worse. Remember the fights? Remember the way you could never say what you were really thinking? Remember how anxious you'd be, waiting to hear if she'd made it home safely?*

Xingxing zhi huo. A single spark starts a blaze.

At a quarter past four, I see her striding down the street, flanked by her usual crew. Her face is ghostly pale, her mouth set in a thin line, her eyes fixed on the sidewalk. She turns toward her house, walking as if there are hungry wolves at her heels.

"Phoenix!" I call, striding forward.

She quickens her pace. Her long black ponytail swishes behind her like it's shaking its head at me.

"Please," I say. I must have some kind of death wish. "I just want to—"

She swings toward me, her eyes flashing. "Do you think I care what you want?"

Up close, her face startles me. I forgot how lucent her eyes are, how sharp her features. How could I already have started to forget her, in a matter of days? What will happen in months, years?

"I told you to leave me alone," she says, voice flat. "I told you to stay away from me."

"I know," I say. "But…"

"But you don't care what I want, do you?" Her eyes narrow to slits. "You don't care about anyone besides yourself. That's why you do what you do."

"Nix…" Her brother looks like he just wants to get her out of here. But Phoenix shakes him off.

"You're such a loser. I can't believe I wasted so much time on you." Her eyes well, but she blinks the tears back angrily. "I was stupid to think I could change you. Only you can do that." Her voice breaks. "But you don't want to."

She turns away from me then. Osprei takes her by the arm and pulls her through the side gate. I can hear her crying before the inside door slams shut. *You're wrong*, I want to say. I do want to change. I'm trying! Why can't anyone see that I'm trying? I'm trying so fucking hard.

It's Saturday, and I'm supposed to head home to Mong Kok, to stay with my father. But I dread seeing him. I dread seeing him on weekends, then seeing the other officers on weekdays. I dread knowing that on Sunday evening I'll have to head back to the academy.

I dread my entire life ahead of me. I have nothing to look forward to.

Without warning, something slams into my shoulder. A full cup of milk tea explodes against my shirt, splashing me in the face. I wipe my eyes as the empty cup falls to the ground and rolls downhill.

Suki glowers at me, her arms crossed as she watches me watch her. Osprei comes back out to stand beside her. She says something that makes him smirk, then throws back her head and laughs as if I'm not worth a second of their time. They have a way of making you feel worthless, don't they? They rub it in your face, so that you can't ever forget how much money they have, and more important, how much you don't.

I can't think about this right now. I wring the hem of my T-shirt, which is sticky with milk tea. The fabric is threadbare anyway; it's probably time to retire this shirt. Ma gave it to me, years ago, when she visited an art fair and bought it as a frivolous purchase just because she liked the artist. Ma was always loose about money that way, though we never had much of it to begin with. Maybe that's why we ended up with all that debt.

When did it become easier to think about Ma than Phoenix?

"Nei go puk gaai, stay away from her, you hear me?" Suki says, forcing me back to the present. "Otherwise, next time it'll be more than a cup of boba." She rubs her fingers together and mimes a bomb explosion.

"You know I actually trusted you?" Suki lowers her voice. "I was the one who argued your case to Ming-lai and Wing-chi that night we went to KTV. I made the others take you on board. You know why?" The empty cup has rolled toward her; she crushes it savagely beneath her shoe. "I saw you that day, before we met. I recognized you on campus. You were carrying your art supplies. You had a fucking sketchbook in your hand. I thought, 'He's just an art student from China. And he's lonely.'"

I evade her eyes. She felt *sorry* for me.

"I underestimated you. I underestimated just how fucked up the ging caat are." She turns to leave, then glances over her shoulder. "I won't make that mistake again. None of us will."

Kai

THAT NIGHT, I FALL INTO A RESTLESS SLEEP.

Ma greets me when I come home. "Aiya," she snaps, and I flinch at her disapproval. I'm in Shanghai, or a facsimile of the Shanghai I remember. The toilet is leaking down the hall, its slow drip reminding me of ancient Chinese water torture. Ma's come back to haunt me, hasn't she?

"Here, have some fruit," she says, forcing a plate of sliced apples on me.

I push aside the apples. "Ma." I clear my throat. "I—"

She interrupts me. "My child, why don't you just leave him?"

"Father?" I ask, incredulous.

She nods vigorously. "He doesn't need you. He left you once."

"I left him once before!" She must know this distinction. "I left with you, Ma."

"Then leave him again." She starts fiddling with a thin paper box, the size of a pack of cards. "He'll live. And if he doesn't, good riddance."

"Ma, he's my father...." Why am I bothering? This isn't Ma. The Ma I know would never speak ill of Father. She would hide her frustration, curb her tongue, and tell me to try my best. She kept her resentments and reservations to herself, and never spoke of him at all.

"You hate Hong Kong," she says. "You want to leave."

"That's not true," I protest. "I—I don't hate all of it."

"Yes," she answers wryly, removing the plastic seal around the box. "The girl. You like her."

She doesn't sound happy about it. This isn't going at all like my usual dreams. In my fantasies, Ma loves Phoenix, accepts her like the daughter she never had. "You two are on separate paths. It is yuan fen that brought you together. And yuan fen will divide you again."

You yuan wu fen. Fated to come together, but not to stay together.

"I don't believe in yuan fen."

"That's why you give up your talent as an artist. That's why you squander away your life for your father. All because of some guilt complex."

This is not *my* ma speaking. I feel a surge of anger at this ghost impersonating my ma, tainting my memories of her. "Bizui! Whoever you are, I won't listen to you."

"My child," she says, clucking her tongue, "you want to remember me as an angel who did no wrong. You want to remember all the good without the bad." She cracks open the box with a practiced motion, pulling back the paper flap. "I asked you to be selfish, remember? I asked you to live for what excites you, not to care what others think of you, to go after your own pursuits and never look back."

"You didn't ask me to kill you."

"But you didn't kill me, child. Why, I did that to myself."

And then she removes a thin white-and-brown cylinder from the box, and I realize it's not a deck of cards; it's a pack of cigarettes. She raises the cigarette to her lips with an arched brow, as if daring me to protest. The smoke she blows in my face dissolves the room into fragments, until the image of Ma is washed away. But I remember now. I remember how I used to beg her to quit, for me, for Grandma, for herself. She would promise to try, but I would wake in the middle of the night and find her out on the balcony, furtively chain-smoking the packet she hid in her sock drawer, or the medicine cabinet, or behind the record player. I used to raid the apartment, looking for stashed cigarettes to toss. But she always had the upper hand. Because I cared about keeping both of us alive. Ma only cared about one of us. And it wasn't herself.

I shoot up in bed with a gasp. My head feels fuzzy as I probe for the light switch, tripping in the dark. I hit the switch and yellow light floods the room. I breathe in, breathe out. This space feels pressingly claustrophobic; the walls ripple and distort in my vision. I crack open the window, despite the raw burning smell in the air. The acrid smoke fills my lungs.

I remembered wrong. All this time, I thought I was living for Ma, for what she would want of me. But that's a disservice to her. She wasn't an angel. She wasn't perfect. She was messy and flawed like every other person.

And she didn't need to forgive me. She just needed me to forgive myself.

I'm still pondering this as I open my door and head out into the kitchen to make tea. I'm not alone, I realize belatedly. Father stands at the refrigerator in the dark, drinking baijiu liquor straight out of the bottle.

I switch on the lamp. He squints at the sudden brightness.

"You just got home?" I ask. It's nearly five in the morning.

He sways. Tian ah, he's drunk. And he probably has duty tomorrow. We're all running on overtime these days.

"Did Ma...did Ma smoke when she lived in Hong Kong?" I blurt out, surprised by my own daring.

He turns his bloodshot eyes on me. "What?"

"When she lived with you. I mean, when you were married. Was she the...same way?"

He wipes his mouth. "She got what was coming to her."

I stiffen. *She got what was coming to her?* "No one deserves—"

"Don't deny it, kid. She wanted to die."

The careless dismissal in his voice shakes me. "It's because she never understood—"

"You know her father died of lung disease too? And her grandfather?" He tosses the empty bottle in the trash; the clang makes me jump. "It was never that she didn't understand. It was that she didn't fucking care." Now that he's started, he won't stop. "I told her to quit, you know that? I gave her an ultimatum." He laughs, leaning against the sink. Liquor makes him talkative. "She said she would try harder. She said she would quit, eventually. Guess what? She *lied*."

Another bottle of baijiu teeters near the sink, but I don't do anything to stop it from falling. It settles by the edge, wobbling precariously.

It feels like we're all on the edge of something.

My throat has gone bone dry. "You want to blame everything on Ma, go ahead." My voice trembles. "She made mistakes, sure, but at least she was there for me. Unlike you."

The blow doesn't land. He brushes off my words like they're nothing but stray dust to him. I watch as he jerks the faucet on and splashes cold water on his face. Every one of his movements is forceful, blunt, overloud. He is the opposite of me in every way. "I've given you what your ma never could—wan ding," he says. *Stability.* "A home, a job—"

"A job I hate!" The truth comes out of me like a river rushing downstream. "Do you know I hate being called by a fucking number?" My voice rises tremulously. "I hate the way they teach us not to think for ourselves. I hate the orders and the obedience and the never-ending violence. Over and over, as if it's the answer to every question. But still, you force me—"

"You are my son. It is *my* right to decide what you—"

"Ma let me draw!"

He slams his fist down on the kitchen counter; the glass bottle clatters into the sink. "Your ma let you waste away your life!"

I suck in a breath. "If *this* is my life, then I'd rather waste it. No wonder Ma had a death wish. I'd rather fucking die than stay here with you."

There's this terrible silence as I realize what I've said. I want to inhale my words and take them back, every last accusation. But I can't.

"You thankless bastard," my father says at last, his voice tight. "Out. Get out. Don't you dare come back here."

I stare at him in shock. He can't mean that. "Ba—"

"Don't call me that," he snarls.

My head feels like it's splintering apart. I grab my backpack and stumble to the door, my vision blurring. When I take one last look back, Father distorts into a warped haze, many-eyed and glaring.

I'm sorry, I want to say. *I didn't mean that. I don't want to fail, not again.*

But I'm a coward. So, I do what cowards do: say nothing, close the door, and walk away.

I move permanently into the dorms. Even on weekends, I don't go home. Amid it all, Hong Kong descends into a hellish summer. Temperatures rise every day; still, more and more protesters flock to the streets. Near the beginning of July, I notice a new billboard spring up outside the Mong Kok police station. It's gigantic—over ten meters wide—and raised over the four-story building on Prince Edward Road.

It's also familiar. It's *Rageland*.

There she is, blown up in size, her face evocative and determined as she runs, her long hair flying behind her. The black Bauhinia flag waves a hundred times bigger, just as desolate and hopeless as I imagined it.

I stare in shock, forgetting where I am until a motorcyclist with anger issues blares his horn at me. I retreat into the shadows of a store alcove, looking out not only at the billboard but at the dozens of pedestrians passing by this busy intersection, the thousands of people who will see this piece, who will see my art, who will know it, but never know me. They will never know that I was the one who drew it.

And they never can.

From then on, I start seeing *Rageland* everywhere. On Lennon Walls all over the city, printed in miniature dimensions as small as Post-it notes, or screen-printed on T-shirts, shared on Reddit threads. I even notice a sticker version, pasted on the laptop of someone working in a Japanese coffee shop.

Phoenix is the one who started this when she posted *Rageland* on her Instagram, encouraging her thousands of followers to like, comment, and share. She believed in my art; at least, she used to.

These days, I'm drawing furiously, painting every weekend. It's hard to say when exactly I started again, but I think it was after my fight with my father. Marco complains about the scent of acrylics in our dorm, so I try to do most of it on the balcony. On my weekends off, I sit by the railing and watch the streets below. People go on with their lives, driving in a hurry, walking in a hurry, talking in a hurry. It makes me wonder if it's just me who's so damn stuck.

I don't want to graduate; I don't want to move forward. It's fucked up—the orders we carry out in the name of peace. But I don't know what there is to do about it. Some mornings it's too hard to drag myself out of bed. It seems like a feat in itself just to make it through the day. I wonder at the lives of normal people, people who can find their "passions" and leave their jobs and apply for something better. How do they improve their lives, like it's easy, like they're following a playbook? Before Ma passed, I never truly understood how hard it is to make your life better. To take your future into your own hands. It feels like reversing the course of a waterfall in mid-air, like trying to fight gravity.

Only people like Phoenix could accomplish something like that. People who believe in themselves, who are strong-willed and confident and vibrant, who don't conform to the world but let the world conform around them. Phoenix could manage anything.

I think of how easily she told me: *I've also had some change in plans. I'm not retaking my SATs. I want to stay here for university.* As if the river can alter its course with the snap of your fingers.

But what if, I wonder, late that night, *what if I saw things like she did?* What if I made myself apply to art school? What if I moved to Berlin? What if I took risks, real ones, ones that changed the shape and course of my river?

What if this life too was worth living? This flimsy life of mine.

But when I wake up the next morning, listening to the familiar rumble of the Wong Chuk Hang train below me, the reality of my future sets in, settles deep in my bones, and I want to laugh at the absurdities I dreamed up. It all seems impossible in the stark morning light, like I'm a ghost trying to live a normal life.

Phoenix

Mr. Tse's dark eyes scan the bookstore one last time. He knows he will never return here again. "I'm a simple man, with small ambitions," he explains. "I prefer books to people. I'm not trying to make a big fuss or overthrow the Beijing government. All I want is to make sure our history isn't erased. I know there's propaganda everywhere these days. I know history gets twisted every day. But there's nothing I hate more than censorship. When people don't know what happened to their ancestors, they forget where they came from. They forget who they once were. Then everyone loses."

I read through the article one last time before emailing it to Wing-chi. Suki recommended I reach out to her; in addition to studying biochemistry, Wing-chi double majors in media studies at HKU. On an afterthought, I email it to Mom too, though I know she'll take one look at the headline and hit delete.

I close my laptop, adrenaline coursing through me.

But my excitement is short-lived. When I check my phone, dozens of notifications flash across the screen, too fast to read. I open Telegram but the group threads are flooded with messages, and I can't keep up. I spot Ming-lai's username—he's raging at people to get their shit together and move fast. He must hate being stuck overseas, out of the center of action.

But he's risked too much here. If he ever returns to Hong Kong, he'll be arrested immediately.

Any one of us could be next.

I can't tell what's happened, only that everyone is panicking. I go to Google, prepared to search for protester-specific stories. But I don't need to do any digging at all. The news is everywhere.

"One-hundred-plus thugs dressed in white descend on Yuen Long MTR station with iron bars and clubs. Protesters were targeted, along with journalists holding cameras."

Yuen Long. My heart drops. That's where Suki lives.

It's close to three AM, but I call her. She doesn't answer.

I don't know what to do. Osprei's out of the country on a business trip with Mr. Fu. Should I tell him what's happened? But he'll see the news himself soon enough. Besides, he's on the blacklist now. He can't risk going out to the front lines.

For that matter, neither can I.

I pace my room, struck with helplessness. I call Suki again. It goes to voice mail.

What if she's injured? They were targeting protesters like her. Despite all her bravado, Suki's only a small girl—

My phone rings. *Kwan Suki.*

"Are you okay?" I demand, my heart pounding.

"I'm fine," she says. "Just fucking pissed. My mom nearly got curb-stomped. She happened to be wearing black." I can hear people chanting in the background. She moves somewhere quieter, then makes a sound between a laugh and a cry. "We got into a blowout fight. My mom called the police and couldn't understand why they didn't show up."

"They didn't show up at all?" I ask, appalled. I try and fail not to think of Kai.

"Not until it was over and the triad gangs were gone. Wing-chi thinks they were colluding with the police."

Bile rises in my throat. They hired *hitmen* against us. They took iron bars and clubs to random MTR commuters, to sow fear and suspicion among us.

What's happened to Hong Kong? I wonder. *What's happened to our city?*

"What can we do?" I ask, my voice thin, angry.

When she speaks, I already know her answer. "We protest."

Despite the hour, the traffic is terrible, and when I finally find Suki in the crowd outside the police station, the sun's started to make its ascent out of the mountains. It's too early in the day for this kind of frantic energy. The crowd is already moving, dispersing like dandelion fluff in the wind. There's dog shit smeared over the police station doors, and the odor wafts over us, mixing with the sickly sweet scent of trash, and something else, something like petrol.

"How are you holding up?" I shout to Suki over the din of the crowd. The first fires flicker and dance in the distance. Someone screams a chant: *"Hong Kong police, you know the law and break the law!"*

Suki's eyes are hollow and rimmed red, and I don't know if she's slept or eaten anything in a while. For a moment, I want to take her to a restaurant with classical music and table linens. We can eat pancakes with strawberries and cream and talk about HKU Law and try to pretend that life will resume in the fall, that we'll be alive and well in the fall, that our lives are guaranteed and that the world will go on.

Instead, I tug on my gas mask and watch as the riot police roll in, as they warn us of "unlawful assembly" through their blaring megaphones. Someone holds up a sign that I take a picture of with my phone, though it makes me wince because the privilege hits home: I AM CARRIE LAM. WHY DO I CARE WHAT HAPPENS TO HK? MY FAMILY HAS BRITISH PASSPORTS.

Suki says something but I don't hear her. I've just noticed the Y-shaped catapult the incoming protesters are wielding down the street, which has something like metal balls inside as ammunition. "They're not planning on using that, are they?" I ask, my voice shaking. "It looks like a war weapon."

"It *is* a war weapon," Suki says, in her unsparing way. "You know the ging caat are bringing in water cannons from China? And revolvers, and sponge grenades, and tear gas." Her eyes are hard. "It's really come to this."

My traitorous mind imagines Kai holding a gun, beating

protesters, binding their arms together with zip ties. Is this what he learns at his police academy? Is this what he spends his time doing these days?

I don't know. I guess I could find out, if I really wanted to. Yesterday, I even took the train to the police academy before losing my nerve. I didn't see him, of course. I told no one about the visit.

Around us, the crowd tries to pick up the next chant, but everyone is shouting off beat, unable to join in unison. People are rowdier, angrier, hungrier for battle. It's because of the Yuen Long mob attack. Like a drug, violence begets violence. It's never sated.

Then the crowd starts shoving, pushing, shrieking. A brick is hurled across the sky, and then another, and another. I hear the screech of a rail getting ripped out of the sidewalk, the twang of a bow drawn, an arrow released, the crackle of fire too close for comfort. I start to retreat, trembling. Suddenly, it's as if I'm back at the night of the LegCo break-in, getting pinned down by that officer, his baton cracking against my skull. If Osprei hadn't shown up . . .

But that's not right. Because Osprei wasn't the one who found me, not at first. It was someone else. *Get the fuck off her!* His voice was low, hoarse. It was familiar.

And now I can't stop shaking. *It was Kai.* He was there that night. Not as a protester as I assumed, but as an officer. He tried to warn me away. I didn't listen.

The memory leaves a gaping wound in my chest. I remember how he held me in his arms, how he whispered my name. Back then, it didn't sound like the voice of a liar. It sounded like someone who cared.

A whistle pierces the air and I come awake. Everyone is talking at once, a cacophony of noise. "Hey!" Wing-chi calls, running toward me. She slaps me on the shoulder. "Phoenix! I didn't know you'd be here," she says. "I liked your writing."

I try to smile. Before I can respond, Suki pushes between us, grimacing. "Apparently someone just bit off the finger of an officer."

"Bit? Like, with their teeth?" Wing-chi's brows wrinkle. I'm trying to picture someone gnawing through skin and bone when a sponge grenade explodes before us.

I lose Suki and Wing-chi in the crush of bodies. The air is smoky and white; I feel strangers press against me, jostling in all directions, screaming. I try to shove my way out of the crowd but I don't know which direction to turn, and everyone else is shoving just as hard. All our base instincts are violent.

Someone trips me and I fall to the cement, crawling on all fours. A sharp boot tramples over my hands and I cry out; my scream is lost in the sounds of the fight. I have to get out of here. I force myself to my feet and run at random until I inhale clean air and take in giant gulps, my lungs greedy for more. I tear off my gas mask, which is broken anyway, and survey the ruined street before me.

There's a lone police van abandoned at the intersection. The windows are smashed, and the exterior is smeared with spray paint. The crowd clamors as a few cops bolt for their lives, their weapons and riot gear discarded. Not all are so lucky. I see another grabbed by three boys, who tackle him all at once, pulling at him from different directions. His helmet is jammed in the fray and ripped from his head. It rolls across the cement....

Before I know it, I'm running, screaming, pelting through the crowd, forcing everyone out of my way. I know it's him, I just know it. In seconds, I reach the intersection. Kai's on the ground, getting bludgeoned by a baseball bat. I scream; there's blood everywhere, pooling on the cement.

"You're killing him!" I shriek, running forward. The boy raises the bat; he can't hear me in the commotion. He swings it down as I run toward him, and I squeeze my eyes shut, knowing I'm about to be bashed in the face—

The boy sees me at the last second and manages to pull back; the bat still catches me in the shoulder. I cry out but don't stop, shoving him off Kai's motionless body. There's confusion and muttered curses, someone tries to argue with me, but I can't hear them, I can't hear anything.

"Kai!" Skies, he's impossibly heavy. I roll him onto his side and gasp as I see the bruises everywhere, the line of blood trailing down his neck. My heart breaks and breaks and breaks. I don't care if he's a monster and he's lied to me every second of every day of our time together—I still care for him and can't let that go. I can't watch him die tonight; I *can't*.

People are shouting as they gather their supplies and rush down the boulevard. "They're storming the MTR station! Jat cai zau!"

I look up, distracted, and almost miss the quiet breath of air that escapes his lips. "Kai!" He blinks, returning to consciousness, and I start to sob. "You're alive. You're alive."

He reaches up and places a cold, limp hand against my cheek, barely conscious. Then his eyes flutter shut. His hand drops, but I grab it.

"Kai, stay with me!" I look around wildly, trying to find

someone to help us, anyone. A black-clad boy runs past me and I grab his pant leg, nearly tripping him. "Help me lift him," I say. "He needs a doctor."

The boy looks at me, then at Kai. "He's ging caat," he says. "Leave him." Then he sprints off.

I swear and shake Kai again, begging him to wake up. I don't know how much time he has left, or how urgently he needs medical attention. For a desperate moment, I wish our roles were reversed, that I was on the ground instead of him. I know the others would help me. But no one will help him.

"Can you stand?" I ask.

He nods, his eyes half shut, then tries to rise to his feet. It's clear his balance is gone. I try to support him, and we totter clumsily along, barely moving at all. What feels like ages later we get to the stations along the side of the road where medical workers in bright vests are administering saline for tear gas victims.

I nearly collapse in relief as one of the medical workers rushes over to us. "He might have broken ribs, I don't know," I say. "I think he's having trouble breathing—"

In the dim light, she squints at Kai, then recoils. "What is it?" I ask, increasingly impatient. She ignores me and goes to her fellow medical worker, and they converse in hushed whispers, as if Kai weren't on the verge of fainting at any minute.

The other woman, older and solemn-faced, approaches me. "I'm sorry, but we can't help ging caat."

"You can't be serious." My voice comes out furious, so choked I barely recognize it.

She looks contrite but unwavering. "Our resources are limited as it is. We're all volunteer workers and the supplies are donated for the protesters. There won't be enough to last the day."

"But—he's just a boy! He—he just turned eighteen—"

"We're sorry," she says, before turning to the new patient just brought in, with blood oozing from his chest.

I can hardly breathe from panic.

"It's okay, Lifeng," Kai whispers, his face bloodless. His hand goes to his rib cage, and his breath catches. I know he must be hurting. He bears it so well. I guess because all his life, he's always been hurting.

Please, God, I pray, for the first time in years. *You can't let him go like this. Not after everything he's been through.*

"Phoenix?" Suki emerges from the gloom. "What the hell...?"

"Oh my God, Suki!" I cry out. "What do I do? Kai's dying, and the med team refused to see him—"

Suki looks over Kai with transparent disdain. "He deserves it."

Kai leans against a wall, then slides to the ground. His face is drained of all color. "Lifeng," he says. "Just...go."

"No!" The tears are coming again, despite all my efforts to stay strong. "I told you—I *can't*."

"God help me." Suki sighs. "You let Tin-lok go, didn't you?" she asks Kai, her eyes turning to slits. "I know you saw us that day. You could've called the cops, but you let him go."

Kai's eyes are closed. He doesn't reply.

Suki takes out her phone reluctantly. "I'm calling 999."

Skies, why didn't I think of that? Because I can't think straight, that's why. I rub my eyes. I can't think while Kai is barely breathing.

Kai's no longer conscious by the time the ambulance arrives. The medics examine him with neutral expressions, their motions clinical and unfeeling. I watch them carry him into the back of the ambulance and I try to climb in behind them.

"Excuse me," the lead medic says, frowning.

"Can I go with him?"

He scratches the back of his head. "Are you family?"

"No, but—"

"Then I'm sorry, miss, but we don't have room."

I watch the ambulance doors shut. Kai disappears from my sight.

"Will he—will he survive?"

"We'll do our best," the medic says before walking away. I watch his receding back, speechless. He didn't even look me in the eye.

"Why couldn't you lie?" I cry out as the medic climbs into the ambulance and the engine revs. "Why couldn't you just lie and tell me he was going to be okay?"

Suki grabs me, wrapping her arms around my trembling shoulders.

"Why did he have to tell the truth?" I ask her tearfully, and I'm not sure who I'm talking about anymore. "Why couldn't he have pretended this was real?"

Suki's voice is bleak with understanding. "Maybe it was real."

Kai

I'M SUBMERGED IN DARKNESS, UNTIL A WHITE light blinks on above me. I make out a faint beeping sound.

"He'll live," a voice says. "He's a lucky one."

"It's a pity, with that beautiful face of his."

"The scar's small, anyway. Could've been a lot worse."

"That's small?"

"The ladies will find it charming."

"He should be prescribed bed rest, to make sure he gets some time off."

"You know how crazy the protests are. I'd be surprised if he even gets a week off."

"Poor kid."

"They're all kids out there."

A door slams shut. Then a face materializes, covered by

a surgeon's mask. My heart starts thudding, and the beeping quickens, as if we're racing, the noise against my heart.

The lower-pitched female voice greets me. "Oh, Mr. Zhang, you're awake!" I try to sit up and she helps me against the sudden dizziness. "Slowly, all right? You just suffered a concussion with a subdural hematoma. That means a pool of blood gathered between the inner layer of the meninges around your brain. Fortunately, we performed a CT scan and a neurosurgery consult, and it looks like the bleeding was minor and no neural surgery is needed. You're lucky." She pauses, cringing at her choice of words. "Well, as lucky as you can be. You also have two broken ribs, extensive ecchymosis in the upper and lower extremities, and twenty stitches in the face."

All I can do is blink in response. My hand goes to my cheek, which is smarting.

"Don't worry," she says, handing me a compact mirror. "You're still a pretty kid."

I take it with confusion. At first, I think she wants to point out the bags under my eyes, or the bruises on my jaw and throat where the protester tried to strangle me. But then I turn my head and notice the long gash going down the side of my left cheek to my jawline.

"The scar will shrink, with time. You're lucky it missed your eye. You can come back to the hospital in four or five days to have the stitches removed."

"What was it?" I ask, my throat dry. I'm imagining a knife in the dark, someone carving up my unconscious body. I don't remember the wound at all. In fact, I hardly remember anything. Except...Lifeng.

I lurch off the bed. Where is she? Is she safe?

"We think it was glass on the ground. Your left cheek must've landed in it with considerable force."

I'm hardly listening. I struggle upright, determined to find Phoenix right away.

The doctor goes to the door. "Your clothes are on the chair."

Someone's bothered to fold them. The sight makes my chest pang. "Th-thank you."

She gives me a small nod before leaving. "We're glad you made it out alive."

My body feels foreign to me. Simple things become hard to do, like sliding a foot into my pant leg. Everything is creaky and burning and sore.

I can't find my phone, but I head out anyway, after grabbing my wallet and signing some release papers. I hope they didn't notify Father. It's not worth troubling him. Besides, I'm already up and walking. All the injuries are internal—well, except the scar, but he'll hardly look me in the face anyway.

"Oh, and Mr. Zhang!" a nurse calls, her voice echoing down the hall. "There's a visitor waiting for you in the ICU waiting room. She's been there all night."

Tian ah. I feel as if time stutters and grinds to a halt. I forget to thank the nurse, limp toward a map of the hospital, and search for the waiting room. When I finally find it, I stride inside, pushing past other patients in my hurry to enter.

She's right in front of me, sitting in the foremost row of chairs closest to the door, her legs tucked in and her head resting on her knees. She's still wearing her protest clothes from earlier. That means she hasn't gone home since.

"Lifeng," I whisper, and when she doesn't stir, I realize

she's asleep. I soak in the sight of her: the curve of her nose, the dark of her lashes. Her eyelids flutter and I wonder if she's dreaming. I hope they're good dreams.

Then her head shoots up. She rubs her eyes blearily, looking around. "Kai?" she rasps. "You're . . . okay."

I nod, lost for words. I forgot the sweetness of her voice, the mellow timbre of it. "Because of you," I say at last.

She stares at me, her eyes wide, then reaches up to touch the scar on my cheek. "Does it hurt?" she whispers.

I shake my head, though it does. "I know it's ugly."

"No," she says fiercely. "You couldn't be."

I want to reach for her, to tell her everything. But then she turns away, and I see the mottled purple-green bruise covering almost her entire left shoulder, creeping up to her collarbone. "You're hurt," I say, my throat closing. "What happened?"

"It's nothing," she says, covering the massive bruise with her other hand. "Nothing like what you went through."

"Did a cop . . . ?" I trail off, my chest constricting at the thought.

She laughs, a humorless sound. "No, it was from a protester, actually."

"But, why would a . . ." To protect me. To stop that frontliner from hitting me.

I can't speak. She's been in this hospital for skies knows how long, waiting for me to wake up. She brought me here, even though she knew the worst of me. And still she saved me.

"Lifeng," I say, my voice low and hoarse. "I'm sorry. I'm sorry for what I did. I'm sorry for lying to you, for using you, for not knowing what was really important until it was too late. I—I know I don't deserve your forgiveness."

I don't really know what I'm saying, if the words even make sense. Maybe I'm delirious from exhaustion, or maybe it's the sight of her overbright eyes, like twin wells, shining pools of light. She is so lovely to me. She always will be.

"Kai…" She trails off. "I'm sorry too. I didn't mean what I said, that day you came to my house. I know…I know it was real for you too."

She takes my hand, and for a second I feel airborne. *She forgives me*, I think, *in spite of everything*.

"My mom told me something once, after her divorce," Phoenix says. She tugs at her earring, a nervous habit. "She said, 'You both need to be happy on your own first, if you want a chance of being happy together.'"

I stare at her, uncomprehending. "You aren't happy?"

Phoenix meets my eyes, and abruptly, I understand—she means *me*. I'm not happy here; I never was. And I brought that into our relationship.

"I don't regret our time together," Phoenix says, her voice tremulous. "I want you to know that. But Kai…I don't think this can work. Not now. Not yet."

I know I should say something, but I can only look away. Across the waiting room, I watch a nurse approach a family with news. The grandmother breaks down in tears. I can't tell if it's from happiness or sadness. Humans are such fragile creatures, aren't they?

"Nix!"

We both turn. "Mom?" Phoenix exclaims. Her mother rushes through the doors and throws her arms around Phoenix, who winces. I edge back to give them space.

"I was so worried," she's saying. "Robin said you went to Yuen Long. Then you didn't come home last night...."

"How did you know I was here?" Phoenix asks, voice muffled.

"Dr. Hua called me, thank God," her mom says. Her voice sounds accusatory, but then she adds, "I'm just glad you're all right."

Phoenix hugs her back.

I'm intruding on their private moment, but I can't look away. I want to observe them, study them. What would it be like, I wonder, to have a family that understands you, or at least one that wants to try?

Father was in Yuen Long last night—I noticed him there briefly, before I got separated from the others. Is he all right? Did he make it home last night?

"Mom," Phoenix says, disentangling herself. "Can we have a minute? Alone?"

Her mom dabs at her eyes with her silk scarf. She cries like Phoenix does, I think, silently, so that you don't even notice until you see the tears. "Don't be too long," she says, shooting me a baleful look before heading out the doors.

"How come your dad's not here?" Phoenix asks, glancing around the waiting room. "They didn't notify him?"

I swallow. "We're not exactly on speaking terms right now."

Phoenix frowns, absorbing this. "You could...you could come stay with me. In the interim." At the look on my face, she laughs. "Not like that. You'd have your own bed. We have, like, three guest rooms for you to choose from."

I know what I want to do—I want to follow her. I want

to convince her that we can make this work. But I remember what her mother said, about needing to be happy on your own first. Then I think of Ma and what she once wanted for me—what I want for myself.

I looked up the Berlin art school last week, when I couldn't sleep. Phoenix was right about the full scholarships they offer.

She's right about a lot of things.

Phoenix watches me. She gives me a small, sad smile. "You're not coming with me, are you?"

I shake my head, trying to ignore the growing lump in my throat. "I have to talk to my father," I tell her. "I have to try."

A tear wells at the corner of her eye before slipping down her cheek. I wipe it away without thinking, then remember I can't do that anymore.

She stands so still it's like we're frozen in time. "I guess I just wanted to put off saying goodbye," she admits, voice soft. Because goodbye is inevitable between us.

I put my hands in my pockets to keep from touching her again. "Take care of yourself," I say quietly. I already miss her, right this moment. I didn't know it was possible to miss someone who's standing in front of you. "Don't study too hard. You need sleep too, just like the rest of us."

She laughs, a strangled sound. "You should listen to your own advice."

I nod, and she starts to turn away.

"Don't forget to carry a jacket with you," she says quickly, glancing back at me. "It gets cold at night here, even in summer. And be more mindful in restaurants. Watch out for pickpockets." Her lips quirk in a hint of laughter. "And strange girls who steal your phone, then track you down with it."

"I'll watch out," I say, trying to smile. "One of them might just change my life."

The old ladies on Father's street recognize me, clucking at my injuries as I walk into the lobby. I punch in the code for the door, and it works; Father hasn't changed his lock. I don't know if that's because all along he wanted me to come back, or because he thought I wouldn't dare try.

He doesn't even look surprised when I come inside. He's standing in the kitchen, staring at his microwave dinner, which sits on the counter like a still-life painting—untouched, cold.

"Father," I say quickly, because I'm afraid he's going to kick me out at any second. "I know you don't want me here. I'll leave soon. I just want to talk to you."

He nods, uncharacteristically amenable.

"I'm sorry for what I said to you. I wish I could take back my words. I am grateful to you for giving me a home, a job. I'm grateful to you for paying off Ma's medical bills."

He fidgets with his chopsticks. His eyes linger on the stitches on my face.

"I wasn't always truthful with you when I should have been. So I'm trying to be now. I care about my art. A lot. It matters to me."

"I know," he says tersely.

I'm taken aback by this; it's not how I planned this conversation to go. Still, I forge on: "So I guess, that's why, what I mean to say—"

"Zai," Father interrupts. Splotches of scarlet rise on his cheeks. The lines on his forehead crease, a pale purple. *A face for watercolor*, I think. "You should know that I...I read your phone," he says. And then, to my infinite disbelief, he takes my scratched-up phone out of his pocket, handing it to me with notable reluctance. With slow understanding, I realize another cop must have found my phone in Yuen Long and passed it on to my father. "I read your texts. To your ma."

Cold fury courses through me at his sheer temerity. That he would dare read my innermost thoughts, meant for no one, not even Ma if I'm being honest, that he would dig through my secrets like a thief pillaging an ancient tomb, with no respect for the history, the artifacts, only mining for stupid gold.

"You should get a password lock on your phone," he says, scowling.

I reel back. I'm about to lash out at him when I feel a hand on my shoulder, a firm touch.

I whirl around; there's no one there.

The breeze blows in through the open window, scented with the fragrance of blooming jasmine. Ma's favorite flower.

I take a deep breath. It's as if I feel her voice in my ear, asking me to give him another chance. "Go on."

Father eyes me grudgingly. "To be honest, I saw your art from the beginning. You left your notebooks lying around the kitchen, like you thought I wouldn't notice. And then, the billboard. Outside the Mong Kok station. I knew immediately that was your work."

I have to grip the table to steady myself. "I didn't put that up there, I swear."

He shakes his head. "It doesn't matter. I saw that billboard every day on my way to work, as if you were shouting in my goddamn ear how much you hate what you do."

I thought no one would recognize *Rageland*. No one but Phoenix. I pitied myself, famous and yet known by no one.

But my father saw it. He saw it and saw me.

"I know you want to apply for art school. I read your texts. It's foolish but...I'll support you as I can."

"Father—"

"Your ma never wanted this life for you. I'm sure you know that." He glowers at the floor, his shoulders coiling with frustration. But I'm beginning to understand that his constant irritation is a mask, to hide the undercurrent of less straightforward emotions beneath. "She never wanted you to end up in Hong Kong. That's why she got out when she did. It's a shame, what happened to her. But she raised you right. She did, in the end."

I take a step back. I feel as if Ma is here with us, a third presence, not a hungry ghost but a benevolent one, radiating light and warmth into this lonely place. Father's been on his own for so long, and yet he's letting me go again. He's letting me leave even though I'm not what he wanted for a son, even though he hoped for an obedient one, a dutiful one, someone who followed orders and rose through the ranks because of his discipline and loyalty.

Instead, he got me. More interested in paintings than people. Vain and pining away, head lost in the clouds.

Still, he tried to help me. I tried to help him. I guess we're all just trying, in the end.

Through the open window, birds caw below, intrepid as they dive and swoop straight into incoming traffic. I spent all my time trying to earn Ma's forgiveness, when all along I already had it. I spent so many sleepless nights thinking Phoenix would never forgive me, but in the end, she did. I thought Father would not accept me, and so I never even let him try. I thought my dreams were futile, thin as tissue paper, and so I hid them away, never bothering to hold them to the light. Now I see the only one standing in my path is me. Zhang Kai En. The way to the ocean is clear, if only the river chooses to run.

"Zai, what I'm trying to say is, I'm…I'm…" He seems to choke on his words, his face reddening with effort. "Never mind. You need to start packing now and submit your letter of resignation to Lieutenant Chan." He makes an irritated tsking sound. "He'll try to convince you otherwise. Don't let him talk your ear off. And make sure you collect your last paycheck. They'll cheat you if you don't."

With my long-lost phone in hand, I nod, my throat too clogged to speak.

"And while you're in Hong Kong, just stay here," he says gruffly, jerking his head at my bedroom door. "It's absurd for an open room in Mong Kok to go to waste. All your stuff's still in there anyway. Your black clothes are so ugly I couldn't even give them away to a pawn shop. I bet no one would take them."

I stifle a laugh, because of course Father would use a time like this to complain about my wardrobe choices.

He stands to throw away his dinner, then shoos me away. Before he can catch sight of my watery eyes, I hurry into my room, closing the door behind me. Then I slide to the ground, dizzy with feeling.

What a mess of a family we are. Yet I don't think I'd give this one up, not even for a rich one like Phoenix's, as picture-perfect as she and her siblings are. We are never going to be the type of family that dives into deep long talks on the meaning of life, or hugs each other as if it's the easiest thing in the world. Touch is unnatural, praise is unnatural, even eye contact is unnatural. But we're trying. And right now, that's all I could want.

I write down my schedule for the next few days, because Professor Ng told us that if we put it down on paper it might give us some semblance of control. There's so much I have to do, but the thought isn't exhausting anymore. It's a relief instead to have something to look forward to.

I have to apply for the Berlin scholarship before the deadline next week. I should apply by tomorrow at the latest. Then I have to get my stitches removed on Friday. Then I should visit Ma one last time in Shanghai, clean her burial site before I leave.

I don't know if I'll be coming back for a long time.

It's taken me three months to adjust to Hong Kong, to not get lost in the streets or forget everyday Cantonese. It's taken me three months to understand that my life is not a static thing, frozen and fixed as a fossil. My life is ever-changing, nebulous, something precious and rare. Three months ago, I couldn't have guessed I would meet someone like Phoenix. I couldn't have guessed I would leave her. I couldn't have guessed a lot of things. But I see now that the trick is not in the holding fast. It's in the letting go.

I turn in my resignation letter at the academy. Marco gives me a pep talk and his last egg tart. Lieutenant Chan reminds me to be a filial son and visit Father during my holidays.

At the hospital, the nurse tells me about her German brother-in-law as she removes my stitches, going on and on about the currywurst in Berlin. When I leave, she presses more medicine into my hand. I'm surprised by her kindness. Most medical staff don't sympathize with the police, and I understand why. There are too many horror stories of police brutality out there. It's true that I hate it too—the violence. It's true that the officers like the one who assaulted Phoenix are far too common, and the ones like Marco are few and far between. But the good ones, they exist. They're out there too, trying to protect their city.

But do we do more harm than good? Why do some people need protection, while others need imprisonment? Why do ging caat deploy tear gas and rubber bullets; why are we *encouraged* to use violence as the answer? I know these are questions too big for my father, who is, at the end of the day, just trying to do his best. But I'm also beginning to understand that you can love someone and still hurt for them; you can hold these dualities separate. My father grew up in a different time, one that prized obedience above all, one that never questioned authority and those in power.

But I am not my father.

And perhaps this is the key to growing up: to love the one who raised you, to care for them, and yet, to use their history and their life to reach further, to grow further, and to become something more.

34

Phoenix

I WAKE TO ROBIN POUNCING ON MY BED LIKE it's a swimming pool and she's doing a cannonball. "Up!" she yells in my ear. "Dad's here."

I make an unintelligible noise and roll over in bed. My eyes are crusted shut with dried tears. I fumble for my water bottle, which Robin passes to me in a rare fit of mercy.

"Dad's going over divorce stuff with Mom. But apparently he wants to stay for brunch." She gives me a furtive look. "He probably wants to talk about Yale."

I slide back under my sheets and moan. Now I absolutely don't want this day to start.

It's been easy enough to dive back into academics, studying so hard every day that I barely have time to process my emotions. It's only at night, when I can't keep my eyes open any longer and am forced to bed, that the tears flow.

I remember the night Kai and I broke into the country club pool, the way he looked at me when I unbuttoned my shirt, like the yearning was a living thing inside him.

I remember how lost he looked when he came to my house. The way his face would close off when my friends spoke in English, and he could hardly keep up with the twists and turns of conversation. I remember a dark street, riddled with glass and tear-gas canisters.

I remember our fights. How I screamed at him, called him a brainwashed puppet of China. There were so many things we never understood about each other.

I remember *Rageland*, the painting he made for me. We tried, didn't we? We tried our very best.

It just wasn't enough.

I sit up on my knees and crack open the window. The tip of the Repulse Bay water is visible through the sycamore leaves, casting a brilliant gold hue where the surface of the water scatters the light. It's a beautiful day, and I'm still alive, despite all that's happened.

"You shouldn't wear this now that you've broken up with Kai." Robin holds up his jacket from where it was buried beneath my pillows. "Do you want me to take it for you?" She tries it on. The hem falls to her knees.

I sigh. "Robin—"

"Thanks!" she cuts me off, running out of the room before I can stop her.

Osprei yawns, meandering inside just as Robin rushes out. "Morning, ladies."

I look up, surprised. "You're up before me." Normally, Osprei isn't a functioning human being before noon.

"Technically, I didn't sleep last night," Osprei replies, checking his reflection in my vanity mirror. He's dressed in full black. I remember today's Saturday; we're supposed to head to the Kowloon protest with Suki in an hour.

"Mom told me you two made up," he says, with a flippant smile. "Guess you're not going to Yale. Bummer."

"I still have to tell Dad."

Osprei shrugs. "You wanna do photography instead, right? Especially since your Insta is blowing up. I mean, you could even monetize it at this point. Become an influencer."

I wrinkle my nose at him. "To be honest, I'm not great at photography. I think it was just a hobby," I admit. "My account got big because I was at the right place at the right time, and the protests needed to be captured. But still…I like the idea of someone across the ocean looking at my work and being able to understand a different perspective through it, to see a world different from their own. I'm still working on Tin-lok's article. I think maybe I'll major in law and journalism. Like Suki and Wing-chi."

I don't know if Osprei heard me; he's studying his reflection like it's the next *Mona Lisa*. But my idea is novel to me, and I like the way it sounds on my tongue.

"You care too much about finding your passion in life, Nix," he says, yawning again. "You'll find it eventually anyway. You don't have to be on the hunt for it 24/7. Relax a little."

"But I want to be *someone*," I say. "I feel like I'm always just living in relation to someone else." At his bemused look, I explain: "Charlie's dumber friend. Osprei's younger sister. Mom's good kid."

"Kai's clingy girlfriend," Osprei adds, unhelpfully. He's watching a video on his phone now. It sounds like a football match.

The door opens and this time it's Suki, her hair freshly dyed silver. She heads to my bathroom to use my face wash.

"You get my point," I say, turning back to Osprei. "I want to have something I'm proud of, something that I can point to and say, this is who I am."

"You're already your own person," Suki calls from the sink. "Who else would join me on the front lines and even make the first move on Kai? You have a personality and it's your own. You're pretty assertive, you know."

"That could just be an American thing," I say, tugging at my earlobe.

"Or not," Osprei smirks.

"Brunch is ready!" Robin bellows from downstairs. (That girl should take up tuba with her lung capacity.)

I grab my protest gear and head downstairs. Robin and Dad are seated at the kitchen island, playing chess. Dad's remaining king is slowly getting cornered by Robin's web of pawns.

"Dad," Robin says, "if I win this game, can I take over the family business instead of Osprei?"

Mom looks aghast, but Osprei laughs. Dad looks…surprised. I hope he's beginning to see that even though Robin's a girl, and the youngest, she's shaping up to be the smartest one. (And the only one who actually cares about profit margins and brand equity, though we'll see how long that lasts.)

"Morning, Phoenix." Dad pointedly ignores Osprei and Suki behind me. (Osprei's still in Dad's bad books after his run-in with the law.) "You're heading into your last year of secondary school soon," Dad says, as if this is some revelatory scientific discovery.

I nod cautiously. When Dad said he was staying for brunch, I knew immediately what that meant—he was here to play parent for a day, to convince me to give up on HKU and apply to Yale instead.

"Robin tells me your photography account is gaining traction. That will come in handy for college apps," he says. "College admissions love a good story. You can play up the whole 'fight for democracy' angle. Americans will eat that up."

"Should we have brunch?" Mom asks in a stiff voice.

But I don't take the easy way out. I face Dad head-on, squaring my shoulders. "Actually," I say, trying my hardest to keep my voice level, "I'm not applying for university in the States anymore. I'm going to stay here."

Dad is sipping his mimosa and barely seems to hear me. When he raises his head a beat later, there's a vague smile on his face. "Oh, really?" he asks, like Mom hasn't already briefed him.

"Yes, *really*." I lift my chin. "We've had a discussion within the *family* and agreed this is the best course of action."

Osprei grins at me, mouthing, *Good one.*

I wait for Dad to reply, but for once I'm not readying my defenses. Yes, I have rational motives and goals behind wanting to apply to HKU. I have a four-year plan and a multidisciplinary course of study outlined, not to mention high scores to back up my argument. But the real reason I'm confident is because I've given up. I've given up trying to please him and win his approval, as if it's the most coveted prize in the world. Mom's already said yes. So has Osprei, and Robin, and even Suki, and all the people I truly love and who love me.

Dad puts his mimosa down and stands. I brace myself for his anger, but instead he just studies me. "It sounds like you've made up your mind."

"I have," I say. Then I turn to Osprei. "Ready to go?"

He nods. "Let's do it."

Dear Instagram friends and followers, this is not goodbye forever. I'm still supporting the protests actively, and I still stand with HK, but I'm going to start putting my focus elsewhere. This photography account was always meant to shine a small light on the nitty-gritty of what's happening in this city, but I know now there are other ways to do that. Thank you to the followers who translated my captions into Spanish, Vietnamese, even Finnish. Thank you to the followers who shared these posts with everyone from relatives and coworkers to news outlets. And thank you, most of all, to the Hong Kongers who stand together, who sacrifice so much for this city we love and call home. Gaa jau, HKers. Add oil!

EPILOGUE

Phoenix

WE'RE ABOUT TO HEAD OUT OF THE MTR STA-
tion when I get an incoming call. My heart nearly falls out of
my chest. It's Kai. I stare at my phone, wondering if this is a
cruel prank from the universe.

"Aren't you going to answer that?" Suki asks.

I draw a shaky breath and bring the phone to my ear.
"Hello?"

"Hey...it's Kai. Are you busy right now?"

"No." I step into an alcove as a crowd of protesters streams
past. "Why?"

"I'm leaving Hong Kong." He hesitates. "I wanted to see
you before I leave, if that's all right."

I don't remember how to form words. I press my hand
against my sternum, as if checking to make sure it's still
intact.

"Hello?"

"Yes," I say quickly, making a decision like I always do—in a split second. "I would love to. Where?"

"I can come to you."

Ten minutes later, Kai turns the corner, parting the Kowloon crowds as he strides down the street toward us. Even in ripped jeans and a long-sleeve tee, he still turns heads. The way he walks, it's like he knows you can't help but stare.

Osprei's watching my expression. I put on a smile and wave, calling out Kai's name. He slows as he spots us, coming to a halt a few feet away. "Hey, you," he says, trying for lightness. But his eyes are pensive.

"Wanna grab claypot rice first?" Suki says to Osprei. "Phoenix, we'll meet you at the march later?"

I wave, and they leave us. Kai looks at me, keeping his distance until I nod at him, and he steps closer. It used to be so easy between us, I remember, like a dream.

But all dreams pass.

"Let's take a walk around the block?" Kai suggests. He glances at the frail, wispy clouds overhead, then at me. From the way his eyes squint, I can tell what he's thinking—he's capturing this moment to draw later. This makes me smile, how naturally I can read him now. It wasn't always this way.

Maybe not everything's lost between us.

"You were right about art school, and about my mother," Kai says at last. "I was trying to pay penance with my life, as if that would bring her back." He laughs softly, looking up at the pigeons roosting patiently on the telephone lines. "I'm applying to art school in Berlin. My father gave me his blessing." I suck in my breath, but he forges on, not looking at me. "I'm going back to Shanghai first. To say goodbye to Ma." His eyes meet mine at last. "I leave tomorrow."

"I'm—I'm so happy for you," I say.

He smiles down at me, his eyes bright, and my lips unconsciously widen to match his, as if I'm a mirror and I can't help but reflect him. His happiness is infectious.

These are probably our last moments together, I realize. I study his profile and remember a time when I considered him my enemy. It's funny, what time does to you. Everything really can change course in the blink of an eye.

Kai lowers his voice. "I want you to have this," he says, taking his sketchbook out of his bag. "They're mostly of you. All the best ones, anyway."

I start to open it, but he stops me. "Not yet. Wait until I'm gone."

"I'd rather have pictures of you," I confess. "I already see myself in the mirror every day."

"There might be one or two self-portraits in there, but I don't like drawing myself, sorry," he says. His mouth curls in a crooked half grin, one that still makes my heart skip a beat. "Besides, I like to look at you."

Back at the MTR station, I'm not sure how to say goodbye. I hold out my hands awkwardly, not sure if I'm going for a handshake or a hug, but then he pulls me into his chest. I breathe in the familiar scent of his laundry detergent, the warmth of his skin. We fit together, we do. But there was too much else in the way between us. Maybe if Kai hadn't grown up in Shanghai. If I hadn't joined the protests.

But if we'd made different choices, we'd have become different people. And maybe that Kai wouldn't have been brave enough to leave Hong Kong. That Phoenix wouldn't have been brave enough to stay.

Kai leans down and brushes his lips against my forehead. "Another time, Lifeng," he whispers, as if he can read my mind. He releases me slowly; it takes all my willpower to let him go.

He waves goodbye one last time before he disappears into the station. I wave back, smiling as wide as I can. I want to memorize the planes of his face, his dark soulful eyes, his soft, silky hair, the hard curve of his jaw. I know when I remember him years from now, I won't think of the fights, the tears (thousands of tears, really), the grief. I'll think of him in the light: smiling at me, painting, holding his brush lightly, holding his thoughts and dreams lightly.

It didn't work out between us this time, but who's to say what will happen down the road, in the faraway future, in this life or the next? I think of my SAT geometry prep, of parallel and perpendicular lines. I think of falling leaves that return to their roots, and constellations that drift across whole galaxies as one. I can't say with confidence what our paths hold for us, and yet I know with my entire being that someday, somewhere, our paths will cross once more.

There's so much uncertainty in our future. There's so much we must hold close yet know that any second it can shatter. Who knows what will happen to Hong Kong once the handover happens in 2047? Who knows if China will wait that long, if it will force control in five years or five months? The truth is, none of us have singin ziming, none of us can say with the certainty of a magician, *Let me tell you, this is what will happen*. And yet, we go on, because of the hope that things will get better.

We go on.

AUTHOR'S NOTE

Phoenix and Kai's story began for me in early 2019 after reading international media coverage that depicted the Hong Kong extradition bill protests in a black-and-white, one-dimensional light that I felt lacked nuance. While Western media outlets depicted brainwashed Chinese cogs in a wheel, Chinese state-run media cast protesters as immature kids behaving like rioters and terrorists. What most of these pithy soundbites failed to capture were the real people behind the headlines—people who were anxious yet determined, conflicted yet resolute. Villains and heroes alike, both brave and afraid.

That summer, in Hong Kong, I started writing what would later become the first chapter of *An Echo in the City*. And yet, I scrapped the story soon after starting. Repeatedly, I was advised not to write this book. Writer friends in the publishing industry worried that it would be too niche, that US publishers would not buy an international story without an American (read: white) protagonist. Nonwriter friends and family worried about the backlash over the controversial subject matter. I, too, was concerned. And yet, as I continued to receive updates from friends and family still in Hong Kong, the seed of the story took root, quietly but insistently, demanding water and light. I decided to write just one chapter. I told myself it wouldn't become a book. But the chapter wrote itself. So did the next one. Slowly, the story grew. Though the moments when words flow like a downhill stream are, in truth, few and far between, this was one of those moments.

It is important to note, particularly to Western readers, that Phoenix and Kai's story is *not* representative of the entire Hong Kong population. In fact, there is a vast range of perspectives, experiences, and opinions about the city and its protests that are not captured in this novel; to attempt to do so would be to write a never-ending story. In imagining *An Echo in the City*, my aim was not to offer a definitive conclusion on history but rather to open a doorway, to capture a transient moment in time, and to ask a question, or several. It is my hope that readers will come away from this story inspired to seek more, to listen more; that they will see this not as an end but as a beginning.

Further Reading

Chan, Holmes, ed. *Aftershock: Essays from Hong Kong*. Hong Kong: Small Tune Press, 2020.

Choy, Jeffrey, and Karen Wong, eds. *Umbrella Uprising: A Visual Documentation of the 2019 Hong Kong Protests*. London: Design Media Publishing (UK) Limited, 2020.

Dapiran, Antony. *City on Fire: The Fight for Hong Kong*. New York: Scribe US, 2020.

Loh, Christine. *Underground Front: The Chinese Communist Party in Hong Kong*. 2nd ed. Pokfulam: Hong Kong University Press, 2019.

Further Viewing

Do Not Split (2020), directed by Anders Hammer

Revolution of Our Times (2021), directed by Kiwi Chow

ACKNOWLEDGMENTS

Writing is often considered a solitary process, but this book provided me invaluable company and solace during a time of widespread isolation.

To Alice, Theodora, Nocus, and many others, thank you for answering my thousands of questions and bearing with me through the time zone differences and the unexpected challenges that life threw at us. This story is infinitely better because of you. And to the many, many, *many* individuals interviewed for this book who cannot be named—I am forever grateful to you. Your courage, grace, and resilience sustained me.

Thank you to my editors, Sam Gentry, Hannah Milton, and Hallie Tibbetts, who each championed this story with care and embraced its messy complexities.

Thanks to my agent, Peter Knapp, for rolling with the punches beautifully.

Thanks to Lauren Spieller, without whom this book would not exist.

To the entire team at Little, Brown Books for Young Readers, but especially Jenny Kimura, Hsiao-Ron Cheng, Karina Granda, Annie McDonnell, Jane Cavolina, Anna Dobbin, Nicole Wayland, Patricia Alvarado, Stefanie Hoffman, Alice Gelber, Savannah Kennelly, Cheryl Lew, and

Victoria Stapleton, thank you for working so tirelessly behind the scenes and between the lines.

To my first readers, Adriana De Persia Colón, Grace Li, and Rona Shirdan. Your encouragement kept me going when I was on book number seven with no finish line in sight. And this acknowledgments section would be remiss to not recognize Laura Weymouth, my fairy godmother and author mentor extraordinaire. Truly God packaged all things light and warmth and sunshine to form you.

I am deeply grateful for the support of the Highlights Foundation, with special thanks to Alison Green Myers and George Brown, for their tremendous kindness and generosity. To the Highlights Fellows—Jae, Nathalie, Daria, Pam, Narmeen, Jess, Gerry, and Adriana—from writing sprints to tea sessions, we've formed our own little family, haven't we?

To Xuan Juliana Wang and Justin Torres, for teaching me the power of words. I entered your class trying to conform my work to be liked by all. I left with the understanding that writing, at its worst and at its best, is an act of violence.

To early mentors Sarah Perry, Padma Venkatraman, and Sarah Aronson, your belief in me and my premature work was an invaluable gift.

To my fellow creators-of-worlds—Joan, Diana, Yixuan, Joseph, Amanda, Marianna, Yuqi, Aleese, Gloria, Heather— it is an honor to create alongside you.

To Naz Akbari, mentor, life coach, friend, and much more.

To Max and Linda, my chronic lunch-ditchers— Crepeville, soon?

To my 姐姐們—Audrey, Iris, and Rebekah—I'm so lucky to have a second set of sisters.

To Uncle Hon, for paving the way as an artist.

To Auntie Kwok, for the nuanced advice and the unwavering encouragement. The themes of this story were sowed during my summer with you.

To my mother, who signed me up for my first library card. To my father, who humored my obsession with geodes by accompanying me to the neighborhood ditch on Saturdays, to chip away at sewage rocks and find the occasional (much celebrated!) quartz. To my sister, who subjected me to her intricate, one-hundred-plus-hour-long make-believe games, and to my brother, who was subjected to mine. How could an imagination fail to grow and abound in an environment such as this? My early love for stories is thanks to you.

Lastly, this book is for my grandparents. To my 外祖父母 and my 祖父母, I was and am privileged to have you in my life. From Hong Kong to Shanghai, from revolution to abject poverty. Because of you, I gamble for the hope of a better future.